**Praise for the delectable Culinary Mysteries
by Nancy Fairbanks . . .**

"Clever, fast-paced . . . A literate, deliciously well-written mystery."
—Earlene Fowler

"Not your average who-done-it . . . Extremely funny . . . A rollicking good time." —*Romance Reviews Today*

"*Crime Brûlée* is an entertaining amateur sleuth tale that takes the reader on a mouth-watering tour of New Orleans . . . Fun." —*Painted Rock Reviews*

"Fairbanks has a real gift for creating characters based in reality but just the slightest bit wacky in a slyly humorous way . . . It will tickle your funny bone as well as stimulate your appetite for good food." —*El Paso Times*

"Nancy Fairbanks has whipped up the perfect blend of mystery, vivid setting and mouthwatering foods . . . *Crime Brûlée* is a luscious start to a delectable series."
—*The Mystery Reader*

"Nancy Fairbanks scores again . . . a page-turner."
—*Las Cruces Sun-News*

Holy Guacamole!

Nancy Fairbanks

BERKLEY PRIME CRIME, NEW YORK

THE BERKLEY PUBLISHING GROUP
Published by the Penguin Group
Penguin Group (USA) Inc.
375 Hudson Street, New York, New York 10014, U.S.A.
Penguin Group (Canada), 10 Alcorn Avenue, Toronto, Ontario, Canada M4V 3B2
(a division of Pearson Penguin Canada Inc.)
Penguin Books Ltd, 80 Strand, London WC2R 0RL, England
Penguin Group Ireland, 25 St. Stephen's Green, Dublin 2, Ireland
(a division of Penguin Books, Ltd.)
Penguin Group (Australia), 250 Camberwell Road, Camberwell, Victoria 3124, Australia
(a division of Pearson Australia Group Pty., Ltd.)
Penguin Books India Pvt. Ltd., 11 Community Centre, Panchsheel Park, New Delhi—
110 017, India
Penguin Books (NZ), Cnr Airborne and Rosedale Roads, Albany, Auckland 1310,
New Zealand (a division of Pearson New Zealand, Ltd.)
Penguin Books (South Africa) (Pty.) Ltd., 24 Sturdee Avenue, Rosebank, Johannesburg 2196,
South Africa
Penguin Books Ltd, Registered Offices: 80 Strand, London WC2R 0RL, England

This is a work of fiction. Names, characters, places, and incidents either are the product of the author's imagination or are used fictitiously, and any resemblance to actual persons, living or dead, business establishments, events, or locales is entirely coincidental.

HOLY GUACAMOLE!

A Berkley Prime Crime Book / published by arrangement with the author

PRINTING HISTORY
Berkley Prime Crime mass-market edition / November 2004

Copyright © 2004 by Nancy Herndon.
Cover design by Elaine Groh.
Cover illustration by Lisa Desimini.

ISBN: 0-425-19922-3

Berkley Prime Crime Books are published by The Berkley Publishing Group,
a division of Penguin Group (USA) Inc.,
375 Hudson Street, New York, New York 10014.
The name BERKLEY PRIME CRIME and the BERKLEY PRIME CRIME design are
trademarks belonging to Penguin Group (USA) Inc.

PRINTED IN THE UNITED STATES OF AMERICA

10 9 8 7 6 5 4 3 2

Grateful acknowledgment is made to W. Park Kerr and Norma Kerr for permission to reprint copyrighted recipes from the *El Paso Chile Company's Texas Border Cookbook*, William Morrow and Co., Inc, 1992

Author's Note

Opera at the Pass and its members and singers are all fictitious, as are the plot and all characters except historical figures mentioned in passing. However, El Paso, its restaurants, and its chefs and food writers, except for Carolyn, are real people who have kindly agreed to contribute their names, recipes, and establishments to this book, for which they have my profound thanks: Lionel Craver for his sangria recipe; Annette Lawrence, owner and chef at The Magic Pan for her recipe for Tlapeno/Tortilla Soup; Jose Nolasco of Desert Pearl for his Crab and Lobster Enchilada; Mr. and Mrs. Henry Jurado of Casa Jurado for their recipes for *Enchiladas de Calebacitas* and *Pescado al Mojo de Ajo*, and especially to W. Park and Norma Kerr for permission to reprint recipes for guacamole, Green Enchiladas, *salpicon,* and crepes with *cajeta* and pecans from their wonderful cookbook, *The El Paso Chile Company's Texas Border Cookbook.*

Books I used for research in writing *Holy Guacamole!* are: Cleofas Calleros, *El Paso's Missions and Indians;* Paul Horgan, *Great River/The Rio Grande in North American History;* W. Park Kerr and Norma Kerr, *The El Paso Chile Company's Texas Border Cookbook;* Leon C. Metz, *City at the Pass/An Illustrated History of El Paso;* C. L. Sonnichsen, *Pass of the North/Four Centuries on the Rio Grande;* Reay Tannahill, *Food in History;* W. H. Timmons, *El Paso/A Borderlands History;* Maguelonne Toussaint-Samat, translated by Anthea Bell, *History of Food;* James Trager, *The Food Chronicle;* and Alan Weisman, photographs by Jay Dusard, *La Frontera/The United States Border with Mexico.*

NFH

Prologue

El **Paso, Texas,** the city to which my husband, Jason, and I moved several years ago, has always seemed an exotic place to me, but I'm adjusting. The city is beginning to feel like home. It's not a small, dusty border town, as you might think if you've heard the Marty Robbins song. El Paso has over 700,000 people and Ciudad Juarez, across the river, over a million, maybe even two million. So many people from the interior of Mexico flood in yearly to work in the twin plants and to immigrate, not always legally, to the United States, that Juarez officials have no idea how many people live there.

El Paso has developed during the twentieth century into a city with tall buildings, a university, museums, a symphony, opera, and drama, but its history is Spanish, rather than English. Here at the intersection of Mexico, New Mexico, and Texas—a land of desert and mountains—the first Caucasians were Spanish conquistadors coming north from Mexico to look for land and riches and Spanish friars in search of new souls to convert.

We may now have a wide variety of restaurants, but the food we miss when we are away from home is Mexican food, the ingredients and recipes for which are descended from the Aztecs, Mayans, Incas, and North American Pueblo Indians. Our newspaper articles and conversation often circle around subjects such as the disappearing water supply, our stepchild status in our own state, and the third world diseases that come across the border or fester in our own *colonias*. We discuss the violence of the drug trade, which results in execution-style murders in Juarez and in El Paso because the cartels use our border to transport their product.

On the other hand, I feel quite safe here. El Paso has a low murder rate and an excellent record of catching killers and shipping them east for execution, Texas being a state that carries out a lot of executions, although less cruelly and more judicially than the rustler hangings of the old days. But violence is not new to El Paso. Our history is blood soaked, and our written history began in 1598 when Don Juan de Onate and his troops arrived at the Pass and claimed all the land drained by the Rio Grande for Phillip II of Spain.

Then he and his men continued north to found Santa Fe, and the El Paso area became, for two centuries of Spanish rule, the mid point for the caravans freighting supplies from Mexico City to northern New Mexico. The men and wagons took six months to reach Santa Fe, six months to distribute the goods, and six months to return to Mexico, and on the Camino Real, the route they took, they were always in danger of attack by Indians, particularly Comanches and Apaches. Las Cruces, only forty miles north of El Paso, is named after the crosses raised over the graves of those who died on the trail.

Mission Nuestra Senora de Guadalupe, which still stands in downtown Juarez, then named Paso del Norte, was founded in 1659 and completed in 1680, but it was the Pueblo Revolt in northern New Mexico ten years later that led to settlements here. The various tribes under their leader, Pope, rose on the same day and slaughtered Spanish colonists—men, women, and children. Unable to fight off the rebels, the Spanish governor, Don Antonio de Otermin, gathered those Spaniards who survived and those Indians who wished to come and fled down the Camino Real. These survivors settled in Paso del Norte, and at new missions, Ysleta, Socorro, and San Elizario, each built for different Indian tribes. Before the end of the century, the Spanish returned, took back the New Mexico colonies, and resumed the long journeys from Mexico City, through Paso del Norte, to Santa Fe.

Along the Rio Grande the settlers and Indians dug ace-quias for irrigation, built haciendas, raised herds of sheep, cattle, and goats, and crops of wheat, corn, chiles, melons, beans, European fruits, and especially grapes, from which they made wine. But even as trade grew and the land was cultivated from the eighteenth to the mid–nineteenth century, the Apaches rode out of the mountains and the Co-manches from the plains to the east to raid and kill the Spanish and their Indian converts.

In 1821 Mexico fought for and won its independence from Spain, but life went on much as before, continuing the transformation from the European ways brought over by the settlers to the Pueblo ways of New Mexico and Mexico as Spain became a distant memory. And then the Anglo traders came and brought a new era of bloodshed after Texas won its war with Mexico and Alexander Doniphan's Missouri Volunteers defeated the local Mexi-can army and took Paso del Norte in 1846. For a time the U.S. Army settled here to protect settlers and travelers from raiding Indians, who didn't care what country claimed the land.

The Civil War, the local Salt War, the crime wave brought in by the arrival of the railroads, and the era of the gunslingers kept the blood flowing in the second half of the nineteenth century. Then the twentieth century turned El Pasoans into violence-voyeurs as the Mexican Revolu-tion brought attacks on Juarez by Orozco, Pancho Villa, Huerta, and others. The shellings, dyamitings, and rifle charges played out across the river while our citizens watched from the top stories of buildings, railroad cars, and the river levees. There are photographs of ladies in white dresses with large hats and parasols and men in suits and hats enjoying the show, but some of the spectators were killed by stray bullets, and finally the U.S. Army returned in strength to pursue the bandit revolutionary Pancho Villa, no longer a hero in the United States. They never caught him.

Prohibition initiated another wave of crime and violence as liquor was smuggled across the river, and finally the drug wars began in the '60s and '70s and continue today, mostly across the river, but here in El Paso as well. Illegal immigrants, seeking a better life in the United States, drown in the river and die of heat, thirst, violence, and asphyxiation in the desert and in locked railroad cars and trucks.

We are a city with a long history of violence and death, which I had, heretofore, found a matter of interest rather than a cause for alarm. It didn't occur to me that history could catch up with us, especially at a festive celebration after a production of Verdi's *Macbeth*. We opera lovers enjoyed the hors d'oeuvres, the margaritas, and the cultural chitchat, but we also saw the beginning of a violent death.

The next day my amazing, cross-border adventure commenced—me: food columnist and faculty wife Carolyn Blue. But then, I'm getting used to adventure, just not at home.

It all began with the guacamole.

1

Après Macbetto

Carolyn

Jason and I were invited to join the Executive Committee of Opera at the Pass last spring, just before we went to France on a tour. They didn't seem to care that we are so often away from home, all summer in New York, for instance, not to mention the various scientific meetings we attend because of Jason's research on environmental toxins and our excursions for my syndicated food column "Have Fork, Will Travel." My initial supposition was that the invitation stemmed from a desire to recruit someone for the committee to provide refreshments at parties and fundraisers (little did they know that currently my interest lies more in eating than cooking).

Jason, however, served on a university committee with Vladislav Gubenko, the opera guru of the university music department and the artistic director of Opera at the Pass, which explained, according to Jason, why we were chosen, aside from our love of opera. It certainly wasn't that we're big donors, having given only a hundred dollars. After all, with two children in college and retirement staring us in the face twenty years or so from now, we try to be thrifty—well, Jason is thrifty, and he tries to keep an eye on me.

At any rate, we had attended a performance of Verdi's *Macbeth* that Saturday night at the Abraham Chavez Theater, which is part of our local civic center, a rather impressive and very modern curved structure with five long, rounded windows deeply inset into thick walls. From the side, the building presents the appearance of crisscrossing slopes. Unfortunately, it has suffered from a leaky roof and other problems ever since it was finished in the 1970s. I myself have noticed stains on the curved wooden walls of the 2,500-seat theater, every seat of which was filled for *Macbeth*.

Instead of chandeliers, long curtains of crystals with lights behind them hang from the ceiling in the theater. Since I'd been reading El Paso history, I couldn't help but think of the much-admired chandeliers improvised for an all-night party at the home of trader James Magoffin in 1849—sardine tins attached to the hoops of pork barrels with lights attached. It must have been something to see. The historian even mentioned food served at the party—an imported "cold collation." At most historic fiestas and banquets in El Paso history, much more notice was taken of the available beverages. For instance, when the Southern Pacific came to El Paso in 1881, historians tell us of speeches, cannons, a banquet, and a dozen bottles of champagne, seventeen gallons of wine, four hundred glasses of lemonade, and so forth. They must have had a good time, but did they get anything to eat? I knew, because I'd fixed some of the refreshments, that *Macbeth* was going to be celebrated with both food and alcohol.

And it was. Soon after the final bows, we attended the party with its gala postperformance crowd of singers, donors, members, and El Paso persons of importance. Dr. Peter Brockman, President of Opera at the Pass and wealthy neurosurgeon, gave a long-winded speech of thanks to those who had made the performance of *Macbeth* possible and promised that future productions would be less avant-garde. Obviously, he hadn't cared for Vladik's Tex-Mex version of Verdi's tragic opera, in which the

Scots had metamorphosed into contemporary drug dealers competing for control of the cocaine market, and the witches' chorus was whittled down to three sopranos, further disappointing Verdi purists.

The artistic director actually interrupted the speech at one point to say that his production was calculated to bring in donors and ticket purchasers among Hispanics, who make up most of the city's population. "University last year say I do zarzuela, no grand opera, or nobody buy tickets," said Vladik, combing blonde locks away from a high forehead. "This year no money for any production at university. So Vladik save Opera at Pass from bankrupt."

Dr. Brockman glared at him. Francisco (Frank) Escobar, member of the opera board and prominent community banker, who happened to be standing next to Vladik, said quietly, "On behalf of the Hispanic community, I'd like to say that we support grand opera and deplore drug dealing." He is a slender, handsome man with ascetic features and silvering hair.

Vladik shrugged. "More Hispanic names on ticket list for *Macbeth* than last spring *Abduction from Seraglio*. I look."

Dr. Brockman cleared his throat and introduced "our own opera-loving Father Rigoberto Flannery, who will lead us in prayer."

Father Flannery, who had done a fine job singing Banquo but was now wearing his usual clerical collar and black suit instead of his rival drug-dealer costume (tight pants, alligator boots, unbuttoned silk shirt, and gold chain nestling on a hairy chest), took the microphone and beamed at the crowd. They in turn stopped eating hors d'oeuvres and drinking margaritas in order to join in prayer. I'd heard that Father Flannery is the son of a devout Hispanic mother from San Antonio and an alcoholic Irish father, who was killed while trying to escape family responsibilities by hopping a freight train to Houston. The Church had provided Father Flannery with schooling from boyhood on.

Well loved by his congregation at San Isidro and by opera enthusiasts, he has an excellent bass singing voice and has been known to tie his homilies during mass to operas and urge his flock to attend opera performances. Last year I heard a rumor that the bishop reprimanded him for comparing Mascagni's *Cavalleria Rusticana* and the high rate of teen pregnancies in El Paso during a sermon on sexual morality. Funny, I never thought of Santuzza as a teenager; she's the unwed, pregnant heroine, whose lover, Turridu, is killed in a duel at the end of the opera—divine retribution, according to Father Flannery, and an object lesson for boys who seduce innocent girls.

"Blessed Holy Father, we thank you for granting the joy of opera to humankind," he began in a booming voice, "for surely opera is as close to the singing of the heavenly angels as we can hope to experience before you accept, as we pray, our souls into your blessed company. We ask you to look favorably upon this gathering of opera-loving El Pasoans, and upon our city, which is peopled by so many faithful Roman Catholics.

"Lastly, Holy Father, we ask your blessing on the fine food and drink provided for this occasion by our ladies."

At that moment Adela Mariscal, a music graduate student at the university who had sung one of the three witches that night, approached a table loaded with food, bottles of champagne, and punch bowls filled with margaritas. She was carrying a large cut-glass bowl of guacamole, which looked delicious enough to make me consider asking her for the recipe. Of course, I'd have to try it first.

The priest spotted her too and added to his prayer a presumably extemporaneous blessing. "Particularly, Lord, bless our Juarez songbird, Adela Mariscal, whose guacamole is treasured on both sides of the border, a gua-camole so ambrosial that even the Holy Mother could hardly make it better."

Adela blushed and looked alarmed as she clutched her bowl, forgetting to place it on the table.

"That's sacrilege," gasped Frank Escobar's besequined wife loudly enough to be heard by the priest.

He looked up from his prayer and said to the banker's lady, "Hyperbole, my dear Barbara. I'm sure we all realize that the Holy Mother is much too busy for cooking these days. After all, she has to intercede with her Son for the forgiveness of our sins and the granting of our prayers." Father Flannery is a Marian Society supporter. He then bowed his head again and finished, "In the name of the Father, the Son, and the Holy Spirit, bless this food, this drink, and this company. Amen."

The crowd murmured, "Amen," and Vladik Gubenko hustled straight for the guacamole. "Priest is right about delicious Adela's guacamole. Is very tasty. As artistic director, I eat it all," and he snatched the bowl from Adela with a charming smile.

"You can't," she cried.

"Sure, I can." He dropped a kiss on her cheek and reached behind her for a large handful of tostados, which he scattered over the pale green surface of the avocado dip. "You make for me, no?"

"No! I—I made it for everyone!"

"In opera I am most important of everyone in El Paso. I get guacamole." And he walked off holding the bowl, dipping a tostado into the guacamole, and savoring his prize.

Of all the nerve, I thought. Poor Adela looked as if she might cry. And no wonder. It was a lot of guacamole. She must have spent hours chopping and squishing and stir-ring to produce that much dip. And when she was singing that night, too. She probably chopped all the ingredients before the performance and mashed the avocados in a blender or food processor after changing out of her costume.

"Don't be upset, Adela," I said to her as I helped myself to a margarita. "It's not your fault that Vladik decided to make a fool of himself. You should take it as a compliment to your recipe."

"Everyone ees supposed to eat some, not just Vladik."

"Yes, I want some myself," I agreed. "It looks wonderful, and the priest certainly thinks it's spectacular."

"He should not say ees better than Virgin Mary's. Ees bad luck."

"Well, I know they grow avocados in the Holy Land now, but that's a new thing. I'm quite sure the Virgin never made guacamole in her day, so you really shouldn't feel that you've been thrown into some sort of sacrilegious competition. Personally, I'm going to get my own tostados and share Vladik's bowl. In fact, I'll urge others to do the same. No reason he should make a pig of himself while the rest of us are left out."

"*Gracias.* I hope you can get others to take from him. He is peeg," Adela added angrily. "Probably no one want to eat from same bowl with him."

I had to laugh. "A pig, maybe, but talented, certainly. He did a beautiful job of turning that witches' chorus into a trio, and I have to tell you, Adela, that you sounded wonderful, the other two girls, as well. It's hard to believe anything so beautiful could also seem so ominous. I think you have a promising future in opera."

"Gracias, Senora Blue. You make me feel happier." Tears actually rose in her eyes.

"Now, cheer up," I urged, smiling. "If Vladik actually eats all that guacamole himself, he's going to have one killer stomach ache."

The poor girl looked horrified, although I'd been trying to make her feel better.

Adela's Guacamole

Aztecs and Mayans were very fond of avocados, not only with chile and spices as guacamole, but as food for dogs, which were fattened on avocados before being eaten as a special treat at feasts. Does that seem slightly disgusting? Just remember that pate, that expensive favorite of gourmets, is made by stuffing grain down the throat of a goose and then harvesting the liver. Why not a tasty, avocado-stuffed dog?

Although Spanish conquistadors brought back avocados from Central America as early as 1527, they were little known in Europe until after the Second World War. Now we grow them in California and Florida and have since the early part of the twentieth century; they are popular all over Europe, Israel makes money exporting them, and Mexicans eat fifteen kilos a year per person. The Aztecs made avocado bread, modern cosmetics manufacturers use avocado oil, and in Zaire they make beer from avocado leaves.

But the best use for an avocado is a delicious guacamole. The main ingredient is extremely healthy because it contains linoleic acid, which breaks down cholesterol and fat globs in the arteries and prevents our blood cells from clumping together in the first place. You might get fat eating avocados, but you're less likely to have a stroke or heart attack.

Note that this recipe calls for Miracle Whip as a preservative—not lime juice, which makes the guacamole slightly acidic; not avocado seeds stuck back into the mixture, which some gourmets say is an old wives' tale; and definitely not the mystery herb provided by Adela's Tia Julietta.

- In a blender or small food processor, puree together until smooth *1 cup roughly chopped cilantro;*

2 fresh jalapeno chiles, stemmed and chopped; and
1 teaspoon salt. (If your blender isn't doing a good
job pureeing the ingredients, add the Miracle Whip
and turn the machine on again.)

- In a medium bowl, roughly mash *4 large buttery-
  ripe, black-skinned avocados (about 2 pounds), pit-
  ted and peeled.*

- Stir in cilantro puree; *1 pound (5 or 6) ripe plum
  tomatoes, halved, seeded, and diced; ½ cup peeled,
  diced red onion;* and *¼ cup Kraft Miracle Whip
  Salad Dressing (unless it was added to the cilantro
  puree).*

- Adjust seasoning.

- Cover with plastic wrap, pressing the film onto the
  surface of the guacamole.

- Store at room temperature for up to 30 minutes, or
  refrigerate for up to 3 hours.

  Makes 3 cups.

Permission to reprint given by W. Park Kerr and Norma
Kerr from their *El Paso Chile Company's Texas Border
Cookbook.*

Carolyn Blue, "Have Fork, Will Travel," *Seattle Times.*

2

In Search of Guacamole

Carolyn

The other two witches, both Russians if I was any judge of accents, came over to talk to Adela. After being introduced and congratulating them on their performances, I filled a plate with tostados and went off in search of my husband. Jason was chatting with a professor from the English Department, Howard Montgomery. Being the resident Shakespeare scholar, he was delighted with the change from a witches' chorus to a trio.

"The first time I heard Verdi's *Macbeth*—of course, I've seen Shakespeare's play more times that I can count—I was appalled at the witches' chorus," said Professor Montgomery, a round, middle-aged cherub of a man, who was devouring my canapés with gusto. "All those women squalling oompah music. 'What was the composer thinking?' I asked myself. 'It's an abomination.' It was a Met broadcast, and I turned it off. Didn't actually see the opera until twenty years later, and I must say that, aside from the peculiar notion of casting the Scottish nobility as drug dealers, I highly approve of this version. Three witches. That's what Shakespeare had, and it worked just beautifully in the opera. Gubenko is to be congratulated."

"That's an excellent idea!" I agreed. "Let's go do it. I happen to have picked up some tostados, so we can sample the guacamole while we're supporting our artistic director."

"My dear, I'm perfectly happy with these delicious canapés, which your husband tells me you provided. I hope to convince you to give Dolly the recipe." He looked around vaguely. "I wonder where she is. Wasn't she with us just a minute ago, Jason?"

"I don't think so," said Jason. "I haven't seen her yet this evening."

"Oh well. She is here. I distinctly remember that we came in the same car. She was complaining that the orthopedic boot, which she's wearing because she broke her ankle, looks bad with her dress. The boot is black—a sort of suitcase fabric with Velcro straps—and her dress— um—I've forgotten what color it is, but I asked why she didn't wear a black dress. She has one, and it's long. It would have covered the boot, but she said her black dress—"

"I'm so sorry to hear that Dolly broke her ankle," I interrupted, afraid that he'd meander on about his wife's dress forever when I wanted to get us over to the guacamole. I linked my arm with his and urged him in that direction, nodding to Jason to follow. "I'd be delighted to give Dolly the recipe, but it's so simple you can just tell her."

My husband was trying to stifle laughter at my manipulation of the kindly Shakespearean scholar.

"That's very good of you, Carolyn, but I'd be sure to forget," Howard replied apologetically. "All those measurements and whatnot. It's amazing that I remember long passages from the plays, but if Dolly sends me to the grocery store, I always come back with the wrong thing. Still, I'm sure the English faculty would love some of those delicious canapés at the annual Christmas party. Would you consider them festive enough for the holiday season? I know you're an expert on food, so I'd value your opinion on the suitability of—"

"Very festive," I assured him, "and easy to make. You

just go down to the El Paso Chile Company—it's on Texas Street, has trees in front of it, and is painted in bright colors. There you buy some of the hot pepper-fruit preserves. I used the peach and the raspberry tonight, but you could probably use jalapeno jelly as well. Then you'd have red and green." We were threading our way through the mob, which was all the jollier for the infusion of margaritas. "Then you buy some Philadelphia cream cheese and crackers at the supermarket, spread the cream cheese on the crackers, and dab on the preserves. Nothing to it." I pulled Howard into the circle around Vladik Gubenko and held up my plate of tostados.

The artistic director was hugging the guacamole bowl in one arm and eating with a spoon, having evidently finished off the chips he'd snatched from the refreshment table. There were still a few tostado crumbs in his thin, blonde goatee, but no more tostados on the surface of the dip, and evidently the crowd of adoring ladies around him didn't want to cause him any discomfort by asking to share. I had no such qualms.

"You clever Russian," I said, kissing him on the cheek and then flicking a few crumbs from his beard. "We've come to congratulate you on your production of *Macbeth*."

He beamed at me.

"And to share the guacamole." I dipped the largest tostado I could find into the bowl and scooped up a big glob of dip. Then I offered the plate to Jason and Howard.

"No share," protested Vladik. "Was made for me by one of my pretty sopranos, no?"

"No," I said, savoring the guacamole. It was, as Father Flannery had said, heavenly, and I had to get the recipe. "I've brought Professor Montgomery over to meet you. He's our Shakespearean scholar, and he loves what you did with the witches." I helped myself to another chip full. Adela should patent it. But not before I got it into a column. Mexican food is popular all over the country now. My readers would love it.

"Shakespeare much loved in Russia," said Vladik solemnly. He had to put the spoon into the bowl in order to shake Howard's hand. "Many translation, many read in English. Both plays and opera put on. Russians love Shakespeare."

Howard nodded nostalgically. "I remember as a graduate student—what happy days those were. I took my doctorate at University of Virginia. Met my dear Dolly there. She was an undergraduate in the Shakespeare class I graded as a graduate assistant. Lovely girl. Still is. Reminded me of Viola in *Twelfth Night*. You'll have to meet her—Dolly, not Viola."

As he rambled on and Vladik looked puzzled, I managed to devour three more helpings of guacamole, while Jason dipped two chips and turned to talk to a fellow who was employed by the city to do environmental things. He'd been a student of Jason's last year.

"But as I was saying, I was amazed as a graduate student at the numbers of critical papers written in Russian on the bard. Unfortunately, I didn't read Russian, still don't, but I knew one fellow who did, and he said many were very good. No doubt, it's your love of England's best dramatist that led you to redo the witches' chorus. I found the singing of just three witches, as called for in the play, quite lovely."

Vladik nodded enthusiastically and said, "And my witches very pretty too, no? Two is Russian, one from Juarez. All got very nice titties." Professor Montgomery looked taken aback. "Have costume lady make dresses to show off. Can't have big titties hide under baggy black dress. No reason witches can't be young and pretty."

"I was referring to their musical talents," said Howard, "and your arrangement of the music."

"Sure." Vladik winked. "Verdi envy Vladislav Gubenko

for fixing that scene and picking pretty girls, no old uglies. Maybe I take Mexican *Macbeth* to Broadway, to Met. No?" As pleased as he was with himself, he had now noticed that I was eating his guacamole. "So Carolyn Blue, you meet yet my stars? No? I introduce." And still clutching his guacamole, he insisted that I follow him to a group that included the Chilean soprano, Maria Ojeda-Solano, aka Lady Macbeth; her murderous opera spouse, baritone Wang Zhijian; and a passel of hapless El Pasoans who were trying to converse with them.

It's easy to give a fiesta if you have access to the El Paso Chile Company, which happens to be in my hometown. If you live elsewhere, as most people do, the company has a website. The owner, W. Park Kerr, has written books of recipes for spicy border dishes and knockout border drinks, and the store has all kinds of lovely and exotic spices and foodstuffs. Favorites of mine are the fruit and hot-pepper preserves, which you can spread over cream cheese on crackers for easy and tasty canapés.

Preserves have a long and interesting history. Feasts given by Roman and Byzantine emperors featured preserves made of fruit and honey. The Valois kings of France loved their preserves; Francis I favored quince paste and once took some along when he went to visit his mistress. She, unlucky woman, was entertaining another lover, who dove under the bed, but the sophisticated king passed some of the treats to the terrified lover and said, "Here you are Brissac, everyone has to live!" He may have had the fellow killed at a more convenient time; the story doesn't tell us. Nostradamus, when not foretelling the future, wrote a book on making jellies and preserves, and Louis XIII of France went into the royal kitchen and cooked up his own. Mr. Kerr follows in an elite tradition and is fortunate enough to have sugar for his creations. Sugar did not become available for preserving fruit until the eighteenth century.

Carolyn Blue, "Have Fork, Will Travel,"
Pittsburgh News-Journal.

3

Vladik in Trouble

Carolyn

"**Carolyn, here is** Lady Macbeth, Senora Maria Ojeda-Solano, and Macbeth, Wang Zhijian," said Vladik, taking away my chips and dumping them on top of his guacamole. "Not need these when have fine jelly crackers," he added when I looked mutinous. Then to his stars, "And this is lady, Mrs. Carolyn Blue, whose crackers you are enjoy."

The two singers stared at me, bemused. Perhaps they hadn't understood the introduction.

"I go talk to president of board. Rehearsals closed, even for big shots. My *Macbeth* surprise for everyone but cast." Vladik took himself and the guacamole off in the direction of the neurosurgeon, and good luck to Opera at the Pass's artistic director, I thought, if he believed that he could convince the very conservative Dr. Peter Brockman that the drug-war *Macbeth* had been a cultural triumph and should be followed by more, not less, avant-garde productions.

What did Vladik have in mind? I wondered. *Carmen* set among the cardboard shacks in the squatter *barrios* of Juarez with the smugglers transformed into coyotes sneaking illegal aliens across the Rio Grande? *La Boheme* in a New Mexico '60s hippie commune? Actually, that might work. Even my *Carmen* idea might work. In fact, I had rather enjoyed the weird *Macbeth* but mostly because of the voices.

"What an honor to meet you, Senora Ojeda-Solano," I

said, shaking the Chilean soprano's hand. She had an empty flute of champagne in the other hand and was wearing a very regal garnet satin gown and a tiara. I'm not sure I've ever actually met anyone wearing a tiara. "Your Lady Macbeth was wonderfully powerful." She nodded in queenly acceptance of my compliment. Didn't the woman speak? "I see that you need another drink. Would you like to try a margarita?"

"I dreenk only champagne," she replied. "Mexican cactus dreenks ees bad for the throat. So ees strange—" She looked disapprovingly at a tray of my canapés. "—theengs on plate." She touched her throat as if to ascertain that it had not been damaged by our humble border offerings.

I waved a waiter over to refill her champagne flute and turned to the Chinese baritone. Initially I had thought a Chinese Macbeth even stranger than a drug lord Macbeth, but Mr. Zhijian, a stocky man with thick black hair, had proved to be not only a fine singer, but also an excellent actor. By the end of the production I had accepted him as a Juarense with a desire to garner the whole drug trade for himself. "What a pleasure to meet you, Mr. Zhijian. I enjoyed your performance so much." I'm sure I butchered the pronunciation of his name.

"Not Mr. Zhijian. Wang my family name. Zhijian mean *firm in spirit*. In English you, Carolyn; I, Firm in Spirit. You, Blue; I, Wang." He nodded cheerfully. "I like you food things." He popped a jalapeno-peach canapé into his mouth. "Vely good taste, like dragon fire on tongue." He consumed another and then tossed down the margarita a waiter had just provided.

Noting that Mr. Wang was not only very cheery but also somewhat glassy eyed, I said, "Margaritas taste better if you sip them."

"Yes," he nodded with a wide, loopy smile. "Taste vely good. I have another." And he did. If I had drunk two, or however many, margaritas straight down, I'd have fallen flat on my face, which is almost what Mr. Wang did. Luckily, those of us in the circle, excluding Senora Ojeda-Solano, caught him before he could hit the floor, after which several male members of the chorus helped him away, while the Chilean soprano looked on with raised eyebrows and sipped her champagne. I noticed that the bottle the waiter poured for her was Tattinger's, while the bottles on the table for the rest of us were some American brand I was unfamiliar with—perhaps of the five-dollar variety.

With Mr. Wang gone, I told Senora Ojeda-Solano how fond I was of the novels of Isabel Allende, especially *The House of the Spirits*. Although Allende was a fellow countrywoman and a famous author, the soprano had never heard of her and didn't seem receptive to my recommendation. She turned and began a conversation in Spanish with Barbara Escobar, the banker's wife. I went looking for Vladik in case there was any guacamole left. I almost caught up with him, but he had flitted off with the bowl, leaving me to catch a conversation between Dr. Brockman and Frank Escobar.

"We've got to get rid of him," said the neurosurgeon, shaking a very long finger in Escobar's face. "It's bad enough that he snuck that atrocious staging of *Macbeth* in under our noses, but now he insists that more of the same is just what El Paso needs. We'll be the laughing stock of the opera world when this gets out."

I wasn't convinced that the greater world of opera was that cognizant of what we were doing in El Paso, but I didn't say that.

"I did not participate in establishing Opera at the Pass to be made a fool of by some upstart Russian," the doctor continued. "I have to wonder now where the university found him. Probably some place like Uzbekistan."

"Or Chechnya," suggested Frank Escobar. "They're a group of troublemakers. I think the university suckered us when they suggested we take him on. I've heard that the new fad there is zarzuela, not grand opera. Not that I don't like a good zarzuela. Barbara and I always attend the performances at the Chamizal. But imagine what Gubenko would do to a zarzuela."

"I heard him say that he doesn't like zarzuela," I told them. I didn't like it that much myself. The one I saw was a sort of Spanish operetta without subtitles or program notes. I had no idea what was going on.

"He won't even be able to ruin that program," said Brockman. "I'm sure you're aware, Carolyn, being connected by marriage with the university, that state budget cuts are hurting spending on education. I'm told the music department took a severe hit."

"Scientific research funding too," I agreed. Jason had been complaining, although a lot of his funding comes from outside sources, thank goodness. Otherwise, I'd never hear the end of the blow to science dealt by short-sighted state legislators and a penny-pinching Republican governor.

"Let's hope the music critic from the *Times* is still sick," said Frank Escobar. "I'd just as soon not have this production reviewed."

"Yes, I was very upset when I initially heard there'd be no review of the Friday night performance, but it turned out to be a blessing that the critic is the first reported flu case in the city," Brockman agreed.

I murmured my excuses, having spotted Vladik with a group of university people. He'd only managed to finish half the guacamole. I accepted another margarita from a passing waiter and joined the new circle. My husband was trying to convince Vladik that the administration wasn't singling him out for unwarranted budget cuts.

"President hate me," said Vladik stubbornly.

I thought he looked rather sickly, but then who wouldn't after eating a half-vat of guacamole. I helped myself to some in the interest of his health.

"Vice president for Academic Affairs hate me," he persisted. "Music chairman hate me. All jealous of Vladik. My *Macbeth* make them give money. They see many Hispanics come. Many applaud loud and shout, 'Bravo'."

I personally thought that if the upper administration had been in attendance—I hadn't seen any—that they'd take away his budget entirely.

Melanie Collins, who is married to a geology professor, said, "I thought it was wonderful. My first opera, and I was absolutely enthralled. I think the university is treating you dreadfully, Vladik. It's shameful." She laid a sympathetic hand on his arm and smiled at him like a girl with a teenage crush.

"You would say that," snapped her newly arrived husband, who, instead of a tuxedo, was wearing dusty khakis and heavy hiking boots.

"Why Brandon, I thought you were still on a field trip," said his wife. "Couldn't you have changed your clothes before you came to the party?"

"And give you time to trot off with this Russian puke? You think I don't know you've been sleeping with him?" Brandon Collins turned on Vladik and snarled, "I ought to break your scrawny neck, you communist son of a bitch." He actually put his hand on a pointed hammer that was holstered on his heavy leather belt—some geological tool, no doubt, but it did look dangerous.

Those of us in the circle were, needless to say, both embarrassed and alarmed at this turn of events. The opera's artistic director, who had turned a sickly shade of green, said, "Vladik sick. Very sick." He thrust the guacamole bowl into my hands and stumbled away before Professor Collins could smack his head as if it were a rock of scientific interest.

"Some lover you picked," Collins said to his pink-faced wife. "He didn't even have the guts to stay and fight for you, did he?"

"It might have been the guacamole," I murmured, "or even the margaritas."

The simplest recipe for a margarita, according to the authors of *The El Paso Chile Company's Texas Border Cookbook* is *3 ounces gold tequila, 3 ounces orange liqueur,* and *3 ounces lime juice* shaken with ice and poured into a cold glass, the rim of which has been coated with salt. But what of the tequila? It first became popular in the United States when Mexican Revolutionaries and their American counterparts across the border favored the drink. However, tequila did not gain a wider distribution in our country until the Second World War, when European liquors became hard to get. It has gained steadily in popularity since then.

In Mexico it dates back into Indian history before the Spanish Conquest when pulque was distilled from the agave cactus and drunk at religious ceremonies by priests and nobles, who were working themselves up to the high point of the event when a person or persons were sacrificed on the altars. The lower classes were not allowed to drink it unless they were to be sacrificial victims. Then presumably their fears were muted by drunkenness.

Later Mezcal wine or brandy was distilled from the agave, and finally tequila, which was produced from huge cactus plantations, where the sap is harvested and then distilled—in early days in rawhide containers—latterly in barrels of oak and even plastic. The distilleries are mostly in the state of Jalisco, and the processes are closely kept secrets. An interesting footnote is that women are not welcome in the distilleries. They are still considered "unclean" and "bad luck."

Carolyn Blue, "Have Fork, Will Travel,"
Charleston, Southern Messenger.

4

"Our Cultural Establishment Has Suffered A Great Loss"

Carolyn

Jason and I were ensconced comfortably in the padded lounges on our patio, drinking coffee and reading the Sunday papers. Last month we discovered that we could have the Sunday *New York Times* delivered right to our door, so Jason was reading that while I browsed through the *El Paso Times* before going into the kitchen to fix brunch—*eggs ranchero*. Sometimes we have mimosas with them, but after the margaritas last night, I didn't feel like drinking alcohol. The truth is, I'd been sick during the night, a rare event for me, and I didn't think I'd had *that* many cocktails.

Ah well, I felt fine in the morning, and it was such a beautiful day. Blue skies, sunshine, temperatures in the 60s. El Paso can be quite lovely in the winter—at least when there's no inversion layer to trap toxic air in the river valley. Today the air was so clear that the city below us and the mountains across the border in Juarez stood out in sharp delineation. A house with a view. I felt extremely contented and picked up the newspaper again.

There was no review of the opera—I'd looked—but there was an article on the editorial page, of all things. "Listen to this, Jason." And I read him the editorial, which was titled "Insult Shrouded in Beauty."

"For those of us attending an opera for the first time, the Opera at the Pass production of Verdi's *Macbeth* at the Abraham Chavez Theater was an eye-opener in more ways than one. We were an audience dressed in seldom-used finery, El Paso being a casual sort of town. Having spent as much on tickets as a big-name rock star might command, we were prepared to be bored by a stuffy, classical experience or, for the more optimistic, amazed by the talents of the composer and singers. We were certainly amazed.

"Ms. Ojeda-Solano and Mr. Wang Zhijian, from Chile and China respectively, are possessed of voices both beautiful and loud. They rocked the auditorium without the aid of microphones—eat your heart out, Ricky Martin. Local singers and instrumentalists from the university and the city distinguished themselves as well. And the music was melodic, sometimes even foot tapping. My wife came away humming one of the arias. For those of us who suffered through *Macbeth* in school and then promptly forgot the whole thing, translations in English and Spanish, projected above the curtain, kept us apprised of what was happening on stage.

"On the basis of what I have said so far, you might think that El Paso has come of age, has joined the mainstream, culturally speaking. Not so. Instead of spending our expensive evening watching tragedy evolve among Scottish kings and thanes, Artistic Director Vladislav Gubenko served up his own inappropriate revision of the story. El Paso was treated to a distasteful and demeaning tale of murderous drug dealers. Perhaps Mr. Gubenko thinks that we are incapable of appreciating anything more uplifting. Perhaps Opera at the Pass needs a director with more respect for the local audience.

"Although our proximity to Mexico certainly gives us a front-row seat for the violent activities of the drug cartels, we do not need to be entertained with the spectacle of contemporary lawlessness when better things are available. If we want the drug culture dramatized for us, we can go to the movies. Many of us may be cultural Philistines, Mr. Gubenko, but we are not all drug dealers, and we bought enough tickets to sell out the theater. Your made-for-El Paso version of Verdi's and Shakespeare's classic tale is an insult to the city."

"What do you think of that?" I asked my husband.

"I think Vladik's going to be upset. He was pretty proud of that staging."

"I know, but did you like it?"

"Macbeth and Lady Macbeth were excellent," said Jason. "Never heard of either of them, but we were lucky to get voices like that, and I kind of liked the trio of witches, but the drug-dealer theme was over the top. I can't say it worked for me. Still, I doubt that Vladik meant to insult anyone."

He leaned over to rustle through sections of the *New York Times,* probably looking for the sports pages, or possibly the travel section. Personally, I like the wedding section. It's so different from wedding descriptions in my youth. The New York paper offers us strange brides and grooms, too old to have stayed single so long, and avantgarde weddings. It's very entertaining. Still, I wish Jason wouldn't drop the paper on the cement. By the time I get to it, I often find ants scurrying over the news item I want to read.

"Weren't you going to fix eggs ranchero this morning?" Jason asked hopefully.

I glanced at my watch and got up. "Ten minutes," I promised and went into the kitchen. Eggs ranchero aren't hard to make, and they are delicious. To think I'd never tasted them before we moved here. Obviously I was getting acclimated, which is not all that easy for a lifelong

Midwesterner transplanted to the border. I turned the radio to KTEP, National Public Radio in El Paso, or so I thought, and poured vegetable oil into a large frying pan. Instead of classical music, I got a news bulletin:

"We interrupt our programming for this local news item just in. Vladislav Gubenko, artistic director of Opera at the Pass and Professor of Music at the university, was found dead in his condo at Casitas del Paso this morning by a neighbor walking her dog. Retired El Paso Police Lieutenant Luz Vallejo discovered the opera director in his bedroom after following an unpleasant trail from her front yard through the open front door of his house.

"A preliminary statement from the coroner indicates that Gubenko may have aspirated his own vomit during a violent attack of stomach flu. Sergeant Arthur Guevara of Crimes Against Persons suggested that the deceased overindulged in alcohol the night before, as there was a distinctive odor of tequila at the scene.

"Gubenko's innovative staging of Verdi's *Macbeth* received its second and final performance last night at the Abraham Chavez Theater. Dr. Peter Brockman, president of Opera at the Pass said, during a telephone interview, "In the death of Professor Gubenko, our cultural establishment has suffered a great loss." I was so shocked that I broke the yolk of the third egg into the frying pan and had to scrape it out of the oil I had used to soften the tortillas.

Carolyn's Easy Eggs Ranchero

As a Middle Westerner, I always thought of breakfast as hot oatmeal on cold winter mornings, cold cereal with milk and fresh fruit in season, eggs and bacon occasionally, never spicy sausage (I didn't know there was such a thing), and an occasional venture into the exotic—cinnamon toast. Then I moved to Tex-Mex land and discovered that breakfast can be spicy enough to turn your ears pink and clear your sinuses. I highly recommend, for instance, huevos rancheros. *For brunch, you might even add margaritas or mimosas.*

- Assemble *vegetable oil, 6-inch corn tortillas, eggs, Pace Medium Picante Sauce or similar product, a wedge of longhorn cheddar cheese,* and *cilantro sprigs (optional).*

- Warm a thin layer of oil in a frying pan large enough to hold four fried eggs.

- Soften the tortillas one by one by dipping on each side in the oil. Lay the tortillas flat in a shallow grilling or roasting pan.

- While frying the eggs over easy in the remaining oil, grate the cheese. Then place one egg on each tortilla, while frying more eggs if necessary.

- Spread hot sauce over each egg and almost to the edge of any uncovered part of the tortilla.

- Sprinkle grated cheese liberally over the salsa.

- Place the pan under the broiler until the cheese melts.

- Lift each tortilla carefully onto a plate—one or two per plate—garnish with cilantro sprigs, and serve hot.

In 1947 David E. Pace set up a business in the back room of a San Antonio liquor store, where he whipped up his picante sauce and other Tex-Mex delectables, which he spent the afternoon selling around town from the back of a truck. From this folksy beginning, Pace

Foods became the top producer of Mexican salsas. Campbell Soup paid $1.115 billion for the business in 1994. Those of us who occasionally want to make easy guacamole, *chile con queso*, or eggs ranchero at home, love Pace Picante Sauce.

Carolyn Blue, "Have Fork, Will Travel,"
Milwaukee Daily News.

5

Adela Distraught

Carolyn

My huevos rancheros were very tasty. With the sun high in the sky and the temperature hovering at 70, we raised the green and white striped umbrella on the patio table and ate there, discussing the news report I'd heard on the radio. Jason had liked Vladik, mostly because of their mutual interest in opera, but also because Vladik had as little patience with long academic committee meetings as my husband. Therefore, Jason was understandably upset to hear of Vladik's death.

"And it was an undignified way to go," said my husband. "I'm not surprised all that guacamole made him sick, but I wouldn't have thought he was so drunk he couldn't keep from choking to death." He poured more coffee and took another appreciative bite of his huevos rancheros. "Opera in this town is going to take a hit. We can't expect any more performances from the university, other than degree recitals and the dinner theater, which pays for itself. Even if the funding revives, they've decided they want zarzuela, not the real thing, and God only knows how his death will affect Opera at the Pass."

"Maybe it won't. The board president didn't like the *Macbeth*. I heard him say that they should get rid of Vladik."

"Stupid," said Jason sharply. "They may not have liked the staging, but look at the principals he brought in. Can they do that on their own?"

While this conversation continued, I had other thoughts. Jason and, evidently, the police thought Vladik had succumbed to too much alcohol, or perhaps as the coroner suggested flu, but Vladik definitely hadn't had the flu, and I too had been sick—only once, but *I* hadn't had so much guacamole. The look on Adela's face when he claimed the whole bowl kept coming back to me. She'd seemed almost panic stricken as she told him that he couldn't eat it all, that it was for everyone. I had to wonder if others had been ill last night, if something had been wrong with the guacamole, and Adela had known it.

My suspicions were probably foolish, I told myself, but when a graduate student having problems in the lab called Jason to the university, I decided to pay a call on Adela. I knew the young woman well enough from the fund-raisers at which she'd sung to know that after 9/11 she'd moved from her family home in Juarez to a dorm room on campus. Security at the international bridges had become so tight that it could take hours to cross when the national alert was raised. Our students from Juarez, and there were several hundred, sometimes had to leave home in the middle of the night to insure arriving for morning classes on time.

I left a vague note on the kitchen table in case Jason got home before I did and drove over to the university dormitory. Because it was Sunday, there were no guards stopping cars without permits from entering the campus, and parking places were easy to find, unlike those near the science building or the library during the week. A student on duty at the first floor desk called upstairs and got Adela's permission to send me up. She was in her room studying for a history test.

"Adela, I loved your guacamole and just had to come over to ask for the recipe," I said disingenuously as I took a seat on her bed. "You know I write a food column."

The young woman looked uncomfortable but stammered that she could provide a recipe. "Thank you so much," I exclaimed. "Do you want to dictate it to me or—"

"I could write eet down. Ees my mother's, but she be excited eef you put eet een the newspaper."

Actually, Adela herself looked more anxious than excited, so my suspicions were reinforced. I'd have to pursue this further. While she took a piece of paper from the drawer of her desk and began to write, I asked casually, "Were you sick after the party?"

She looked up and shook her head without speaking.

"I was. But not much," I added. She looked relieved. "Still, it made me wonder. I made those canapés ahead of time, and now I'm afraid the preserves or the creamed cheese might have developed bacteria. And then, of course, there's Vladik. I suppose you heard about him."

Adela finished the recipe and handed it to me. "I have not heard from Professor Gubenko," she said very formally.

"Oh, my dear, I'm so sorry to be the person to have to tell you this, as I'm sure you were fond of him."

"I am not!" she exclaimed, and then bit her lip. "I mean—well—he ees good voice coach, but he—he—"

"He what, Adela?" I asked, concerned. What had he done to her?

"He promise me the part of Lady Macbeth, and then when I—well, later he breeng een woman from Chile."

Good grief, had he lured her into bed with promises of the leading role and then reneged when he'd had his way with her? That was an old-fashioned way of putting it, I suppose; no doubt Gwen, my daughter, would giggle if she heard my phrasing. Young people these days don't think twice about hopping into bed with one another. Not Gwen, I hope, but a professor and a student—that was another matter. Still, I was getting ahead of myself.

"I'm sure you were very disappointed," I said gently.

"I am furious. Men should not—not make the promise and then—then forget all about eet when—when a person's career may depend on—well, I was angry at heem. But I get over eet."

"Of course, you did," I agreed. "You were wonderful last night. I imagine he did that witches' trio just for you. And after all, it may have been for the best. Lady Macbeth is a very difficult role. It demands not just a lovely voice, which you certainly have, but maturity and experience. I'm sure you'll sing it one day."

"You really theenk so?" she asked wistfully.

"I certainly do, and in the meantime, you distinguished yourself last night." Good grief. I'd completely forgotten what I came for, which was not to reassure a young singer of her potential, no matter how sincere my reassurances might be. "The thing is—about Vladik."

"I suppose he ees sick too," she mumbled.

"Worse than that, Adela. He died last night."

"Died?" Her face went pale, and her lips trembled. "Ees *dead?*"

"Yes, I'm afraid so. They think he became very sick and aspirated—"

"What ees aspirate?" she demanded anxiously, wringing her hands.

"He was throwing up and choked to death on it. At least that's what the initial police report said."

"Police?" Her voice faded. "Oh, dear Holy Mother!" she whispered and dropped her face into her hands. "No one ees supposed to die," she said, sobbing. "A little sick, maybe *si.* But no dying."

"Adela?" I asked in the calmest voice I could manage. "Did you put something in the guacamole?" She nodded her head, face still covered with her hands, sobs coming faster.

"What was it?"

"I don' know," she moaned. "I tell Tia Julietta about heem. Never could I tell my mama. She would be so ashamed. I say to my tia I hope his *Macbetto* ees big failure, an' his party—eet ees horrible. An' Tia Julietta, she geeve me these powder. Herbs. *Verdad?* Just herbs. To make people a leettle sick. So they hate his party an' he get sick too. But no one meant to die!" she wailed.

"Ees not my fault. He should not eat all, an' even eef he eat all, he shouldn't die. An' Father Rigoberto, he should not offend the Holy Mother by say I make better the guacamole than her. Ees a curse on me." Her English and her common sense seemed to deteriorate as she became more upset.

"Now, I be arrest for kill him. An' the Texas, they kill me for kill Vladik when I only mean for Vladik be a leettle sick, like you gringos say—Montezuma's revenge. *Turistas* not die from Montezuma's Revenge."

"Well, Adela," I said, sighing, "you're not going to be executed. After all, as you say, you didn't mean for him to die. His dying was sort of second hand to whatever you put in the guacamole."

"You not tell police about Tia Julietta?"

Personally, I thought her aunt had no business giving an angry, hurt young woman a dangerous herbal potion. What was she, this Julietta? Some sort of witch? "We don't know that the police are going to start questioning people about the food. Maybe they'll take his death as completely accidental. But, if they do question you, Adela," I advised, "I think you should get a lawyer and let him supervise any conversations you have with the police."

"*Abogado? Si, Tio Javier es abogado.*"

"Maybe an American lawyer would be best. Unless your uncle practices in this country."

"Maybe I just go home to Mama's."

"Wouldn't that look suspicious?" I suggested.

She began to cry again.

It occurred to me that if the medical examiner did a toxicology screen on the contents of Vladik's stomach, which would surely be part of the autopsy, then the police would be questioning everyone who had provided food. That included me.

6

Questions Abound

Carolyn

Having had my appetite for Mexican food whetted by huevos rancheros at noon, I stopped by Casa Jurado, which is near the university, and ordered two #2 Mexican plates to go, a bag of tostados, and a container of salsa. A taco, a *chile relleno*, and an enchilada each in the combination plates, not to mention rice and beans, should do for dinner. Needless to say, Jason beat me home.

"Where have you been all this time?" he asked. "I've been fielding telephone calls ever since I got home."

"And I've been getting Adela's recipe for guacamole." I put the recipe and my purse down on the console in the hall. "Look, I brought dinner from Casa Jurado," I added, holding up the Styrofoam containers and the white paper bag and heading for the kitchen with our dinner.

"I'm not sure that's such a good idea," Jason muttered, following behind.

"Since when don't you like the #2 combination plate?" I took two bottles of Dos Equis from the refrigerator, poured them into the frosted mugs I keep in the freezer, and balancing the dinners on the mugs, carried them out onto the patio. Sunset in El Paso is a lovely sight—a bold wash of colors on the western horizon that never ceases to amaze me. Of course, Jason says that it's the result of dust and other pollutants in the air, but then what can you expect from a scientist? My scientist followed with napkins and tableware.

"I wasn't talking about dinner. I meant the guacamole," he said.

I eyed my husband sharply. How could he possibly know that Adela had tampered with the guacamole? "You didn't like it?"

"It was great, what little I got, but people from the party last night are calling each other to exchange stories about how sick they were when they got home. If I'm not mistaken, you were sick yourself."

I hadn't realized that my one trip to the bathroom had awakened him.

"Has to have been the guacamole," he reasoned. "The person who had the most is dead. The rest, who had less, got sick but survived, and those of us who had hardly any are okay."

Ah, the scientific mind at work, I thought, doused my taco with salsa, and ate it quickly, before dribbles of tomato and chili could fall all over my blouse or the grease from the meat make the bottom drop out of the taco and into my lap.

"It must have spoiled," said Jason. "We had an evening of avant-garde *Macbeth* and food poisoning."

For the time being I didn't enlighten Jason.

"Some police sergeant called, as well as the opera aficionados," Jason continued. He was well into his chile relleno. "Asking questions about who got sick and who provided the food. Of course, I had to tell him about your canapés, but I also mentioned that I thought it more likely the guacamole was the culprit. Pass the chips and salsa, would you? He's coming by to talk to you."

"Really? Are we suspects?" Although I usually prefer wine with dinner, there's nothing like an icy beer with Mexican food, and Dos Equis is very tasty. I heard recently that it's coming out in cans. I wonder if people will then sprinkle the can with salt and lime juice as they do Tecate, another Mexican beer. I don't care much for drinking from cans myself.

"Suspected of what?" my husband retorted. "The man choked to death on his own vomit."

"Maybe they know something we don't know. I wish I'd thought to get some of the Mexican crepes at Casa Jurado."

"They'd be soggy by the time you got them home," said Jason, and pushed the chips and salsa back in my direction. "Look at that sunset, will you? We never saw anything like that in the Midwest. Wonder what a sunset would look like if you could keep heavy metal particles suspended long enough to have an effect?"

Needless to say, I had no idea.

"Did I tell you about this article I read—think it was in *C & E News*—about how many diamonds you can produce by burning a corpse under high enough temperatures and pressures?"

"How many?" What a strange idea.

"Hmmm. Maybe five half carats for a woman, six for a man."

"That's wonderful. We should specify in our wills that our bodies be turned into diamonds. Think how thrilled Gwen would be. Someday she could tell her friends that her earrings were Mother and her bracelet—"

"It would be too expensive," said Jason, dashing my macabre fantasy.

Another round of calls began after dinner—members who had provided food and been questioned by the police. I took one from Barbara Escobar, who was in tears because she had the impression that the authorities thought she'd poisoned Vladik Gubenko with her tuna-salad-stuffed pastry puffs, her motivation—his insulting drug-dealer *Macbeth*. I assured her that their hypothesis made no sense whatever. After all, I said, she had made the puffs before she'd seen the opera, the theme of which had been kept secret from everyone but the cast. Therefore, she'd had no reason to poison the artistic director until *after* the performance.

"You're right," she cried. "I'll sue. Frank, I want you to call our lawyer."

I didn't mention that being questioned by the police wasn't grounds for a lawsuit.

Sergeant Guevara and Detective Gomez arrived at our house just after eight. Was the sergeant related to Che Guevara? I wondered after asking if they'd like to sit out on the patio and have a glass of iced tea. I presumed that it wouldn't be proper to offer beer.

They opted for the living room, being, no doubt, El Paso natives and, therefore, wimps about any temperature from the low 60s down. Jason and I sat on one blue love seat, and they sat on the other, which was placed perpendicular to ours and bordered a nice rug I'd bought in San Francisco and had shipped home.

"We understand you made some food for the party," the sergeant began.

"Yes, crackers with cream cheese and jalapeno-fruit preserves from the El Paso Chile Company," I replied.

"Oh, man," said Detective Gomez. "You tried their barbeque sauce?"

"No, is it good?" I am always interested in new food products that don't require production by me.

The sergeant glowered at his detective and reintroduced his line of questioning. "Now, folks, we'd like to know what kind of relationship you had with the deceased."

It occurred to me that I could shock the sergeant by saying, "Ménage à trois." Of course, I'd never say that, and if I did, Jason would be horrified. I restrained myself. Jason said he'd served on a university committee with Gubenko.

"And you, ma'am?" asked the sergeant.

"We all liked opera," I replied. "Did you find something lethal in his stomach contents?"

"You thinking of taking over my investigation, ma'am?"

"Well, I realize that you are being facetious, Sergeant, but as it happens I have some experience with investigatory pursuits. Just last summer, my mother-in-law was accused of murder in San Francisco, and I myself helped to find the actual murderer, who, while still on the loose, shot at me, I might add." A source of anger every time I think of it. "You have my heartfelt sympathy. It must be very trying when miscreants attempt to kill you for simply doing your duty."

Jason had rolled his eyes and leaned back against the cushions. The sergeant, who evidently suspected me of some kind of joke, cast me a flinty-eyed glance. "Would you folks call the deceased a heavy drinker?"

We looked at each other. "I don't think either of us could say," Jason answered.

"Well, you was at the party with him. How many drinks did he have that night, would you say?"

"Three, maybe four," I guessed. "Margaritas."

"Over six feet, over two hundred pounds. He couldn't have been that drunk," said the detective.

"Especially since he consumed a pound of guacamole while having his three or four drinks," Jason agreed.

I'd have preferred that he not bring up the guacamole, but there was nothing I could do about it.

"Either of you get drunk? Or sick?" asked the sergeant.

"Carolyn was sick when we got home. I wasn't," said Jason, "and neither of us was drunk."

"I'm a food columnist," I added. "I'm more interested in food than alcohol, and Jason was driving. You didn't have more than two drinks the whole evening, did you, Jason?"

"Why bother?" he replied. "The champagne was atrocious, and—"

"Did you notice that they had Tattinger's for Lady Macbeth?" I asked indignantly.

"Not in my glass," said Jason.

"Well, I guess that wraps it up," muttered the sergeant, looking disgusted.

"That wasn't very arduous," I remarked once we had seen them to the door.

Jason grinned. "What did you expect? Bamboo shoots under your fingernails?"

"I expected to be *grilled*. Obviously they don't think they're investigating a homicide."

"They don't have any reason to," said Jason. "I can't imagine why they're bothering people when they don't even know yet what they're dealing with."

"The first twenty-four hours of a case are the most important," I said knowledgeably. "If you ever watched police dramas on television, you'd know that, Jason."

"My wife, the busybody detective," he muttered.

Jason doesn't approve of my recent, if minor, involvements in amateur criminal investigation, for which reason, I seldom mention such activities to him. He just gets upset, which takes his mind off his research. Although never for long.

7
A Meeting of Incompatibles

Carolyn

Jason, of course, began Monday by leaping out of bed, donning sweats, running briskly up and down the mountain, fixing and eating a healthy breakfast, and leaving for the university. I, on the other hand, would have happily slept away the morning. I had stayed up late reading *Desert Queen*, the wonderful biography of Gertrude Bell. She was a Victorian lady who charmed Arab men and shared information on the Middle East not only with her British colleagues but also with Arab kings, sheiks, and holy men. What an astonishing and eerie book. Her experiences in Iraq before, during, and after the First World War bring a shiver to the spine of the modern American reader because it seems that the same things are happening to us that happened to the British in the Middle East eighty or so years earlier.

Be that as it may, I did not get to make up for my lost sleep because Adela called to say that the police were sure she had murdered Vladik. "What did you say to them?" I asked reproachfully.

"Nothing," she assured me. "I say I want a lawyer. They say I don't need lawyer because they are investigating Vladik's death, which ees probably the natural causes."

"So there's no problem. They really have no idea what they're investigating, Adela. They're talking to everyone who brought food to the party. Mrs. Brockman, Mrs. Escobar, me—we've all been interviewed."

"But they take my passport and my student visa," she wailed. "They say I cannot cross border, even to see my mama."

That didn't sound good to me, but I repeated my assurances and pointed out that if we (Mrs. Brockman, Mrs. Escobar, and I) had been citizens of another country, the police would have taken our credentials too. Then I advised her to attend her classes, talk to her friends, and stop worrying.

Adela immediately found a new cause for dismay: Who would be her voice coach now that Vladik was dead? I was very tempted to say that if she needed his coaching, she shouldn't have spiked the guacamole. However, I held my tongue. Even if the guacamole had made him sick, which it probably had, at least according to Jason's reasoning, Adela couldn't have foreseen that he'd eat so much, and she hadn't meant to kill him. If she'd actually meant to kill him, she wouldn't have told me that she'd put some foreign substance into the guacamole. That was *my* reasoning.

By the time I got off the phone, I was wide awake, so I had breakfast and read the newspaper, where I discovered a very interesting quotation from the neighbor who had discovered the body, a quotation resulting from a later interview by the newspaper. " 'It's possible,' said Luz Vallejo, former police lieutenant, 'that he died because someone put a pillow over his face and held it there while he was throwing up. He did the rest of his vomiting in the bathroom and over the side of the bed. So why was there vomit in the middle of the pillow? You don't bury your head in your pillow to throw up.' "

She made a good point. The police investigating the death must have seen the pillow. What did *they* think? That one of us ladies had poisoned him at the party and then snuck into his house to finish him off? I wanted to talk to Luz Vallejo. The problem was, would she talk to me? A police person, which she had been, probably wouldn't, but a retired person—well, older people, retired people, like an audience. I just had to find out where she lived.

Luz Vallejo

A blonde, white female, mid-forties, 5 feet 6 inches, 110 to 120 pounds, teal-blue pants outfit and Reeboks, arrived at my door at 10:23 Monday morning. Reporter, I surmised, although I didn't recognize her, but then I'd been retired three years so there were probably new faces at the *Times*. "My name is Carolyn Blue," she said, and she held out her hand. "I wonder if I could speak to you for a moment."

"Reporter or Avon lady?" I asked, ignoring the hand.

She looked embarrassed and took it back. "I wanted to ask you about the—crime scene? Vladislav Gubenko, the man whose dead body you discovered. I saw your name and opinion in the paper this morning and, since you aren't listed in the phone book, I just took a chance on asking around your neighborhood. You're my second try. The man on the other side was very pleasant, but didn't know you, or your husband."

"How did you get past the security guard?" I asked. Damn rent-a-cops weren't worth squat.

"I said I was visiting you," she answered.

"I didn't get any call. Did you climb over the rock wall?" I didn't think she had, but it was fun to ask. She looked pretty surprised. The call probably came while I was in the bathroom. Turn the shower on, and you couldn't hear it if a stray rocket from White Sands landed across the street.

"Me?" Carolyn Blue gave it a few seconds thought. "I don't think I could climb a rock wall if I wanted to, and I've been told that dangerous spiders lurk in El Paso walls and jump out at you. Black widows and fiddler spiders, not that I've seen either, but I certainly wouldn't care to be bitten by one. It's frightening enough to spot a scorpion in the bathroom."

"So he just let you in because, being a white Anglo, you looked harmless enough. Why do you want me to tell you about Vladik?"

"Well, I knew him—he was an acquaintance of my husband's at the university and a fellow opera lover, and the police are questioning all us opera ladies who brought refreshments to the party. I don't think my canapés made him sick. I don't even know if he ate any of mine, but I guess dangerous bacteria can grow on anything. Then I read that you thought someone might have caused the aspiration of vomit that killed him by holding a pillow over his face. Sergeant Guevara and his detective didn't say anything about that, so—well, here I am. I'd hate to think someone did that, but on the other hand, I'd hate to think my jalapeno-fruit canapés made him sick."

The woman looked at me hopefully while my knee throbbed and it occurred to me that she might never stop talking if I didn't let her in. And it would be interesting to see her expression when I described the crime scene. Talking to "opera ladies," were they? Guevara was obviously screwing up the investigation, piddling around while he waited for tox screens when he should be checking to see who hated Gubenko, besides me and the guy who wrote the editorial in the *Times*.

That must have been some performance. I read some of *Macbeth* in high school and faked the rest with the Cliffs Notes my sister had in her bookcase in college, and I couldn't picture Macbeth as a drug-dealing scumbag. Singing opera no less. *Madre de Dios,* but opera is hard to take. I never realized how bad until that asshole Russian moved in next door and turned his speakers up extra loud every night.

"Come on in," I said, holding the door open and leading her into my living room. I sat beside the little table with the drawer that holds my gun, not that I thought she was carrying, but all those years in Vice make you careful.

"This is very kind of you, Ms. Vallejo," she said sweetly.

Anything to get the weight off my knee, I thought, not so sweetly.

8

Was He Murdered?

Carolyn

Once **we were** seated in the ex-lieutenant's living room, which was sizable but didn't contain much furniture, I looked expectantly at my hostess. She looked back, but said nothing. A tall woman with medium-brown skin, a little lined at the eyes and mouth, gray-streaked, black hair cut short, wearing a denim shirt and jeans, she looked somewhat older than I, possibly fifty. Why had she retired so early? I'd read about police officers that took their retirement pay from one position and then became chiefs in small towns with a second salary, but she was home on a weekday.

"It's very kind of you to talk to me," I said, although she wasn't talking to me and I wished she'd start. "Did you know Vladik well?"

A huge police dog padded in and eyed me suspiciously. "Over here, Smack," the lieutenant said, and snapped her fingers. The dog sat down by her chair and stared at me. "I didn't want to know Gubenko well," she replied. "He tried to come on to me when he first moved in, which I didn't like and put a stop to."

Well, she was a handsome woman, although somewhat older than Vladik, I thought.

"And he played that damned music turned up past the point of pain night after night."

"I take it you don't like opera," I murmured.

"I reported him to the condo committee about four

times, and then I went over there and offered to shoot his sound system." She smiled tightly. "That made a bigger impression on him than the committee."

"You didn't!" I started to laugh, thinking of Vladik, who had obviously seen himself as a ladies' man, having to back off or lose his stereo set. I had to wonder whether she'd taken Smack with her on that visit. What a strange name to give your dog.

Luz Vallejo looked surprised and then joined me in laughter. "Dumb Russian. He should have known I couldn't shoot up his hi-fi, much less shoot anything within the city limits unless it was in self-defense."

"The police, especially since they're your former colleagues, might accept your right to protect yourself against an opera attack," I suggested.

She grinned. "So they might, but the DA, so I've heard, likes opera. So what do you want to know about the crime scene?" she asked.

"Anything you can tell me. If he simply died from food poisoning, that's one thing. Wouldn't that mean those of us who provided food aren't guilty of a crime? But if someone deliberately killed him while he was sick—well, that's murder, isn't it?"

She stretched out long legs and lit a cigarette. "The best thing about being retired," she commented, "is that you don't have to be in places where smoking's prohibited. Want one?" She offered me the pack.

"No, thank you," I replied politely.

"Hate smokers, right?" She didn't look as if she cared.

"The only time I smoked a cigarette, I threw up, and I imagine that you don't like people throwing up on your property," I answered evasively. I did, in fact, hate the smell of smoke, but I didn't want to offend her. She struck me as sort of scary, both she and her dog.

"Got that right. Gubenko parked his car in front of my place that night, one wheel on the curb, then threw up on my sidewalk and fell into my bushes. Didn't wake me, but it wasn't hard to figure out the next morning when Smack and I went out for an early morning walk. Barf all the way from my yard to the Russian's front door, and on inside, for that matter. The trail took me right to the body."

"Where was the body?" I asked.

"He was lying on his bed, face up, all the signs of suffocation. Want to know what they are?"

"No, thanks. I'll take your word for it," I answered hastily.

"Thought so," she replied. "Place smelled like a drunk tank. Vomit everywhere—in the bathroom, bedroom, hall, on him and the bedclothes. Green vomit. Were your canapés green?"

She was trying to, as my daughter would say, "creep me out." "White, red, and peach," I replied. Green was for guacamole, obviously.

"So maybe you're in the clear, unless you held the pillow over his face. As sick as he was, I suppose a woman could have held him down till he inhaled in the middle of the next retching episode."

I felt a little green myself. "And that's what you think happened? Someone held a pillow over his face instead of him dying in the—more or less natural course of things? How did they get in his house?"

"They didn't break in, if that's what you're asking. I checked while I was waiting for the medics and cops to arrive. Either the killer had a key, or the Russian left the door open. Probably the last. It was open when I got there the next morning. If the killer had a key, he'd have been smart to lock up after himself, so it would look like Gubenko died alone. And that's not what I figure happened. The pillow was on the floor, vomit-side up, the indentation of his face still in it, and he was on his back."

"Then why aren't the police investigating that instead of chasing after us?" I asked.

"One, what Guevara is doing is the easy way, talking to respectable ladies while he waits for the tox screens to come in. Two, I told him what I figured happened, and he brushed it off because there's bad blood between us. If I told him there was a guy with a knife behind him, he wouldn't turn around or run. He's lazy and stupid." Her dog started to growl. "It's okay, Smack," she said, patting his head. "Just because I'm pissed off doesn't mean you have to bite someone."

"Is he dangerous?" I asked nervously.

"She. She's a retired narcotics dog. Her partner couldn't keep her when she got too old for duty because the partner had to get a new dog, so I took her in. But old Smack here could do some damage if I told her to, and if you'd come in with pot in your pocket, you'd have seen some action."

"How fortunate that I don't use illegal drugs," I murmured weakly.

"Right. She jumped a kid at a high school the other day. I was there giving a talk. Kid was dealing coke and had a couple of ounces on him. Smack held him up against the wall, while I called in the troops. Of course, they had a cop undercover there who had enough to arrest him, so the dealer just got caught a little early. Any more questions?"

"I guess not," I said.

"And what are you going to do with the information?"

"Well, since you don't seem to think Sergeant Guevara is going to catch the killer, I guess I'll ask around about any enemies Vladik might have had. I'd hate to see people harassed by the police when a real criminal actually killed him."

Luz Vallejo laughed. "You're going to investigate this yourself? Well, that's a hoot."

I could have told her that I wasn't inexperienced when it came to investigation, but I didn't. She'd hurt my feelings, and I didn't care to be laughed at again.

9

Indignant Ladies Unite

Carolyn

I drove home to think about my next move, if, in fact, I wanted to make a next move. Lieutenant Vallejo had thought the idea "a hoot," and Jason would be upset if he thought I was getting involved in another murder investigation. On the other hand, my life had been much more exciting of late, much more interesting. Writing about food is all very well, but one doesn't really use one's powers of logical thinking, and one doesn't really make a difference in the world, only in a meal or two somewhere in the country.

Not that I'm ungrateful for the syndicated newspaper column on eating out that I more or less fell into and the book on eating out in New Orleans that I recently sent off to the publisher. I pulled into the driveway and started toward the front door, thinking of whom I might interview if I decided to look for the person who held the pillow over Vladislav Gubenko's face. Before I could even sit down to make a list, I noticed that my answering machine was blinking. I pressed the Play button and heard the following:

"Carolyn, this is Vivian Brockman. I'm getting the women who made refreshments for the party together. I think we should protest this ridiculous harassment by the police. Lunch at the Magic Pan on Doniphan at twelve-thirty. I'm reserving a table on the patio. If you get this message in time, please come."

I glanced at my watch and left the house, calculating that I'd only be five or ten minutes late, which would leave me time for their wonderful tortilla soup and a half sandwich. What did Vivian have in mind as a protest? Letters to the editor of the *Times?* Picketing the police station? Confronting Sergeant Guevara? Hiring a lawyer? One of the women who had provided food was married to a lawyer, so maybe we could get pro bono representation. And what would our suit against the police allege? Interfering with our civil rights? Slander? I've never sued anyone, so I had no idea.

Five women had preceded me, ordered, and were sipping iced tea. I sat down after greeting them and took in the ambiance. I'm very fond of the Magic Pan. Their patio has vines, greenery, ceiling fans, and a mister, so you can eat outside, even in hot weather—although not during high winds and dust storms, or when it turns cold. On those less frequent occasions, you eat inside where they sell interesting "antique" doodads and jewelry. I love jewelry so was glad to be outside and away from temptation. Bad enough that I was surfing the Internet for an area rug to put in the family room. I hadn't mentioned this pursuit to Jason yet. He was still muttering about a rug I bought in San Francisco, although I'm delighted with that purchase. I love colorful rugs, and our floors are tiled here in El Paso so they need a bit of softening underfoot.

Now who, among the food providers at the opera party, had come to the meeting? I glanced around the table. Vivian, who had provided a mountain of shelled shrimp (available at the Albertson's for a price) and a spicy sauce; Dolly Montgomery, little rolled sandwiches with a chile-cheese spread inside (Jason said he thought they'd come from the university catering service, about which I wish I'd known); Barbara Escobar, tiny pastry puffs stuffed with tuna salad; Olive Cleveland, a cauldron of very good chile con queso with a burner to keep it warm; and Maria-

Reposa Hernandez, mixed hors d'oeuvres from the Portable Fiesta. Her husband was the lawyer.

I ordered, as planned, a cup of tortilla soup and a half Lone Star sandwich. If I'd ordered a bowl of the soup, I wouldn't have been able to eat dinner. It has a rich, spicy broth and is crammed with veggies, chicken, tortilla strips, and melted cheese. I'd have eaten every delicious bite in the bowl and been uncomfortably stuffed. Not that the Lone Star sandwich isn't good as well. The Magic Pan has an array of sandwiches with a wonderful raspberry-chipotle sauce slathered on the buns. The meat in the Lone Star is, as you might expect, beef.

I'm told that cattle, not to mention sheep and goats, once grazed on long grass in our area. There are still ranches, but the cattle now have to walk their poor legs off to find enough grass to get them through the day. As far as I know, cattle don't eat cactus. People do, but I have yet to treat myself to that pleasure. For all I know, some of the prickly things in my yard are edible and I should be harvesting them and putting them up like a good pioneer woman. Ha!

"I want to go inside," said Barbara Escobar, the youngest among us. She has that heavy, dark hair with absolutely no split ends to disturb the patina. Her skin is smooth and quite light; I've heard her make disdainful remarks about Mexican Americans with dark skin and obvious Indian heritage, like Luz Vallejo, who is a handsome woman, in my opinion. How determined people seem to be to distinguish themselves from others on the basis of the smallest differences in skin color.

"It's freezing out here," Barbara complained.

She probably enjoyed the summer heat, although I couldn't imagine it. I'd heard that August had produced a temperature of 106 degrees. Fortunately, I wasn't in El Paso last summer to experience it. I'd probably have turned my thermostat to seventy and refused to leave the house. Peter Brockman claims that his solar house, situated properly in relation to the sun, heavily insulated, and possessed of thick walls and deeply overhanging eves, doesn't need air conditioning at all.

I'd been fascinated to hear this, having read that the Spanish colonists had oriented their haciendas by jamming sticks into the ground and studying the shadows before placing a house that would fend off both heat and cold. My interest, based on our high electric rates for refrigerated air conditioning, had dissipated when Vivian Brockman said, "No matter what Peter thinks, I keep the air conditioner on from April to November."

"Well, are we going to move inside?" Barbara demanded. The others had continued to chat while she complained.

It was only in the mid 60s, bracingly comfortable to my mind, but they agreed with Barbara, so we picked up our glasses and moved into the big room with its huge stone fireplace and plank tables supported by the bases of antique sewing machines. All the chairs were mismatched, the tables sporting flowered place mats, the windows ornamented with shutters and stained glass insets, and the decor finished off by a dark red carpet spotted with tiny white flowers. It is a charming room, but I had to turn my head as we passed the jewelry counters.

"I think we should start the meeting," said Vivian, taking what appeared to be an old oak library chair and patting her densely curled gray hair. If she'd only known, her coiffure resembled a mini afro. "The only others who provided food," she said, "are working women or students, so they probably won't be coming."

That explained why Adela Mariscal hadn't answered the summons.

"Are we all agreed that the police have treated us outrageously?" Most of the ladies nodded. The several, including me, who had been served sandwiches, were distracted by the difficulty of keeping the ingredients inside the rolls. Raspberry-chipotle sauce is yummy, but also very slippery. I always hold my sandwich in two hands, which leads to sticky fingers but spares my clothing.

"We've committed no crime," Vivian said indignantly. "It's not a crime to provide refreshments for a fund-raising event."

"Still, Martin says we could be sued by Vladik's estate," warned Maria-Reposa. "Well, Opera at the Pass can be sued, as well as the rest of us. In my case, Portable Fiesta could be sued, and the university through Dolly. Carolyn used preserves from the El Paso Chile Company, so they might be liable. It depends on what made Vladik sick. But it's a civil action I'm talking about. I don't know about criminal actions; Martin doesn't do criminal."

A hubbub of dismay arose among the ladies. They couldn't imagine being arrested for a crime, but they could imagine being sued; professors, doctors, lawyers, all kinds of people could be and are sued. Anyone of us, except Maria-Reposa, could be sued by her husband, or represented by him. What a putative windfall for the Hernandezes. I certainly hoped Jason and I wouldn't fall into Martin's clutches. I didn't even like the man. He had once told me that if Jason were ever sued for sexual harassment, he'd be glad to take the case. I was more insulted by him than by Sergeant Guevara and his disappointingly short interrogation.

"Actually," I said, speaking above the babble of female voices, "although Vladik may have suffered from food poisoning, that was undoubtedly inadvertent." Shame on me because I couldn't resist adding, "Which would be manslaughter rather than homicide, wouldn't it?"

They all looked alarmed.

"Or maybe negligent homicide. I haven't lived in Texas long enough to know what the terms are." So much for my little moment of antic humor. I wouldn't have said those things to Adela. She'd have died of fright, since she was the person guilty of inadvertent poisoning—she and the greedy victim.

"However, there's another possibility, or perhaps I should say added possibility. If you read the morning paper, you'll have noticed that a retired policewoman, his neighbor, found the body, and she thinks someone put a pillow over his face while he was throwing up, whether to suffocate him or to cause what actually happened, the aspiration of his own vomit, she wouldn't know, I suppose, but that *would* be murder. Unfortunately, the sergeant in charge of the case either doesn't believe it or is too lazy to pursue a more complicated investigation."

"I move that we confront the sergeant and insist that he find out who really killed Vladik," said Barbara Escobar.

"We could make a list of people who might have hated him enough to do that," I suggested. *Since I'll be making such a list myself, I might as well get their input,* I thought. *They all knew him to some degree.* "Can anyone think of a name?"

Barbara laughed. "Well, Peter comes to mind. He said to Frank at the party that they really needed to get rid of Vladik. I don't think any of us liked the *Macbeth.*"

"Howard liked it," said Dolly. "He was pleased to see three witches instead of a whole chorus."

"Then we won't put Howard down," I said, smiling and taking a pad and pen from my purse in case anyone came up with another name. "And Jason was friendly with Vladik, besides which Jason was in bed with me when the deed was done."

"Good gracious," exclaimed Olive. "We're looking at our own husbands first? Well, mine was in Chicago. He was supposed to see the Friday performance, but I had to go by myself, and I only came over to the party Saturday long enough to leave the chile con queso and chips."

"That reminds me, Olive, your pot is in my car," said

Maria-Reposa. "As for Martin, I don't think he's met Vladik. I don't remember introducing them at the party."

Maria-Reposa was the committee member, not her husband. She had also donated a seamstress from Juarez to work on costumes, not to mention quite a bit of money.

"Frank, who couldn't stand either Vladik or the performance, was at my side, snoring like a recalcitrant mule all night," said Barbara.

"Perhaps he has sleep apnea," suggested Vivian, the doctor's wife. "You should send him to the sleep clinic at Providence Memorial. As for Peter, poor man, he was called out for emergency surgery shortly after we got home. Some drunken driver, not wearing a seat belt, who smashed his car into a telephone pole and his head into the windshield, I think he said. And of course, that wasn't what Peter meant by 'get rid of.' He meant fire the fellow, revoke his contract, something civilized."

"I know someone," said Dolly. "This may sound ridiculous, but Howard told me that a geologist actually threatened to kill Vladik for sleeping with his wife. I didn't hear it myself and don't remember the name, but I'm sure we could find out. He should make an excellent suspect and distract the sergeant. I was digging up spring bulbs when the police came to my house, and I was so upset by Sergeant Guevara's attitude that I never did get back to the bulbs. I'm going to send them to my daughter. What with water rationing, it's just too much trouble, not to mention wasteful, to get them going in the spring."

"Oh, that was Brandon Collins, the geologist, you're talkin' about, honey bunch," drawled Olive. "He's all bark an' no bite."

Olive is from East Texas and has that distinctive Southern accent and golden curls, probably rinsed to keep out the gray. I've been rinsing my hair so long that I'm not sure whether or not I have any gray hair yet. Olive's husband calls her Olive Ann.

"Professor Collins did have his hand on a nasty-looking, pointed hammer when he made the threat," I murmured, and I wrote his name down after Peter Brockman, which I'd crossed out. I'd forgotten all about the geologist.

"Let the police go looking for people who had reason to kill Vladik," said Vivian. "They can talk to his colleagues in the music department at the university, his students, maybe fellow Russians, if there are any. Obviously, none of us would be involved. All in favor of confronting Sergeant Guevara as soon as we have dessert, say, 'Aye.'"

We all said 'aye' and studied our dessert menus. I was torn between the chocolate brownie and the lemon square, but settled for the latter. Very tasty too.

10

Indignant Ladies vs. Sergeant Guevara

Carolyn

Vivian Brockman called ahead to police headquarters at Five Points to announce that a delegation of six ladies would arrive within the half hour to talk to Sergeant Guevara. She was told that if he were called out in the interim, she'd have to talk to someone else. Fine, she said; the committee would talk to his commander, whoever that was, but the committee *would* be heard. I listened in on this conversation while jotting notes on people to interview if Guevara didn't take the hint: the geologist, music professors and students, fellow Russians. There were some at the university. I didn't know about the rest of El Paso.

Then we all went to our separate cars; no one uses public transportation in El Paso if they don't have to because the buses and bus air conditioning break down during hot weather. I imagine historical modes of transportation in El Paso would have been more comfortable in hot weather than a sealed, unairconditioned bus—the Butterfield Stage, for instance, which first arrived here in 1858, or the mule-drawn streetcars starting in 1882. They circled the downtown here and in Juarez until 9:00 in the evening, although their drivers felt free to get off in mid trip to deliver messages and shop. The streetcars were eventually mechanized and then discontinued entirely in the 1970s. The economic benefits anticipated by Mexico did not materialize, but maid service in El Paso became a thing of the past for some years because the women couldn't get over here from Juarez. Thank goodness there are other means to get across the border now.

It seemed that ladies going to lunch not only don't use public transportation, but also don't carpool, at least not these ladies. Six cars pulled out of the parking lot and headed in different directions. Evidently there was a way to get to Five Points without turning left across traffic on Doniphan. I wished that I had followed someone who took the easier route, for I was the last person to arrive at the police parking lot.

It was fortunate, I thought, while driving up North Mesa, that Vivian hadn't gotten hold of the sergeant himself. *The committee would be heard?* He'd have taken that amiss, not being, in my experience, a very pleasant person. And he'd be angry that Luz Vallejo had talked to the newspaper, although that was her problem, and that we'd read her opinion and been moved to bother him with our concerns.

I arrived in the area of the university and wondered where to turn left. Montana seemed like a good idea. It was a main thoroughfare. Of course, I got lost and had to stop at a gas station to ask for directions. The attendant didn't speak English and looked very irritated that I spoke so little Spanish. *"Donde está policia?"* I asked. He shrugged and pointed to a police car passing by. Stymied, I ran after it and caught up at a light, where I skirted a car in the right lane so that I could knock on the patrol car window. I hate running, but the officers did know how to get to Five Points. In fact, they were headed there and waited so that I could follow them, right to the entrance of the area for police parking. Officer Cobos then got out and walked back to tell me that I couldn't follow any further; I'd have to circle around to the public lot. Ah, me.

Then, of course, there was the crowded situation in the public lot and the questions about where I had been when

I got inside and the complaints from the ladies about being kept waiting while Sergeant Guevara was located. I imagined that he was hiding out in the men's room, or had escaped out the back door as the ladies filtered in. However, he did appear after ten minutes or so and eyed our group with disfavor.

"Can't get the whole bunch of you in my office," he said. "What's this about? Someone come to confess and needs moral support from the girls?"

What a rude man. "I'm sure you have a conference room," I suggested mildly.

"What's going on here?" asked a uniformed, middle-aged man, who had just entered the reception area. He had lots of military bits and pieces sewn to his shirt.

"Just about to chat with a delegation of civilians, Commander," said Guevara.

"Use my office if you want. I'm on my way to City Hall." Then he smiled at Maria-Reposa and asked jocularly, "Martin planning to sue the city again?"

She smiled and replied, "If the city behaves itself, he won't have to, will he?"

And that's how we overcame the sergeant's objections to seeing us and ended up sitting on blue chairs with the sergeant seated uncomfortably behind the commander's desk and keeping a wary eye on Maria-Reposa, whom he took to be a person of influence.

Vivian launched, none too tactfully, into our mission. "It seems, Sergeant, that while you were out harassing ladies who donated food to raise funds for opera in El Paso, an excellent cause I'm sure we'd all agree, and one supported by a good many influential people, my husband among them . . ." She lost track of her thought or her sentence structure at that point, so she glared at him while she recollected herself. "Mrs. Blue—" She nodded in my direction. "—noted an interesting story in the *Times*. It seems, Sergeant, that Vladislav Gubenko, our late artistic director, died not of refreshments we provided, but because someone entered his house and smothered him with a pillow."

"Bull," said the sergeant, offending a number of us. He was very angry. "He died from choking on puke, and he was puking because someone food-poisoned him, and the food he'd been eating was stuff you ladies brought."

"The contents of his stomach have been analyzed, then?" I couldn't help asking. Even if they found the substance that made Vladik sick, could the tests tell them which party food had contained it? If so, poor Adela. This buffoon with his unpleasant language would keep harping on the food and ignore the pillow.

"Tox screens aren't back yet, but they'll show he was poisoned."

"Will they show that the food poisoning, if any, was inadvertent, Sergeant?" asked Maria-Reposa softly. "I'm sure that no person in this group would deliberately cause injury to another person. We're all perfectly respectable." She smiled at him. "Wives of a doctor, a lawyer, a banker, two university professors, and the owner of several local businesses."

"Yes, ma'am," he said, more polite because he knew that the commander thought well of her, or perhaps the sergeant was impressed by the credentials of our husbands. Obviously the police end of justice is not necessarily blind. "But you mustn't pay much mind to what you read in the papers, ma'am. That's just guesswork."

"The person who was quoted is a retired police lieutenant," I pointed out.

"It was a woman," snapped the sergeant.

"So are we," said Vivian. "Are you saying that women are not to be trusted?"

I was afraid that he might answer that and interrupted to say, "Her expertise was evidently in Vice. Surely, a Vice lieutenant would have seen a good deal of violence and have opinions that can be respected."

"And I'm in Crimes Against Persons," he retorted, "so I'd take my opinion over someone else's because I know what I'm doing. Now, you ladies don't have anything to worry about until the tox screens come in, and I've got a lot of cases to investigate, thirty on my desk at this minute, so unless you know for sure someone attacked that Russian with a pillow and can give me a lead on who it was, I need to be getting back to my desk." He stood up, an irritatingly smug look on his face.

We glanced at each other, and then Dolly Montgomery said, "Well, I hate to be a snitch, but my husband told me about someone who threatened to kill Mr. Gubenko the night of the party."

Guevara looked somewhat taken aback. Evidently his investigation hadn't turned that story up. "How did Gubenko react to the threat?" he asked suspiciously.

Dolly looked to us because she didn't know. "He said he felt sick," I replied, "and then he went home."

"Sounds like a couple of guys having an argument. Don't necessarily mean anyone meant to kill anyone else. Like you said, Gubenko was already sick. You think this guy put something in his food and *then* threatened to kill him?"

"The man accused Vladik of sleeping with his wife," said Barbara Escobar, obviously relishing the scandal. "Isn't that a motive for murder? Don't you even want to know the man's name?"

"Okay," Guevara replied sarcastically. "What's his name?"

"I don't know," said Barbara. "Carolyn, what's his name?"

Like Dolly, I hated to rat on a professor, even if he had been carrying a dangerous-looking hammer. I hesitated, and Olive said, "His name's Brandon Collins. He's a geology professor, an' he wouldn't hurt a flea. He leads our amateur rock-huntin' hikes into the Franklins. A lovely man. He can't be blamed for bein' a little bit upset now an' then when his wife is a silly twit like Melanie."

"Brandon Collins," grumbled Guevara, writing it down. "He with the university?" Three of us nodded glumly. "Any other suspects?"

No one answered, so Vivian said sharply, "It's your job to find suspects, not ours. We came to see that you do it."

"I know how to do my job, lady," Guevara retorted. "I just gotta be left to get on with it."

"Then do so, sergeant. And I must say, I don't like your attitude. Doesn't our El Paso training academy teach officers to be courteous to the tax-paying public?"

Tortilla Soup

One of my favorite soups is tortilla soup, and one of my favorite places in El Paso to eat it is the Magic Pan in Placitas Santa Fe, a colorful shopping center full of boutiques where you can buy interesting things or just window shop. Owner-chef Annette Lawrence provided this recipe.

- Cut *2 white corn tortillas* in ¼-inch x 2-inch strips. Deep-fry strips in *vegetable oil* until crisp and set aside.

- Place *3 boneless chicken breasts* in 4½ cups *boiling water* with *1 teaspoon salt* and ½ *teaspoon black pepper*. Boil 10 minutes; remove from pot to cool, and dice when breasts can be handled. Reserve broth.

- In a medium-sized pot, sauté *1½ cups peeled, chopped white onion* in *1 tablespoon olive oil* until onions are translucent.

- Puree *2 canned chipotle peppers with sauce* (more if you like your soup very spicy) in 1 cup of reserved chicken broth.

- Add puree and rest of reserved chicken broth to sautéed onions.

- Add *1 cup chopped tomatoes (seeds and juice removed)*, diced chicken, and *½ cup chopped cilantro.*

- Bring to a boil and simmer 15 minutes. Test for seasoning.

- Ladle into four bowls, add tortilla strips, sprinkle with *1 cup shredded Monterey Jack or cheddar cheese,* and top with *1 peeled, sliced avocado* (optional unless you're making tlapeno soup). Serves four.

Carolyn Blue, "Have Fork, Will Travel,"
Burlington Daily Register.

11
Sources of Information

Luz

You'd think with all the frigging medication I take, I wouldn't have to resort to smelly creams, but there I was, middle of the afternoon, hadn't done anything but walk the dog and surf the web, and my knee was swollen and aching, so I was rubbing in some damn goop made from jalapeno chiles, hoping to get a little relief.

Of course, I shouldn't have cut back on the shots, but the stuff costs a frigging fortune, and I was doing so well, I thought I could afford to take fewer. Now I'd have to go out bounty hunting again, catch myself someone with a big reward on his head, that or sell the condo, or end up a cripple like the first time.

"Get away, Smack. You know and I know that I'm not rubbing cocaine into my knee, and you're not getting a reward for finding capsaicin cream." The dog hung her head and sank down beside my chair.

Given the circumstances, I wasn't in a very good mood when the phone rang and that asshole Guevara wanted to know what I thought I was doing screwing with his case by talking to the newspaper and siccing a bunch of dumb women on him when he had work to do. "Not like I get to sit around the house, watching TV and living off my retirement," he snarled.

"Up yours, Guevara," I replied, but I had to wonder who the dumb women were who'd come to visit him.

Maybe the same one who came to visit me. She was the only person who'd shown any interest in my theory of Gubenko's death. At the time Guevara had sneered and told me to mind my own business because I wasn't on the force anymore, and good riddance. Nice guy. I should have shoved his ugly face into a puddle of vomit. God knows there was plenty of it around that morning. Problem was I know better than to screw up a crime scene. "I don't suppose you thought to take fingerprints from his condo—just in case I got it right, and he had an unfriendly visitor that night," I added.

"I got fingerprints up the wazoo," he snapped. "They just don't match nothin'."

"So ask around," I snapped back. "That wasn't any ordinary barf-in-the-windpipe death. Either the killer gave him something to make him sick and then made sure he died of it, or it was a crime of opportunity, but it sure as hell wasn't some bad-luck death. I saw that pillow. What'd you do? Throw it out so you wouldn't have to work the case?"

"Screw you, Vallejo."

"Back at you." I was tired of this conversation.

"Say, how's the joints? Looked to me like you was limpin' Sunday. Hate to think you're getting worse." He laughed and hung up.

I threw the phone across the room. Smack, thinking the game was on, ran after it and brought it back, then shook her head playfully when I tried to retrieve the sucker. I raised my hands in surrender. "Keep it," I said. She didn't know what to do. I was changing the rules.

Carolyn

As I pulled out of the parking lot, I assumed that Sergeant Guevara wouldn't even question Professor Collins, which was, perhaps, just as well. Although the geologist had threatened Vladik, it seemed to me that he was much more likely to have gone home and yelled at his wife than followed her lover to his condo and smothered him with a pillow. The couple had continued the argument after Vladik's departure, at least for a while. All the rest of us escaped as fast as we could because the incident was so embarrassing. And maybe—what was her name?—Melanie hadn't been unfaithful and had managed to convince her husband of her innocence and—oh well, I didn't even know them. Olive had said the wife was a twit, which was probably true if she'd had an affair with Vladik, who had obviously been a one-night-stand sort of man.

Which reminded me of Adela. Perhaps I should stop by the dorm to see if she knew anyone who had hated him, besides herself, and she'd already confessed to her part in the crime, if it was a crime. I found North Mesa without getting lost again, then turned left at the light at Schuster, and drove to the back university entrance. Without argument, the guard gave me a pass to park and visit the dorm. He probably thought I was the mother of the Adela Mariscal I cited as my reason for coming on campus. Or maybe not. I was blonde and Adela had black hair and darker skin than mine. Also she was a graduate student. My children weren't in graduate school yet, although Chris would undoubtedly follow that path. Who knew what Gwen, a drama student presently studying Miro sets in Barcelona, would do when she graduated. Anything but become an actress, if my mother-in-law had her way.

Adela was in her room and distressed to see me. "Something happen, no?" she cried.

"No. You missed a nice luncheon at the Magic Pan, and then we went over and picked on Sergeant Guevara for bothering us when there's a murderer out there to catch."

"Me?" she squeaked. "You told him that I—"

"The person in Vladik's house. With the pillow."

"Oh. Three, four months since I visit his house. Couldn't be me."

"The thing is, Adela, you did know him. You must have seen him every day." She shook her head. "Well, often. At the department. Can you think of anyone who really disliked him?"

"Me," she replied bitterly.

"Besides you. Maybe someone he got into a fight with. Or someone who complained about him."

She shook her head.

"Can you think of anyone who might know? With whom was he friends? Anyone who might know his business." I was beginning to think that it was hopeless. Adela, although formerly smitten, didn't really seem to know much about the man who had made promises he didn't keep. "Other students?"

She shrugged. "Maybe the Russian girls. Who sing with me in *trio de las brujas.*" I must have looked puzzled. "Witches," she explained.

"Oh, yes. I know I was introduced, but I can't remember their names. Do they live in the dorm too?"

"No, in trailer park, I think. Maybe Vladik get them place and car. They have old car. I don't see them, only at music department. Polya and Irina."

I took out my notebook and looked at her expectantly.

"Polina Mikhailov and Irina Primakov. Vladik get them visas and into school."

As Adela had no more information for me and no address for the two young Russian singers, I reassured her once more about her own situation and went to the music department—what a rabbit's warren the "new" performing arts building is! Once there, I told the secretary that I was a member of an Opera at the Pass committee and wanted to give little gifts of appreciation to the students who had sung in our production of *Macbeth*.

"Oh, wasn't it terrible about Professor Gubenko," she exclaimed. "I couldn't believe it when I heard he was dead.

Those Russian girls must be feeling so sad and lonely. They were his protégés." However, sympathetic as she felt, she wasn't allowed to give out student addresses. She did tell me where they could be found tomorrow after their last class. Evidently they had the same schedule.

Miner's Hall. Where was that? Probably one of the old buildings, the first of the Bhutanese structures suggested by some lady who read a National Geographic article about Bhutan and got hooked, or some such thing. The thick walled structures with their slanting, stuccoed exteriors and tiled roofs do go well with our desert mountain terrain, and the decorative tiling is a bit Southwestern. In fact, the university has a compact and pretty campus, with little gardens of desert vegetation here and there and hundreds of little white lights strung everywhere at Christmas.

I'd catch the Russian girls tomorrow at eleven-thirty and offer to take them out for lunch. Did they like Mexican food? I was doing a series of columns on it, so the lunch would be tax deductible if they were agreeable.

I asked Jason at dinner that night if he'd witnessed the scene between Vladik and Melanie and Brandon Collins. He hadn't. Then I asked if he knew Collins. He did. Finally, I asked if he thought Collins could have murdered Vladik over his wife's alleged infidelity.

"I wouldn't think so. He seems a nice enough fellow," said Jason. "The administration loves him because he does all this community outreach work, but why don't you ask him yourself? Geology is in the old library. The big building across Hawthorne from the Student Union." I must have given him a look of astonishment because he added, "Oh, I can imagine what you're up to. You feel you have to find out just what happened to Vladik."

"Well, I—just thought I'd ask around. The police don't seem to be—"

"Feel free," said my husband, the worrywart, waving a hand. "I've given up thinking I can tell you what to do."

"Well, Jason, it's not as if—"

"It's okay, Carolyn. And now I've got to get back to the lab."

"Again?" I asked, disappointed. I'd had all sorts of historical tidbits I wanted to pass on from my reading of El Paso history—for instance, the fact that students at the School of Mines, an early university incarnation, had crossed the river in 1929 when General Jose Escobar and his rebels were attacking Juarez. The students acted as volunteer stretcher-bearers. Evidently young men, even intelligent ones, just can't resist a war. I'd have to keep my eye on Chris. The students weren't the only people not satisfied to observe the fighting from the north side of the river; reporters and ordinary citizens with Kodak cameras crossed the Rio Grande to get in on the excitement. They had to be quick about it because that particular rebellion was a very short one.

12
Talking Dirty

Carolyn

I was in bed asleep before Jason returned home, which was unusual. *His research must be going badly,* I had thought drowsily before drifting off again. Still, when I awoke, he was already up and gone, as attested to by his cereal dish in the sink. I was up a little early myself and decided to pay a call on Professor Brandon Collins before catching the Russian girls outside their last morning class. After all, hadn't Jason said at dinner, "Why don't you ask him yourself?"

Why not, indeed? I replied to my absent husband, and drove off to the university after a breakfast of toast, yogurt, and coffee, which seemed a better choice to me than the typical ancient Aztec breakfast of maize porridge with chile peppers and honey. They ate this meal at around ten in the morning after having been up working on empty stomachs since sunrise, or earlier. The idea of getting up at sunrise is even worse than their breakfast, in my opinion. I never can understand why people are given to saying how much they'd rather have lived in some earlier century. Obviously, they never read any history.

I found a parking place on the university campus in the area reserved for visitors to the Administration Building and walked across the street to what is now the Geology Building. It has a sort of Florida art deco look, while still retaining some of the Bhutanese features found elsewhere on campus. On one of the floors is a lovely meeting room at which I'd attended a reception. In the building's previous life as a library, that room had been the reference section, or so I'd been told. It must have been very pleasant to peruse reference books in such an impressive setting. The reference section of the new library is rather utilitarian except for some comfortable seating, and the library itself is a large hulk that, for some reason, brings to mind a Southwestern-style prison, albeit decorated in front with a sculpture of organ pipes.

All this architectural ruminating accompanied my search for the geology secretary, who informed me that Professor Collins was in but, she warned, not in a very good mood. Perhaps, in that case, it was not a good time to confront him with questions as to whether he had murdered Vladik. On the other hand, if I delayed when I had gotten this far, I might never find the nerve again, so I followed her directions to his office and knocked on his open door, through which I could see that he seemed to be examining a chunk of nondescript rock with a magnifying glass.

"What?" he asked in answer to my knock.

I advanced into the office and replied, when he looked up, "My name is Carolyn Blue. I wonder if I might have a minute of your time."

"Jason Blue's wife?" He stared at me with a puzzled look, as if I too were a rock of some minor interest. When I nodded, he waved me to a chair. "What can I do for you, Mrs. Blue?"

There was a bigger rock resting on the visitor's chair. I had to remove it before I could sit, but once I had lifted it, with some difficulty, I didn't know what to do with it.

"Oh, sorry," he muttered. "Just put it down—" He looked around his cluttered office space. "Put it down on those papers," he suggested, pointing to a haphazard pile on one corner of his desk. "I've seen you somewhere, haven't I?" He was still staring quizzically. "Oh God, you were part of that crowd at the opera do when my wife and I got into it."

"Yes," I admitted. "When you threatened to kill Professor Gubenko."

"Did I?" he murmured, frowning. "My memory of that night is sort of vague, but I suppose I might have."

Did he mean he might have killed Vladik? Or that he might have threatened to do so? I took a deep breath and came out with my question. "This may seem rather rude, Professor Collins, but I'd like to ask if, in fact, you did follow Professor Gubenko home and carry out your threat."

"You mean kill him?" he asked, looking astonished. "Of course, I didn't kill him, although I do think there ought to be a law against men who seduce women as half witted as my wife. But then there ought to be a law against supposedly intelligent professors who fall in love with their students when they have perfectly good wives at home, especially students dumb enough to make a D in Geology. I must have been out of my mind." He put down his rock and his magnifying glass.

"Now my two perfectly nice children are living in Oxford, Mississippi, in the home of their stepfather, who teaches botany at Ole Miss. Probably studies kudzu. It's a plant that's completely taken over the northern section of the state. And my perfectly acceptable first wife lives there as well and has actually taken an interest in football. The whole family attends the football games of—I've forgotten what Ole Miss calls its football team. Probably Kudzu. The Rampaging Kudzus, or some damn thing. My kids are going to wake up some morning and find they can't get out of the house because the kudzu has walled them in. Then I won't get to see them even two times a year."

He stared glumly at a framed picture on his desk. I couldn't see it but assumed that it might be of his children, or even his ex-wife, children, and the stepfather.

"And in the meantime I'm stuck with an unfaithful wife who has the brains of a prairie dog."

"Are you so sure that she was unfaithful?" I asked.

"Damn right she was. Had that son of a bitch sleeping in my bed while I was out in Mexico with a bunch of students on a fucking field trip. If the Mexican cops hadn't run us off because of bandits or some damn thing, I'd probably never have found out what the dumb bitch was up to. Should have bribed the Mexicans and stayed, but the university frowns on students getting shot by rebels or bandits or whatever they were. If there were any."

"Actually," I said, "Mexico can be quite a dangerous place for visiting Americans. In 1916 when our government recognized the Carranza government in Mexico City, Pancho Villa was so angry that he killed sixteen American mining engineers and shipped their bodies to El Paso. The arrival of the caskets came close to causing a race riot, the Anglos attacking the Mexican American population."

"No shit!" said Professor Collins. "I never heard that story. I wonder if the engineers were from the old School of Mines."

"I'm not sure. I do know that in 1927 the School of Mines and a community college united to add liberal arts courses, and with them female students. The engineers, according to the book I read, were very unhappy with the change because they could no longer attend classes in carpet slippers and undershirts."

"They'd have had better reasons than that to want women kept out," he muttered angrily.

"Just because you were on a field trip doesn't mean that your wife—"

"Mrs. Blue, that's exactly what it means," he retorted impatiently. "I got home two nights early and found a note on my pillow, in Russian, no less. With a translation. 'I am in shower. Wake up, beautiful heart, and we make love all over again with soap and hot water.' I was so pissed I didn't even bother to wash off the sweat and trail dust, just headed out to the opera party and caught him sampling my wife's ear and a bowl of guacamole. And she was embarrassed, for Christ's sake, because I wasn't dolled up in a tux like her fuckin' Russian lover, who deserves—" He stopped his tirade after taking a close look at me.

"I'll be damned. My language embarrasses you, doesn't it?"

"I guess you'll think me old fashioned, but I do prefer not to be sworn at," I responded.

"Hey, I wasn't swearing at *you*. That's kind of nice, you know. A woman who doesn't like dirty language. Talking dirty turned Melanie on. Well, you asked if I followed Gubenko home. I didn't. And I didn't kill him."

I had a terrible thought. "What about your wife?" I asked.

"What about her? Oh, you mean did I follow *her* home and kill her? Hell no. I haven't even seen her since that night. What I did was go over to Jerk's, that's a sports bar and fast-food place on North Mesa. I picked Jerk's because I felt like one, and I ate chicken wings and got roaring drunk. They had to toss me out. Then I decided I was too drunk to drive anywhere, so I staggered off to Jeremy Totten's in Kern Place and banged on his door until he let me in, after which I passed out on his sofa. How's that for an intelligent response to a wife's infidelity?" He was drumming his fingers on the desk and making me nervous.

"The next day I started thinking again instead of just blowing my top. We—Jeremy and I—spent Sunday drinking beer, watching football, and talking about unfaithful wives and rat's-ass divorce lawyers. Jeremy's divorced. He recommended a lawyer who can probably get me out of my marriage with a few pesos left in my pocket instead of buck naked and broke. You want to hear more? Monday— I'm staying at Jeremy's until I get my own place—I went to the bank; took everything out of the safe deposit box, since it's my stuff anyway; and cleaned out half of everything in our accounts, which I deposited in another bank in my name.

"Then I found a realtor and put our house on the market, after which I went back to Jerk's for two beers and another round of chicken wings; it's a place that grows on you. The staff is so rude, they fit my mood exactly. Then—what? I looked up Jeremy's lawyer and told him to file for divorce. With any luck, my cute little wife, who's been calling the department and my office every ten minutes since Sunday, will be served today.

"So that's what I've been doing since Saturday night, not that I know why you're asking. Are you a friend of Melanie's or something?"

I tended to believe him, not that I wouldn't check out his story. After all, he was my best suspect to date—at least until I gathered more information about Vladik. But there was his question to answer: Why was I interested in his business? "Actually, I and all the women who provided refreshments for the opera party are being questioned by the police as people who may have poisoned him."

"No shit. Well, I hope you did a good job and he's still puking his brains out."

"He's dead, Professor Collins. You hadn't heard?"

"Well, no. I've been drunk, passed out, or busy since I last saw him, and he was alive then, although he did say he was sick. I thought he was just a chicken-hearted creep. But I didn't make any food for your party. I don't cook, so the police can skip me."

"I don't cook either, not if I can help it," I said, relaxing. He didn't seem to be about to attack me for suggesting that he was a murderer.

"So he died of food poisoning? Hell of a way to kill someone. There you go wincing again. That's cute." He grinned at me. "If you ever decide to dump Jason, give me a call. I'll ask you out."

"That's very flattering, Professor Collins."

"Brandon," he corrected.

"But don't you think I'm a little old for you?"

He studied me carefully and replied. "Nope. Younger man, older woman. That's the way to go. Then if we get married, we've got a chance of dying around the same time. And think of all the fun we'd have in between. You could come on field trips with me. Nothing more interesting than rocks. You can tell the geologic history of the area you're in by looking at a highway cut. Did you know that?"

"Yes, I did, but I'm not really an outdoor person, and I'm already married and expect to stay that way."

"Okay, but keep me in mind. You never know what's going to happen in a marriage. Jason might get restless, see some cute chick in a class—"

I had to laugh. "He's very good at fending off cute chicks." Still, Professor Collins' suggestion made me uneasy. I glanced at my watch. "Oh my, I have another appointment."

"Someone else you want to ask if he murdered Gubenko. Even if the man's dead, I have to say it couldn't have happened to more deserving guy. Only more satisfying scenario I can think of is that he's still alive and marries my soon-to-be ex-wife and has to put up with her boring company for the next hundred years, but I guess it's too late for that."

"Unfortunately," I agreed, and left to keep my rendezvous with Vladik's Russian students. Before I left, I got directions to Miner's Hall from Brandon. Wouldn't you know, it was up the hill. I hate walking uphill, but I didn't want to lose my parking space, which was downhill. I might never find another and miss the students I wanted to interview.

My goodness, but Professor Brandon Collins was foul mouthed! His language came as quite a shock to me. One

expects more of well-educated people, although I did remember an industrial chemist from New York City, where
Jason consults. That young man had been embarrassingly
profane—even at the Metropolitan Opera. And he talked
during the performance!

13

Lunch with Russians

Carolyn

There they were, two pretty girls with fine soprano voices and good figures, even under their thrift-shop outfits. They were talking to each other in Russian, looking tired and glum, when I approached and reintroduced myself. I had small gifts, art glass fish in different colors, tucked into two gift bags, all of which I'd picked up before my drive to the university. Early rising was bad enough, but climbing stairs in old, high-ceilinged buildings was worse, especially after climbing a hill.

"Polya? Irina? Do you remember me?" I had no idea which girl was which but hoped to find out during lunch. "I'm Carolyn Blue from the opera committee. I'd like to take you out to lunch in thanks for your lovely work in *Macbeth*." You'd think, given their expressions of astonishment, that no one ever went out to eat in Russia.

"Lunch? For us?" they chorused happily. They were clambering into my car, chattering unintelligibly, almost before I could collect myself. One was blonde, Polya, the other dark haired with a slight Asian slant to her eyes. That was Irina, pronounced with two long *e*s. She was definitely a beauty. Could Vladik have chosen them for their looks rather than their voices? Remembering his behavior with Adela and his embarrassing titty speech at the party, I rather imagined it was their looks that had won them their student visas.

They had no afternoon classes so I took them across town with the idea of sampling the *salpicon* at Julio's. Not that I hadn't had it before, but if it was as tasty as I remembered, I'd get a recipe for my column. My guests were happy with anywhere I wanted to go. Obviously, they didn't get around much, poor things. They kept their noses pressed to the car windows all along Interstate 10 East, exclaiming over what they saw. The sights weren't all that picturesque, but if they were happy, I was happy and managed to get off the right exit ramp to Julio's.

Then there were menu problems. Irina and Polya didn't eat in restaurants at all, as it turned out. They ate in their trailer and brought lunches from home, so after two years in El Paso, they'd never tried Mexican food. I had to describe dishes; I had to give warnings about spiciness. After much discussion, they ordered tlapeno soup, mild, a chicken and cilantro soup with avocado slices. After that they got what I was having, salpicon, which is a salad—cold, shredded brisket, marinated and served on lettuce leaves, with cheese cubes, cilantro, and avocado slices.

Avocados were a thrill for these girls. They'd never had any and later wondered whether there were avocado desserts. Actually, I remembered that in the '30s a place in El Paso called the Spinning Wheel had served giant avocado malts to teenagers. How dreadful does that sound? I didn't mention it to my guests lest they want to order that very thing. Of course, they'd never sampled any of Adela's guacamole at the party. In fact, they'd seemed to keep to themselves and had avoided Vladik; and they left early, now that I thought back on the evening. Perhaps they didn't like him. Perhaps he had demanded sex from them.

The salpicon was excellent, and I did solicit a recipe. "You will make at home?" they asked. I probably wouldn't, I replied, and explained about "Have Fork; Will Travel." They thought that a food column for newspapers must be a wonderful job and marveled that the restaurant didn't provide the food free. Since the ethical considerations were too difficult to explain, I introduced the topic of Vladik. They nodded and looked very sad. "Only Russian we are knowing, and one more," said Polya.

"Only person we are calling when car dies," mourned Irina. "He giving money for food and gas and trailer. We don't know what we are doing now. Boris Stepanovich Ignatenko is getting our pay at club now that Vladik dead. Say is being from their partnership."

"I think Vladik owing him money, like we owing Vladik money," said Polya, nodding wisely and rolling another tortilla full of salpicon. "Is very good," she said around a big bite.

"You're waitresses at a club?" I asked. Then it occurred to me that there might be a club in El Paso where opera was sung. If so, Jason and I would certainly have to go.

"No waitress—dancing," said Irina. "Brazen Babes. You are knowing it? Is between university and trailer park. But so far Boris Stepanovich is giving us no money for food. We are wondering what we do. Car is dying again this morning. Nice boy pushes us into parking, but now we are needing push to get started. Need to find other nice boy."

"Brazen Babes?" I asked. What kind of place was that? And what kind of dancing? And when did they get their homework done?

Polya nodded. "Is big surprise for us when we get here. We are not being dancers, not knowing about taking off clothes in front of many men. We are much embarrassed."

"And Vladik is wanting us to have sex with men," added Irina. "I am saying no."

"Irina is not liking men," Polya explained. "Her father was very bad to her, so I am saying okay to Vladik so he don't be mad at us, but sex was very awful. Then we are both saying we rather go back to Russia than have more sex, but we much afraid Vladik making us leave. Only good thing, we think before, maybe we find husbands in U.S. But now we are being women who like women. How you say in English?"

"Lesbians?" I responded in a weak voice. My head was reeling at their revelations. These young women had been forced into white slavery.

"Maybe yes," Irina agreed. "When Vladik think we should both having sex with him, we are saying, we don't do that. We are women who are liking women. So he not bothering us about sex no more, but still we are dancing and taking off clothes on stage and tables. Is very disgusting."

"I imagine." Good grief, I thought. Something had to be done about this.

"Now Boris Stepanovich is saying lap dances. That is wiggling on laps of customers." Both girls moaned and dove into their flan. "We are not wanting to go home, but maybe now losing school visas and degrees. Degree from American university would be very good things, and who will be making us opera stars with Vladik is dead?"

They looked so sad, and I had no idea what the solution to their terrible predicament might be. A good start might be the desecration of Vladislav Gubenko's corpse. What a dreadful man! I shifted in my seat and my foot touched the gift bags. Since both girls appeared to be on the verge of tears, now might be a good time for the presents.

"I almost forgot," I exclaimed. "I brought little gifts for you." I pulled the two bags up from the floor, wishing now that I'd bought something more practical, decent clothes, food.

"For us?" cried Polya, so excited that she came close to dragging the gift bag through her flan.

"So pretty," murmured Irina, after unwrapping the tissue paper and examining the two six-inch glass fish with their swirling colors and tiny bubbles.

Each of the four fish was a bit different, and they seemed to be a hit. Now was the time to ask about Vladik's friends and enemies in El Paso.

Salpicon

Salpicon, which is a shredded-beef salad with chipotle dressing, is a favorite in El Paso and Juarez. Friends who have lived here longer than I said that the ur salpicon is from Julio's in Juarez and that the recipe was printed in the El Paso newspaper. I got this recipe from the El Paso Chile Company's Texas Border Cookbook. *Authors W. Park Kerr and Norma Kerr give credit to Julio's, Rubio's in El Paso, and local caterer Kay Queveda.*

The Kerrs suggest the dish for a cocktail buffet with the ingredients rolled in small tortillas. I've eaten it in restaurants as a communal course for the whole table or as a first course just for me. You can also serve it as a main course for dinner.

- Lay a *5-pound, top-cut brisket of beef,* fat side up, in a 6-quart Dutch oven or flameproof casserole. Distribute *2 large onions, peeled and sliced,* over the meat, pour in *1 quart of canned beef broth* and enough cold water to cover by 3 inches.

- Set over medium heat and bring to a boil; cover, lower heat, and simmer, adding additional boiling water as needed; turn brisket at the halfway point, cooking until it is tender enough to shred easily at its thickest point (about 4 hours total cooking time).

- Remove from heat, uncover pan, let brisket stand in broth until just cool enough to handle. (Warm brisket is easier to shred.)

- Meanwhile, on the open flame of a gas burner or under a preheated broiler, roast the *4 poblano chiles or 6 long green chiles,* turning until they are lightly but evenly charred. Steam the chiles in a paper bag, or in a bowl, covered with a plate, until cool. Rub away burned peel. Stem and seed chiles and cut into ¼-inch-wide strips. (In El Paso during the chile harvest, we can buy charred chiles outside the supermarkets to eliminate the early steps and even wrap and freeze the chiles for winter.)

- Pour off and strain the broth. Measure out *1½ cups* and save the rest for other uses; it's delicious. Trim the fat from the brisket and shred the meat using the tines of two forks, one in each hand, in a downward pulling motion. The meat must be thoroughly shredded, the end result almost fluffy. Combine the meat and the 1½ cups broth in a bowl and let it stand covered at room temperature. (It can be prepared to this point up to 2 hours ahead, but do not refrigerate it.)

- In a medium bowl, whisk together *1 7-ounce can of chipotles adobado, pureed, ⅔-cup olive oil, ½ cup fresh lime juice, ⅓ cup white wine vinegar, 1½ teaspoons salt,* and *2 cloves garlic,* crushed through a press.

- Drain the shredded meat, pressing hard with a spoon to extract any broth that has not been absorbed. In a large bowl, toss together the shredded beef, *8 ounces mild white cheese, such as Monterey Jack,* cut into ¼ inch cubes, and chipotle mixture. Add *1 cup coarsely diced red onion, ¾ cup minced cilantro,* and chile strips. Toss again. Taste and adjust seasoning so that the salpicon is tart, smoky, and fairly spicy.

- Line a large platter with coarse outer leaves from *one head of romaine.* Mound salpicon on lettuce. Garnish with spiky yellow inner leaves of romaine, *3 medium tomatoes,* trimmed and cut into wedges, and *2 ripe black-skinned avocados,* trimmed and sliced into paper-thin rounds but not peeled. Scatter *5 radishes,* trimmed, and sliced into paper-thin rounds over all.

- Serve with warmed *small corn or flour tortillas,* (optional, but not for me; I love these little salpicon burritos).

Recipe will feed 12 as a main course or 20 or more as an hors d'oeuvre.

Carolyn Blue, "Have Fork, Will Travel,"
Wheeling Star-Tribune.

14
Home Sweet Trailer Park

Carolyn

"**Would you like** a cup of coffee, more flan, or perhaps some ice cream?" I asked since they were eyeing their empty flan dishes wistfully.

"Yes, please," said Irina eagerly.

Evidently they wanted both, so I ordered, with coffee for myself. Both girls dove into their ice cream with enthusiasm, and I thought of Pancho Villa, who had come to El Paso when his revolutions were going badly and consoled himself by eating ice cream at the Elite Confectionary. There is a delightful 1912 photo of Villa and several other mustachioed revolutionaries eating ice cream, seemingly from paper cups that fit into cone-shaped holders. When I saw the picture, I wondered whether the ice cream was Mrs. Price's. She was the widow of an Ohio man who came to El Paso in 1905 to make his fortune growing fruit. His trees were killed by a freeze, and he died shortly thereafter. The widow, left with four sons, rented a house in town, bought a cow, and went into the dairy business. Her sons milked and delivered the milk to neighbors in a little red wagon. However, their business grew rapidly, and they were soon providing milk and ice cream from a farm outside the city and a creamery in town.

"It's a terrible thing—Vladik being murdered," I said in introduction to my questions. "Being fellow countrywomen, did you know the names of his friends or, perhaps more important, the names of his enemies?"

"Murdered?" cried Polya.

"He is getting sick and dying," Irina chimed in. "Who would be murdering Vladik?"

"Someone who didn't like him, I suppose," I replied, astonished that they didn't know what had happened to their mentor, or at least what Lieutenant Vallejo thought had happened to him. Didn't they read the newspaper? Perhaps it was something else that wasn't part of their lives since they had moved to this country. "Considering how he treated you girls, he doesn't seem to have been a very nice person. Probably lots of people hated him."

"No one hate Vladik," said Polya solemnly. "For us, he is our only friend in U.S. Is being wonderful opera producer. He is writing the trio for us. Maybe Verdi could writing that, and Vladik, but nobody else. Who would be not liking Vladik?" She was astonished. "Maybe we should now going to trailer. Having homework before go to work, and must finding boy to push car so can be driving to trailer. Many thanks for wonderful lunch and so pretty gifts. Can you taking us back to university? We are not having money for bus."

"Of course," I replied. "And I'll give you a push. Obviously your battery needs to be recharged or replaced." I know about such things because when Jason and I got married, we had a car like that. Our first apartment, when Jason became an assistant professor, had to be on a hill so that he could push the car while I sat inside and popped the clutch, a responsibility that made me very nervous, especially with a baby in the back seat. Then I'd drop Jason off and pray that the car would make it home. A colleague drove him home, so I never knew when he'd be arriving. After I became pregnant with Gwen, Jason ran to school and got a ride home. Adventuresome days.

I did manage to get the girls, in their dreadful, rusted-out car, started. Obviously it had begun life somewhere other than El Paso, where nothing rusts, because rust requires moisture. And thinking about how frightened I'd been, driving home with the baby as a young woman, I offered to follow them to be sure they actually got all the way to their trailer. This offer wasn't completely altruistic. I'd learned hardly anything from them and hoped to give it one last try at the trailer park. They seemed grateful for the offer, rather than suspicious of my motives, so perhaps they weren't hiding anything. How they could not hate their late mentor I couldn't imagine, but they didn't seem to. Polya had cried quietly all the way to the university, murmuring his name from time to time, while Irina, in the back seat, patted her on the shoulder and said occasionally, "Maybe Boris Ignatenko just forget to give us money. We asking tonight."

"Then maybe we having no job either."

"What good is job with no food or gas?" Irina retorted, and Polya began to cry again.

As I followed them to the trailer park, which was on the Westside but not in any area I'd visited, I wondered what they were saying to each other in the privacy of their rattletrap vehicle. Probably deciding how to get rid of me as quickly as possible.

Imagine my surprise when we arrived. They invited me in for tea. Their trailer was as rusty as their car, with a dripping evaporative cooler sagging from a window outside and shabby Salvation Army–genre furniture inside. However, it was clean. It looked dreadful but rigorously scrubbed. The tea, served in jelly glasses, was hot and very, very strong, but I managed to sip it, no small triumph when the glass was blistering my fingers and the liquid my tongue.

On further questioning, both girls insisted that Vladik had no enemies. As for friends, they suggested that he must have been friendly with his fellow professors, and each girl named several with whom she had classes. Then Irina had an inspiration. "Boris Stepanovich Ignatenko. He and Vladik knowing each other in Russia before, always talking and drinking vodka when Vladik coming to club."

"They are being business partners of Brazen Babes," Polya added. "Boris Stepanovich is knowing if Vladik having other friends. You asking Boris Stepanovich. He not knowing Vladik maybe be murder. Maybe you telling him, not us? Is bad we must telling him we need money for eating and gasses. He seeming happy to have our dancing money. Maybe not liking give some back."

"How much do you make?" I asked.

Both girls shrugged. "Money for dancing," said Irina.

"Money men is tucking in our strings," said Polya. "Is much money, I think. What is called tips. Pretty soon maybe we have paying back and keeping it."

I really didn't want to go to a place called Brazen Babes to talk to Mr. Boris Stepanovich Ignatenko. My only contact with exotic dancing had been with a tassel twirler in New Orleans, who sat down at a table full of chemists (and me) and chatted while she drank hot buttered rum at our expense. The rum was my suggestion, and I believe she was reprimanded for not ordering champagne.

Having extracted all the information I could, I thanked the girls for their hospitality, they thanked me for "food and fishes," and I left.

I didn't do too well getting back into familiar territory, but once I did, I decided to make a last stop in the day's investigation. I needed to check out the alibi of Professor Brandon Collins at Jerk's, not a very prepossessing name, but he had felt that it matched his status at the time he went there.

Jerk's seemed a presentable enough place if you like neon beer signs and flocks of TVs turned to sports channels. There were few customers that time of afternoon, and it was hard to imagine it full of reeling drunks, which was how the geology professor had described himself. I did note that the customers at the bar were students, or so I assumed. If that was so at night as well, Professor Collins had set a very bad example for young men of college age. I went to the cash register and asked the waitress manning it if she had been here on Saturday night around midnight. She hadn't, but said the boss would have been. He was always around.

She summoned him, and perhaps taking me for someone who wanted to give a party for a son, he told me that he had a back room for private functions, keg parties and the like. I had to disappoint him in that respect, but he took it well and did, in fact, remember Brandon Collins.

"Big guy. Looked like someone who might be in from working on an oil rig, except that we don't have oil rigs around here. Wanted to arm wrestle all the kids—for money, no less. He was winning too. He had real impressive arm muscles on him. Course, I had to stop the gambling," said the manager virtuously. "I imagine there's some betting going on on the games, but I keep my eyes open. No gambling in Texas, except the little slots and bingo games. Gotta go to Sunland Park across the line in New Mexico for that, horses and a casino at their track. Or over to Juarez. They got the dog races and off-track betting. Used to have gambling at the Tigua casino here in El Paso, but Austin shut them down.

"I do sell lottery tickets. Be a lot more profitable if Texas would bring in Powerball or one a them big jackpot outfits. You ever seen the lines over in New Mexico when there's a big jackpot? Half El Paso's over there, spending their money."

To avoid being a complete nonparticipant in the conversation, I said, "I remember reading about crowds of New Yorkers going to Greenwich, Connecticut, for lottery tickets. Evidently the Greenwich residents didn't think lottery-ticket lines fit their upper-class image."

"Get you a beer, ma'am?" he asked.

"No, thank you. I just drank some very strong Russian tea, so I don't think I'll be drinking any more liquid for a while. I did want to ask you if the gentleman we were discussing got very drunk and had to be ejected around midnight."

"Say, he's not your husband, is he?"

I laughed. "No, I'm trying to establish an—ah—alibi for him."

"You're a private eye, aren't you? Well, I'll be damned. Yeah, he was stumbling drunk. Don't know how that got past me. The kid who was serving him must have been more interested in the football game than his customers. But I wouldn't say I *ejected* the guy. We try to keep it friendly here. I offered to get him a cab, but he had his mind set on walking. I couldn't talk him out of it, but at least, he didn't drive away. His car was still in the lot when we closed, so if he's up for hurting someone on DWI, well, it wasn't 'cause I let him drive. Say, he didn't stumble into traffic and get killed or anything, did he? He said he was going to Kern Place, which meant he'd have to cross North Mesa. I didn't think that was a good idea, but you can't stop a guy from walking. No walking-while-intoxicated law that I know about."

"He's fine," I assured the manager. "He walked to a friend's house and stayed the night. Thank you so much for the information. I hope that I haven't kept you from your work."

"Not like we're doin' a land-office business right now, ma'am, but things'll pick up around five, five-thirty."

In that case, I decided to leave immediately. Not that I said as much to the man. He'd been quite friendly and helpful.

15

On Consulting with an Irritable Spouse

Carolyn

Jason was not home when I arrived, but had left an answering-machine message saying he'd return around seven. He sounded rather grumpy. Obviously, he hadn't really meant for me to visit Professor Collins and had heard that I'd done so today. Well, I'd placate him by cooking something nice for dinner, and in the meantime, maybe I could get hold of the other geologist, Jeremy Totten. Fishing the university phone book out a kitchen drawer, I sat down to look for his numbers. First, the university number.

Happily, he was there, and when I introduced myself, he said, "Right, you're the lady who thinks Collins killed the opera guy. Well, I can vouch for him from around midnight, well maybe a half hour after that, until we left Monday morning to pick his car up at Jerk's and head for the department. Frankly, I think he'd have been too drunk to kill anyone before he got to my place, but at least, he's a responsible kind of guy. He didn't try to drive. I suppose if your victim was killed early enough and lives around here, Brandon might have staggered to the scene of the crime, finished him off doublequick, and then staggered over to my house. But there was no blood on Brandon. How was the victim killed?"

"Well, several things killed him, Professor Totten, neither of which produced blood. And I do thank you for your input."

Of course, he could be lying through his teeth, covering up for his colleague, but I hated to think that an academic would do that. As I could come up with no way to check the veracity of Jeremy Totten, I plucked Park Kerr's *El Paso Chile Company's Texas Border Cookbook* off the shelf and paged through, looking for something Jason might like. Ha! Green enchiladas. I read through the recipe and discovered that I had many of the ingredients, but not the roasted chicken (the supermarket had that), the canned crushed tomatoes with added paste (Progresso made those—I used the product occasionally in soup), corn tortillas (those had to be reasonably fresh but were available at the market), and lots of cheese.

Making a quick list, I rushed off to the grocery store, bought the extra ingredients, and rushed home. I estimated that I'd be able to produce the enchiladas by the time Jason arrived, not that I'd ever made enchiladas before. Wouldn't he be surprised! And I certainly hoped that he'd appreciate all the effort. At least I didn't have to make the tortillas myself—by grinding the corn on a metate, mixing the result with a little water and patting out a round corn cake, then cooking it on a heated stone as Indian women had done for centuries. A Spaniard named de Aguilar, captured by a Mayan chief and rescued by Cortez, told of eating tortillas in 1591. Most Mexican food traces back to Aztec, Mayan, or Pueblo cooking, and flat breads like tortillas have been made for at least five thousand years. There were hundreds of maize varieties under cultivation by the time the Spaniards arrived in the New World.

People who have lived in El Paso a good deal longer than I speak with wistful nostalgia of the *enchiladas verde* at the Hacienda Restaurant in "the old days." The restaurant still exists but changed hands several times before my husband and I moved here, so I didn't expect to sample these warmly remembered delights. Then I found the recipe in the *Texas Border Cookbook,* a gem available for those who want to cook border cuisine at home. Viva la Tex-Mex! It's a delicious dish.

As for the restaurant, I've been there and found it most interesting. It was originally the adobe "mansion" of the Anglo pioneer and Mexican War veteran Simeon Hart. He married Jesusita Siqueiros, after she nursed him back to health from his war wounds, and founded the first flour mill (1849) on the north side of the river where there was a waterfall. No doubt he had some help from her wealthy father in Mexico, who owned a flour mill himself, not to mention a number of other things. Hart's adobe house was built several years after the mill and was much admired by visitors. It even had a library. In a family picture from 1873, I count 7 children and Simeon; Jesusita had died in 1870. Juan, the second eldest of the four sons, founded the *El Paso Times.* His father made a lot of money selling flour to the army, beginning in 1850, and died in 1874.

The restaurant today has long, narrow rooms on the east and south sides that may have been verandas at some time and many smaller rooms inside. In 1880 the government bought Hart's mill and established Fort Bliss there. The water was muddy and caused dysentery, and the soldiers described the place as, "Dismal, dirty, hot, crowded, and full of rattlesnakes." The old officers quarters are now tenements and line the road to the restaurant, which is tucked down below the highway and has a long stretch of wild grass leading to the border. The Hacienda breathes history and is a delight to visit.

Carolyn Blue, "Have Fork, Will Travel," *Denver Times.*

I slaved for several hours, listening to the news, as I prepared the green chicken enchiladas. My husband arrived just as I was drawing the baking dish from the oven. "I can't believe it," he said, nose raised appreciatively in the air. "You've been cooking."

Not only that, but I was still wearing my going-out-to-lunch clothes protected by a ruffled apron. I transferred the enchiladas to heated plates, garnished them with shredded romaine, and carried them into the dining room. Then I took a dish of canned, refried beans from the microwave. Pace may be the big salsa provider from San Antonio, but El Paso has its own factories. From the 1940s Mountain Pass and Old El Paso brands produced canned pinto beans and other Mexican food favorites to comfort El Pasoans both locally and those away from home. After growing into the biggest Tex-Mex cannery in the country, the brands were sold to Pet.

With the enchiladas and beans on the table and margaritas from the refrigerator, we were ready to eat. "What's the occasion?" Jason asked, eyeing my culinary efforts.

"I'm trying out a new cookbook," I replied. I couldn't very well say, *I'm buttering you up so that I can ask your advice on what should be done about the Russian girls.* That would come after the first margarita and first helping of enchiladas, which Jason, thank goodness, thought were very good. In the meantime, I told him that I'd been reading El Paso history and mentioned the powder worn by the ladies of the haciendas at fiestas during the Spanish colonial period. "Their faces were described as glowing lavender white in the candlelight, and their face powder was called 'Mexican white lead' or something like that. Of course, I immediately thought of you, lead being toxic. Do you think face powder could lead to lead poisoning?" I asked.

Jason was intrigued and discussed the subject at length. I'm not sure what he decided because I was nervously anticipating the subject I planned to bring up after a few more conversational diversions.

"Oh, I read a delicious UTEP story," I said, once he'd wound down about toxic face powder. "You know the statue on Mount Cristo Rey? It was done in 1938 by a Spanish sculptor named Urbici Soler. He taught at the university for several years after he finished his statue of Christ, but it seems that he had his classes doing nudes, and the president didn't like it. *His* name was Wiggins. He asked Soler if the nudes couldn't be, at the least, half covered, and the sculptor asked, 'Which half?'"

Jason chuckled, so I told him another story. "Did you know that there was an opera house here from 1887 to 1905, when it burned down? The Myar Opera House. Quite impressive looking—Renaissance in style, and inside it had a chandelier, a blue dome, paintings, frescoes, and tapestries. There's a newspaper article praising the opera house, especially their policy of confining prostitutes to the balcony."

Jason asked what operas they'd put on, but I couldn't give him any examples because none were mentioned. The only performance I knew about was a Dumas play, *Monte Cristo*, with which they opened. I did mention a concert by John McCormack in the '30s. He'd gone to Juarez and come back so drunk or hungover, I wasn't sure which, that he had to lean on the piano to keep himself upright. "Oh, and Arturo Rubenstein came here in that period too," I added, "but the sirens of fire engines and a noisy initiation ceremony in the basement at Liberty Hall drowned him out, and he never came back."

"And now all visiting artists have to contend with," said my husband, "are cell phones, people who come in late, and an audience that always claps in the wrong places."

We both laughed companionably, and I helped him to two more enchiladas and another margarita, thinking, *Well, get on with it, Carolyn.*

"I took the two Russian girls to lunch today. You remember the singers in the witches' trio? Poor things. I thought they would be feeling very lonely and sad over the death of their sponsor."

"That was a nice thing to do," my husband replied, scooping up a long green chile dripping with cheese. "How are they doing?"

"Well, I made some very disturbing discoveries about Vladik and those girls. I know something has to be done, but I have no idea what. Maybe you can suggest something."

"Oh God, don't tell me he's gotten one of them pregnant. I could have kicked him while he was talking about the breasts of the witches. By the end of the evening everyone at the party had been told what he said and complained to me or to Howard or both of us."

"There's worse," I assured him. "It seems that when he brought Polya and Irina over here to study, he told them they'd have to take jobs to pay him back for—I don't know—their transportation or something."

Jason shrugged. "Most of our students have jobs."

"Not in strip clubs with their salary and tips going into a professor's pocket. He evidently provided them with a trailer to live in, a car that barely runs, some second-hand clothes, and money for gas and food. He kept everything else they made. Now they're terrified. The partner in the club has said that they now owe him the money, but he's not giving them living expenses."

Jason was staring at me, aghast.

"They're little better than slaves, Jason, and they had no idea what they were getting into when they came here. Now they're trapped."

Jason put down his fork. "That bastard."

"Jason, your language," I protested.

"Right." He picked up his fork and began to eat. And think. I can always tell when Jason is thinking. He has a certain expression. He finished off his enchilada and drained his margarita. I put more food on his plate and filled his glass. Thank goodness, I had more left in the pitcher. "I really like these chicken enchiladas," he mumbled. "When did you decide to try cooking Mexican food?"

"I'm going to do some columns on Tex-Mex cuisine."

"Good idea." He sipped his margarita. "This mess with the Russian girls is going to blow up in our faces, you know. It's bound to come out."

I nodded.

"So the best thing is to take care of it before the scandal hits."

"How?" I asked.

Jason groaned. "I really hate to get mixed up in this."

"Maybe I can take care of it. If you tell me what to do."

"Maybe you could," he replied thoughtfully. "I think—" He paused and organized his thoughts. "Since you found out about this, you could go to the chairman of the Music Department and explain the whole thing to him. Then while he's reeling from the implications and the probable scandal, you can suggest that, to avoid trouble for the university, he should provide the girls with scholarships to finish out the year. They've got good voices, after all. He or his dean ought to be able to scrape up the money."

"They'll need jobs too," I said, "unless the scholarships are awfully generous. And considering the budget shortfalls this year—"

"Right. Money is tight everywhere. Okay, there may be some jobs open on campus, but I doubt it. Maybe we can talk some members of Opera at the Pass into giving the girls jobs. Without explaining where they've been working up to now. But, damn it, they probably don't have work visas."

We stared at each other, perplexed. "They only mentioned student visas," I admitted. "But gracious, Jason, there are Mexican workers all over the city who probably don't have green cards. They cross the river with something called a *mica*. It's a visitor's permit that allows them to stay for seventy-two hours. Then they work instead of going shopping or visiting relatives. Surely someone would like to hire a nice Russian girl as a—I don't know—nanny or something. Maybe one of the maquiladoras needs a Russian translator. Anyway, I'll go see the music chairman tomorrow. What's he like?"

"Temperamental," said my husband. "Volatile."

"Well, that sounds like fun." I sighed and brought in some vanilla ice cream on which I'd splashed a Mexican coffee liqueur and scattered chopped pecans.

"And Carolyn, much as I appreciate this dinner, I rather suspect that you took those two girls out to lunch to see if they could figure out who killed Vladik and then softened me up so you could bring up what we should do about them."

There are drawbacks to marrying an intelligent man. Such men tend to see through one's little attempts at manipulation.

"By the way, I have to fly to Austin tomorrow for a few days. I'll call you tomorrow night when I get a place to stay, and you can tell me how Dr. Tigranian reacted to the news about his Russian students."

Green Enchiladas a la Hacienda

- Discard the skin from a *roasted chicken* from the supermarket, pull the meat from the bones, and shred it, using two forks.

- In the open flame of a gas burner or under a preheated broiler, roast *9 long green chiles*, turning them, until they are lightly but evenly charred. Steam the chiles in a paper bag, or in a bowl, covered with a plate, until cool. Rub away the burned peel. Stem and seed the chiles and cut them into ¼-inch wide strips. Or if you live in the Southwest and your supermarket has rotating, charring ovens to roast chiles after the chile harvest, you can peel those as above, freeze them, and use them all winter and for this dish.

- Position a rack in the upper third of the oven and preheat to 375°F.

- In a medium saucepan over low heat, warm *2 tablespoons olive oil.* Add ½ cup from *1¼ cups finely chopped onion, 2 garlic cloves, peeled and minced,* and *½ teaspoon dried, crumbled oregano.* Cook, covered, stirring once or twice, for 10 minutes. Stir in *1½ cups canned chicken broth* and *1¼ cups canned crushed tomatoes with added puree.* Chop enough chile strips to equal ½ cup. Add both chopped and whole chiles to the saucepan, stir in *1 teaspoon salt,* and bring to a boil. Lower heat, partially cover, and simmer, stirring once or twice, for 10 minutes. Adjust the seasoning.

- In a deep skillet, warm about *½ inch corn oil (1½ cups)* over medium heat. Using tongs, immerse *12 6-inch corn tortillas* one at a time in the oil; turn them, then transfer them to absorbent paper. The tortillas should be in the oil no more than a few seconds, and the oil should be hot enough to soften the tortillas but not so hot that the edges begin to crisp.

- Spread about ¾ cup of the sauce in the bottom of a large, shallow baking dish (big enough to comfortably hold 12 rolled and filled enchiladas. Or use 4 individual heatproof serving dishes.)

- Using tongs, dip a tortilla into the hot sauce; then lay the tortilla on a plate. Spread about ⅓ cup of shredded chicken across the lower third of the tortilla. Season meat lightly with salt, sprinkle it with about 1 tablespoon of remaining onions, and top it with about 2½ tablespoons grated cheese (from *3 cups, about 12 oz. grated Monterey Jack cheese or medium-sharp cheddar or combination of both*). Roll the enchilada and lay it, seam-side down, in the baking dish. Repeat with the remaining tortillas, chicken, onions, and cheese, leaving about ¾ cup grated cheese. Drizzle the remaining sauce evenly over the enchiladas and sprinkle them with the remaining cheese.

- Bake 12 minutes or until the enchiladas are heated through, the cheese is melted, and the sauce is bubbling. With a wide spatula, transfer the enchiladas from the large baking dish to heated plates, or the oven-plates from the oven, garnish them with *2 cups shredded romaine,* and serve immediately.

Serves 4.

Permission to reprint this recipe was given by W. Park Kerr and Norma Kerr, authors of the *El Paso Chile Company's Texas Border Cookbook,* which I recommend highly to lovers of Mexican food, or even to those who've never had it but want to experiment.

Carolyn Blue, "Have Fork, Will Travel,"
Minneapolis Star Tribune

16

Approaching Brazen Babes

Carolyn

Jason packed his suitcase and then went to bed immediately after dinner, leaving me with a huge mess in the kitchen. No wonder I don't like to cook anymore. The next morning, after he had left, I called Dr. Armen Tigranian at the Music Department. I should have simply barged in. By asking for an appointment, I was put off until three that afternoon, although talking to him was an assignment I had wanted to get out of the way as soon as I could. What had Jason meant by *volatile?* I don't care much for volatile people. You never know what they're going to do.

To take my mind off what might turn out to be a confrontation with Dr. Tigranian, rather than a quiet discussion of what could be done for his ill-used Russian music students, I thought about their place of work and the man they worked for. If I wanted to find out anything about Vladik's associates, Boris Stepanovich Ignatenko seemed to be my only hope. But was it safe or suitable for me to go there? Unescorted women probably didn't. I don't think there were any lone women watching the tassel-twirler in New Orleans. Obviously, I needed advice.

One might think of the police in such a situation, but Art Guevara was not the sort of person I wanted to talk to. Nor was he interested in anything I had to say except whether my canapés had induced sickness in the victim. None of the opera ladies or faculty wives would know any more about places such as Brazen Babes than I did. It was obviously a den of prostitution as well as a performance arena for exotic dancers. I remembered a terrible situation in which I'd found myself in Barcelona. I was actually offered money for my "favors." Not a situation I cared to have repeated; yet going to Brazen Babes on my own might lead to just such a contretemps, should there be any patrons with a fetish for forty-something matrons.

So who did I know that would be knowledgeable about vice in El Paso? I sighed. Luz Vallejo. She had been a Vice lieutenant and could advise me about how and where to approach Boris Stepanovich Ignatenko. She would also be sarcastic about it. Still, better to endure a bit of embarrassment than to put myself in danger. I called her to ask if I could come by that morning. She swore at me. What an ill-tempered woman! Still, when I gave her a hint of my problem, she agreed to see me. She was probably laughing her head off.

Luz Vallejo

When the proper Mrs. Blue called, my first impulse was to tell her to go stuff it. Then she mentioned Brazen Babes. The two of them in the same context caught my interest. The wonder was that she had ever heard of the place. And my knee was aching like a son of a bitch. A little diversion couldn't hurt. I spend too much time around the house feeling sorry for myself, so I told her to come ahead, and she was on my doorstep in ten minutes.

"This is very considerate of you, Lieutenant Vallejo," she said as soon as I opened the door. "I learned some particularly upsetting things yesterday while I was pursuing information on who might have been Vladislav Gubenko's friends and enemies."

She walked right into my living room, with me limping behind, and flopped down on my couch, the picture of perplexity, dismay, and surprised pain. My couch is a rustic Spanish number that doesn't lend itself to flopping, or comfort, or visitors who want to stay very long, which is just why I bought it.

"I took the two opera students he brought over from Russia to lunch yesterday. Poor things, they ate everything I agreed to buy them and still looked hungry, and they cried when I gave them some inexpensive little thank-you presents. During lunch they told me that as soon as they got here, Vladik moved them into a disgusting trailer park, gave them a car that rarely runs, enrolled them at the university, and then put them to work nights at a place called, as I mentioned, Brazen Babes.

"They have to dance partially unclothed on the stage and tabletops, and naked, for all I know, and he wanted them to have sexual relations with customers—all so that he could take their wages and tips in return for his help in getting them to this country."

"Well, I'll be damned," I said. "I never knew old Boris was into white slavery. Naked girls and pimping, sure. He gets arrested. The girls get arrested. Then they all go to court and swear nothing bad was going on, just artistic dancing. What a crock."

"Then you know him?" she asked eagerly. "He's the only person I've found who seems to have been friends with Vladik—they were business partners according to the girls—and who might know anything about Vladik's death."

"Hell, Boris might have killed Gubenko himself," I said. Now this was really interesting. "Did the girls put out?" Mrs. Blue seemed at a loss for an answer. "Did they have sex with the customers?" I added in case she didn't know what *put out* meant or was too embarrassed to answer.

"One did. Once," she mumbled. "Then they refused. They've decided they're lesbians. Small wonder. I gather that her father sexually abused the other one. They also refused to have sex with Vladik. I never realized what a detestable man he was, not that I saw much of him, but I don't think Jason knew either. But then it's not the kind of thing you discuss while waiting for an academic committee meeting to begin."

"How old are they? Are they minors?"

"I don't think so," she answered. "They've been at the university for several years, and they have lovely soprano voices. Vladik evidently promised to make them opera stars here in the United States."

"Well, I'll tell you what we've got here," I said, feeling invigorated, "aside from the possibility of murder: pimping and prostitution on the local level, and the feds could build cases for hiring illegal workers, who worked without work visas, failing to pay minimum wage or any wages, probably nonpayment of social security taxes and worker's comp, nonpayment of income taxes. Too bad the girls aren't minors. That's a good bust. Statutory rape—probably—"

"But I don't want you to have the girls arrested," my visitor exclaimed. "They're victims. We've got to get them out of there and into decent jobs so they can eat and live someplace while they're going to school."

"What's this *we* business?" I asked.

"Well, of course I meant *I've* got to try to do that. I'm going to see the chairman of the Music Department this afternoon, and I'll try to get some Opera at the Pass members to find them jobs, but there's Mr. Ignatenko. He may hold the key to Vladik's murder, or at least have relevant information and—and—" Her face turned pink. "And I don't know how to approach him. I mean can I go into his club, or do I have to have an escort? Where is it? I've never even heard of it. And if I did go in, would it be dangerous?"

"In other words, you want to talk to the smut-bag Russian, but you're scared," I retorted.

"Of course, I am. That's why I came to you for advice. You were a Vice lieutenant. Who else am I going to ask about such things?"

I stared at her, thinking, while she squirmed on my uncomfortable sofa. You couldn't pay *me* to sit on it. Then it occurred to me that I was actually having fun. How long since that had happened? And I hadn't noticed my knee since she turned up at my front door.

"Okay," I said. "If you really want to talk to him without getting kicked out on your ass, or at least having it pinched, be here at, say, ten tonight. You'll have to drive."

"You're going to go with me?" she asked, looking pathetically grateful.

"Yeah, if your husband will let you out of the house. Maybe he'll want to come along."

"He's in Austin," she replied, and gave me a big smile. "It might even be fun," she added. "Going to Brazen Babes. Isn't that a tacky name? What should I wear?"

Jesus Christ, I thought. I was chaperoning Mrs. Brady Bunch to a strip club, and she was right: It might even be fun. But not, I hoped, for Ignatenko. He probably didn't see many prissy faculty wives in his line of work.

17
The Good Works of Opera Lovers

Carolyn

Having lost my own brief and ill-considered optimism with regard to our proposed visit to Brazen Babes, I left Luz Vallejo's house, puzzled at her sudden good humor. In her place, *I* certainly wouldn't be looking forward to that undertaking. I *wasn't* looking forward to it, although having someone to go with was a great relief. I might well have given up the idea if she hadn't offered.

And now it was only mid-morning with no appointment on my schedule until three o'clock. The question was: Should I try to solicit help from the opera ladies before I saw Dr. Tigranian, or hope that he could solve the whole problem? Given the financial straits at the university—all over Texas, for that matter—he probably couldn't give my new protégés enough help. Remission of tuition, that sort of thing, maybe, but jobs, loans? I wasn't even sure whether student loans ever went to foreign students. If I waited too long, Polya and Irina might be reduced to prostitution. I decided to call the other five women, those who had met at the Magic Pan to plot against Sergeant Guevara, and invite them to a charitable luncheon.

Once home, my first call was to Vivian Brockman, the leader of our ad hoc committee. "Vivian," I said, "we have a problem. I think we need to get together with the others. Shall we say Desert Pearl at noon?" I didn't tell her the nature of the problem but let her jump to the conclusion that Sergeant Guevara was coming after us again.

"I might have known," she said. "How many have you called?"

"You're the first."

"Very sensible. I'll call Barbara and Olive. You call Maria-Reposa and Dolly. We mustn't take no for an answer. This situation is outrageous."

I had to agree, although we were talking about different situations. Insisting on attendance was not as easy as Vivian may have expected. Dolly had finally gotten back to her bulb-removal program and didn't want to quit, wash the dirt off, and change clothes. I told her that a tragic situation was developing, a situation that demanded our attention. She gave in. Maria-Reposa was easier. She said, "Desert Pearl? The seafood restaurant? I've heard they have lobster enchiladas."

I assured her that they did, and she decided that lobster enchiladas warranted canceling an appointment to have her eyes examined. "I hate those machines with the little lenses that pop in and out. Of course, Martin complains if he passes me a newspaper article and I can't read it because my glasses are wrong. I suppose I'm getting farsighted. Well, twelve o'clock? Just where is the restaurant?"

"In the shopping center on the left on Resler just before you get to Redd Road."

By noon we were assembled and ordering interesting seafood: Thai shrimp on pasta, Mexican Seafood Pasta, and my favorite, Lobster and Crab Enchilada. Several of the ladies were wearing heels, while I was in tennis shoes, which had been appropriate for a visit to the very informal Luz Vallejo, but perhaps not for Dr. Tigranian later in the afternoon.

I had thought the matter over carefully and decided, as Jason suggested, not to tell the ladies about the unfortunate jobs Vladik had provided for his students. I anticipated a prejudice against hiring former exotic dancers, even though the girls had been reluctant to take up that profession. What I said was that Vladik had provided them with housing and a car, both dreadful, plus an allowance. Now they were alone in this country. The car kept dying, the trailer, for all they knew, would be taken away from them, and they had no money on which to live.

Olive was of the opinion that trailer parks were dangerous places, and that their trailer sounded disgusting.

Vivian demanded to know what Vladik had wanted in return for his largess. Any ideas he might have had of a sexual nature, I assured her, had been shot down by the two girls.

"I just knew he was that sort of man," Vivian responded. "It's a wonder he didn't throw them out in the street when they refused him."

"If he had, the department would have heard and disapproved of the whole arrangement. Those poor girls were terrified to find themselves in a foreign country with no friend but a man who wanted to—ah—avail himself of their virtue. I intend to talk to Dr. Tigranian, chairman of the Music Department, this afternoon and see what can be done for them in the way of scholarship money."

Maria-Reposa said, "The state is no longer doing anything for the poor. Charity is falling to the churches and individual citizens."

"It's the fault of the stingy ole Republicans," said Olive.

"I resent that, Olive," Barbara retorted. "Frank and I are Republicans, and we're as charitable as the next person."

"Which brings us to my idea," I interrupted before a political catfight could ensue. "I think Opera at the Pass should try to help these girls. Surely, we can find them part-time jobs, maybe clothes. I have some of Gwen's at home. You wouldn't believe how shabby their clothing is. I think he outfitted them from a Goodwill store, or perhaps what they're wearing came from Russia."

"I've heard that the wealthier Russians are becoming quite fashion conscious since the communists lost power," said Barbara.

"Not the poor people," Maria-Reposa murmured. "My church gets lots of donations of quite good clothing. We'll have to find out what their sizes are. And food? Do they need food until we can help them financially?"

"I imagine they do," I replied. "When I took them out to lunch yesterday, they were very hungry."

"Mah daughter-in-law could use a live-in baby sitter," said Olive. "It would mean room, board, and a little bitty salary in return for watchin' the babies at night and some afternoons—nothin' very glamorous or challengin'."

"But perfect for a student," I said enthusiastically.

"How's their English? She'd have hired a Hispanic girl, but she wants the children to grow up speakin' good English."

"And why is that?" Barbara snapped. "With the large majority of the population here speaking Spanish, a knowledge of the language is a necessity."

I was embarrassed, because my Spanish is almost non-existent. I'd taken an accelerated night course at the university our first year here, and then found that my maid couldn't understand a word I said. My neighbor said it was the difference between Castilian, which my teacher spoke, and border Spanish, which people in El Paso and Juarez speak.

"Really, Barbara," snapped Vivian. "Your Spanish isn't that good, and I speak better Spanish than your children."

"That's not true," Barbara retorted.

"Does anyone else have a job to suggest?" I asked, relieved that they hadn't returned to the subject of the quality of English spoken by the two Russian girls. It had been peculiar.

"Howard would be over the moon," murmured Dolly, "if he had someone to translate Russian articles on Shakespeare, but I don't know where he'd get the money." She looked quite sad at the thought of the missed opportunity. I tried to imagine what Shakespearean criticism would sound like as rendered by Polya or Irina. And what were these ladies going to think of me if references were asked for and the girls listed Boris Stepanovich Ignatenko of Brazen Babes? Maybe this hadn't been such a good idea.

"What a feather in the cap for Opera at the Pass if one or both of these young women should become famous and we were the group who came to their rescue in their time of need," said Vivian. "I definitely think this is a charitable project we should take on."

Too late. Once convinced, Vivian wasn't likely to give up the idea. She was a very forceful woman. "And I'll tackle the music chairman about funding their education," I said. At least I didn't have to mislead him about their present occupation.

To my mind there is nothing more delicious than a Maine lobster, but lobsters aren't really very friendly creatures. For one thing they don't care much for other lobsters. For another, they're very belligerent. Although they swim backward, they're always happy to turn around and face their enemies, conger eels and octopi, for a vicious fight. Lastly, they have the peculiar habit of sharing their burrows with conger eels. They hope to eat the eel's eggs, while the eel is waiting patiently for the lobster to shed its shell, so that the roommate eel can mount a full-scale attack.

Another tasty denizen of the sea is the Canadian crab, quite possibly another grumpy creature, but even grumpier are the Canadian and Washington state fisheries officers who are trying to keep Canadian crab boats from fishing in U.S. coastal waters. High tech surveillance cameras are in use to spot the boats, global positioning equipment determines in whose waters the crabbers are fishing, and then the international crab thieves are arrested and their boats seized. And the result?

Well, the pearl of the menu at Desert Pearl, a Mexican seafood restaurant in El Paso, Texas, incorporates Maine lobster and Canadian crab in a tortilla with a delicious sauce. Lobster and Crab Enchilada. Somehow the combination of the shellfish wrapped in a corn tortilla works. And the sauce—ah, the sauce. Creamy with a hint of chile and cheese. Not all Mexican food burns your tongue and brings perspiration to your forehead. Some is rich and subtle. Lobster and Crab Enchilada is one of the latter. I tried to make it at home, but somehow it just wasn't the same. My advice is, visit chef/owner Jose Nolasco's Desert Pearl and sample this dish for yourself.

Carolyn Blue, "Have Fork, Will Travel,"
Cleveland Plain Dealer.

18

Dr. Tigranian Hears Bad News

Carolyn

I looked at the faculty list on the wall. Armen Tigranian, Chairman, Room 303. The name was so familiar. I walked down the hall toward the departmental office as I combed my memory for the clue to that name. When I entered, the secretary was at her desk, painting her fingernails metallic lavender. She recognized me from the address-hunting visit and waved me toward the chairman's door, which was partially open and from which issued loud humming sounds, plus others less easy to identify, although they were certainly human.

"Go on in," she said. "He's expecting you."

I edged through the door and was confronted by the sight of a very tall, stout gentleman in a dark, rumpled suit with a tie too narrow for his wide chest. His broad, rosy face sprouted, high on an already high forehead, a pompadour of black hair dramatically streaked with silver, and he was tilted back in his chair, feet on the desk, waving his hands and arms, for all the world like a symphony conductor, but without orchestra, podium, or the customary upright position. And his feet, the soles of which faced me on the desk, were huge and looked from the bottom like big, rubber-ridged paddles. The noises were his personal humming-dum-de-dumming rendition of the music, although I couldn't identify it.

Then information attached to the name surfaced in my

memory like a swimmer popping up out of the water. "Of course," I exclaimed. "Armen Tigranian!"

A ferocious scowl replaced the stern concentration of a maestro directing his players. "So?" he roared challengingly.

"Your name. There's an Armenian opera composer with the same name. Still, you couldn't be he; he's almost certainly dead." I searched my memory for the name of an opera by Tigranian. "*Anoush*. He wrote *Anoush*."

Chairman Tigranian eyed me suspiciously. "You have heard this opera?"

"On record," I replied. "Quite a long time ago. A friend owned it and played it for us."

The chairman sighed. His scowl lightened. "There is an Armenian in the Middle West who is working on *Anoush*. Perhaps it will be performed again. As for me, I am the composer's great nephew; he was my grandfather's brother, but my father came to America before I was born. Although I was named for the composer, my great uncle, I never met him. Not too many people know of *Anoush*. It is not part of the standard repertoire."

"May I sit down?" I asked since he hadn't issued the invitation.

"Of course, of course." His huge feet crashed to the floor like the hooves of a circus elephant that had been standing on its hind legs and gave up the effort too abruptly. Thump. He rose agilely, rushed around the desk, and pulled out a chair for me. Actually, he picked it up and dropped it down beside me.

"So, you are Mrs. Blue, whom I don't know," he announced, going back to his seat. "Have you come to discuss Armenian music? There's not much call for it in El Paso, Texas."

"Actually, I've come about two of your students and Vladislav Gubenko."

"If your daughter has been seduced by the Russian, I

cannot help you. If Gubenko has seduced you, I cannot help you, other than to say that you are old enough to have known better. Gubenko has passed on to his reward, which may well be the fires of hell, but as he is no longer with us, he cannot be sued, charged with sexual harassment, or attacked because of the ludicrous Verdi he produced as his last operatic effort before his death."

I had to bite my lips to keep from smiling. "You saw *Macbeth*, then?"

"I did. If the administration hadn't already ordered that we eschew grand opera and take up zarzuela, they'd have done so when they heard of Vladik's *Macbeth*. What an obscenity to put good singers on stage in such a criminal adaptation. A pun you notice. Eh? Criminal. Meaning offense against good taste, and also depiction of criminals."

"Very nice," I said, assaying a smile. "And I did hear of his death. In fact, there's reason to think he died at the hand of another rather than of a—gastric upset."

"So! Murder? And what else? Did two of my students kill him? They should have come to me with their complaints instead of dealing with problems themselves, but then youth is impulsive, and we live in a city of hot-blooded, transplanted Spaniards who probably raped Indians to produce our students many generations later."

"No one knows who killed him," I hastened to say, although Adela, who was a student, came to mind, if only as a catalyst in the death. Catalyst. So many years in the company of scientists has affected my metaphors. "It's the two Russian girls, Polina Mikhailov and Irina Primakov, whose situation is a cause for worry."

"So, they are sad. That is no surprise. They go to the health services and get antidepressants," he said.

"Vladik has put the department, in fact the whole university, into a position that could cause terrible scandal, perhaps even liability."

"Why am I not surprised? My father always said,

'Never trust a Russian. The only person worse is a Turk.'
But what is your interest in the fate of my department and
the university? Are you a lawyer representing the girls?
Someone I haven't met from the dean's office who has
come to threaten me and take away the last dribble of
money we have to run the department?"

"None of those, Dr. Tigranian," I assured him. And I
told him the story, the unwanted jobs at Brazen Babes, the
sequestration of their earnings, the horrible car and trailer,
not to mention shabby clothes, the demand—although not
met—that they have sex with customers and with Vladik,
and now their frightened dependence on a Russian friend
of Vladik's. Each new revelation turned Dr. Tigranian's
rosy face darker with congested fury.

Finally he exploded, "And you know this how?"

Oh dear, I thought. What if Dr. Tigranian was getting
his cut of the arrangement at Brazen Babes? "I took them
to lunch, and they told me," I replied in a fading voice.
Then I took heart. I'd done nothing wrong. "When I look
back on the conversation, I think they may believe that all
foreign students are turned into slaves in the sex trade in
order to win a degree in this country. He kept them quite
isolated from the university community. They live away
from campus in a trailer park with no university people;
they come to school, take classes, bring their lunches,
study, go home, study, and go out to take their clothes off
at a place that I assume is disgustingly sleazy." A place to
which I was going that night with Luz Vallejo. Maybe she
carried a weapon. Not that I approve of firearms, but there
are times when one wouldn't mind being accompanied by
an armed companion.

While I was anticipating with dread my evening's appointment, Dr. Tigranian was roaring curses. His secretary
stuck her head in the door and backed out hurriedly. I hud-
dled in my chair. Low-voiced conversations could be heard
in the outer office. "Close my door," he shouted. The sec-

retary did that without ever showing herself. Volatile indeed, I thought. It was hardly considerate of Jason to go off to Austin and leave me to break the bad news to this man, who looked as if he'd either knock my head off or have a stroke in front of my eyes.

"Hush," I said.

"What?" he shouted.

"S-sh-sh."

He stopped cursing and gaped at me.

"We have to deal with this, not shout it all over the building. The fewer people who know, the better. If we take care of it before it comes out—"

"How is that possible?" he snapped. "How can this not come out? Accursed Russian! Penis-fixated scum! Son of a whoring mother!"

"Please, Dr. Tigranian, nobody cares if he's well remembered. In fact, the sooner he's forgotten, the better, but we have to do something about the girls."

"What? Buy them a house and a new car? Bribe them with a big settlement held in trust if they're too stupid to—"

"Getting them out of that strip club would be a good start. I don't think your other suggestions are necessary. They just want to finish school. If the department can pay for their tuition and books, maybe—"

"We have no money!" he roared. "We can't buy instruments or music or do performances, other than degree recitals. We don't have paper for the copy machines."

"I know. My husband has been saying the same thing."

"Who is your husband? Someone who wants to get our money, which we don't have, for his department, by sending his wife to blackmail me."

"My husband is a chemistry professor who loves opera, as I do. As weird as that performance of *Macbeth* was, the three young women in the witch's chorus sang beautifully, especially for amateurs. People from Opera at the Pass want to help, but I haven't told them about Brazen Babes or any of that, just that the girls are now almost destitute and don't know what to do. Our committee is going to try to find jobs for them that will allow them to continue their studies, unless you can get them university jobs. That would be even better."

"It's November. There are no university jobs now. They are all taken." Then he stopped snarling at me. "But maybe this can be contained. As you say. Can I trust you to keep this story quiet? Ah, that scheming bastard, Gubenko, may the flames of hell devour him for a thousand thousand years. That cunning, soulless—"

"Sssh," I said, putting a finger to my lips. "I'm not the one who keeps shouting. I just want to help the young women. You need to do the same. Quietly. Without causing even the slightest ripple of interest."

"Humph!" he said. Then he swung his giant feet back up on the desk and waved his hand at me. "Go. Go. Call me tomorrow. We will consult on what can be done."

I doubt that anyone was ever gladder to get out of his office than I. Or maybe everyone fled at first opportunity!

19
Brazen Babes

Luz

Jesus Christ! She looked like she was dressed to attend the meeting of a university alumni group—not the kind gathering to drink beer at a tailgate party, the kind trying to figure out how to fund the museum or the library. Or maybe a group of sorority alumni, meeting to discuss the morals of the active chapter members. I'd been in a sorority. You got to go to more beer parties that way, but you can bet I didn't make any alumni contributions or attend any meetings once I was out of school. The very idea of hanging out with my old sorority sisters was laughable. It was okay to be a criminal justice major in school, but you weren't supposed to join the police force and go out on the streets to catch real criminals after graduation.

And then there was her driving. The best thing you could say for it was that Carolyn Blue would never get a ticket. She was one careful driver. You had to tell her a turn was coming up about a half mile in advance because she wouldn't change lanes if there was anyone in sight on her side of the road. The result was that I'd forget, and we'd have to go back. Of course she wouldn't make a U-turn. It was eleven before we got to Brazen Babes, and then she decided maybe we shouldn't go in there after all. Maybe we could meet Ignatenko for lunch somewhere.

Right. Like I was going to be seen in public eating lunch with that *pendejo*. I dragged her in, and when the bouncer tried to tell us ladies didn't get admitted without escorts, Carolyn said that was discriminatory. I told him to get lost or I'd disable him for life. Then I found us a table. Carolyn didn't want to order a drink. She thought it wasn't a good idea for us to be under the influence of alcohol in a place like this. At that point she was taking surreptitious peeks at the dancers and shuddering. I'm guessing at the shuddering. It was so dark in there, except for the spotlights on the girls, that I couldn't see her very clearly, which was probably just as well. I might have said something more insulting than what I actually said, which she didn't like.

"Don't be a baby," I told her. "Order a drink. It's that or a cover charge. You don't have to drink it if you don't want to. Hell, I'll drink it myself." Muttering to herself, she ordered some frou-frou thing with fruit juice in it. I ordered a shot of tequila, which I shouldn't have been drinking with my meds, but hell, I wasn't driving, so it seemed like a good idea at the time. I hadn't told her yet that we'd have to order two drinks.

I informed the waitress that we wanted to talk to Boris, preferably in his office; that was in case I had to pull a gun on him—not that I told the waitress that last. Our drinks arrived, and Carolyn had, by then, actually watched a whole dance—right down to the buff—the dancer's, not hers. When the drink was set in front of her, she took a gulp and said, "That's disgusting."

"Yeah, well the men don't come here for the great drinks," I said.

"I meant the dance," she snapped.

"That's what they come for," I agreed, and sipped my tequila. I'd ordered by brand, and this wasn't it, so I called the waitress over and said I was going to call the state licensing commission if she didn't get her ass over here with what I was paying for. She mumbled that the bartender must have made a mistake.

"Maybe you shouldn't pick fights with everyone before we ever get to see Mr. Ignatenko," Carolyn suggested in that oh-so-polite tone that raised my hackles.

Oh boy. Table dance coming up, I thought. *The proper Mrs. Blue is going to freak. Oh, Christ, she's waving. If she tries to stop the girl, we'll get our asses kicked out of here even if I do pull a gun on the bouncer.*

No one waved back, and Carolyn settled down for another gulp. The blonde girl, now up on the table with two guys watching avidly, began to do her thing. Carolyn drummed her fingernails on our table loud enough to provide a percussion undercurrent to the music. One of the guys ran his hand up the girl's leg. She stopped dancing and tried to brush it off. Carolyn got up, stomped over to the table, yanked his hand off, and gave it a slap. "Shame on you. I'm sure that's against the rules." Then she said, "Good evening, Polya. Can I help you down?"

"Hey, we paid for a dance," whined the guy who'd kept his hands to himself.

The bouncer showed up and told us to go back to our table or leave. By that time the blonde girl had climbed down, whispered to Carolyn, given her a hug, and left.

"Maybe it's about time you took us in to see Boris," I said, giving the bouncer a killing look. The audience was booing us. "You oughta know that having a proper-type lady in the club during performances is bad for business. What if she goes home and starts calling preachers? Or the cops?"

There was a brief conversation between the bouncer and the floor manager, after which the bouncer, a one-eyed fatty with big arm muscles, told us to follow him. Carolyn insisted on going back for her drink, so I told her to bring mine along too.

"I'm sure I read in the newspaper that the patrons are *not* allowed to touch the performers," Carolyn said to Boris Stepanovich before they'd even been introduced. "One of them just grabbed the thigh of Polina Mikhailov."

"Who are you?" he retorted. "Her mama? And what *you* do here, Lieutenant? I hear you retire."

"We're here about the late Vladislav Gubenko. This is Carolyn Blue. Carolyn, Boris Stepanovich Ignatenko. He owns this dump."

Boris is a scary-looking guy. Real tall. Maybe six four or five. Bony with long arms and big spider hands, wide, bony, squared-off shoulders, and a long face out of a ghoul movie—lantern jaw, thin-lipped mouth, long creases from forehead to chin, a jagged scar across his forehead, and these sunken eyes circled in black. He'd be easy to pick out of a lineup. No way you'd get any other guys looking even halfway like him.

"How you know Polya?" he asked Carolyn.

"I'm a committee member of Opera at the Pass and an opera lover," she replied tartly, "and I don't like to see her mauled by drunken perverts."

Boris let out a big, booming laugh. "You calling my customers perverts? So okay, who else you expect to see here? Pillars of community? Well, we got some of them too. I take you see lap dance. A little hand on thigh nothing. Right, Lieutenant?"

"I hear the city council wants six feet between dancers and customers. That ought to screw up business," I replied.

"Hey, I not near church or school. My girls artists, not whores. City should leave me alone."

"Wonder why nobody believes that crap you're putting out. Artists, not whores, huh? Bull shit."

"Vladik," Carolyn reminded me. "We understand that you knew Vladik Gubenko," she said to Boris.

"Sure, I know him." Boris went to the chair behind his desk, stretched out in it, and smiled widely. "You think man like me wouldn't know a professor? That right, opera lady? I know Vladik since little boys. We climb trees together, sled in snow, go to school, get in troubles together. Good friends, long time. Then Vladik go to Moscow for study opera things, and I get drafted in army, end up in Afghanistan." He touched the scar on his forehead. "Bad place. Bad peoples. Now Americans finding out. Think they go home quick? Ha! Still there. Twenty years from now—still there. Or be smart, give up, go home. Who want Afghanistan anyway? Shit-pile place, I say. Maybe Iraq better, but I think that shit-pile place too."

I smothered a grin. Carolyn was wincing again. "So you and Vladik were boyhood amigos, huh Boris? Where were you the night he was murdered?"

"Vladik murdered? No way. Vladik know how to take care of self. He die from drinking too much tequila. He drink good vodka, he be okay. That's what I hear."

"You heard wrong. So where were you?"

"Where I be? Here. Girls come from big opera party, late for work, but I good boss, let them go sing for fancy peoples. They no say Vladik sick. No say that next day. I read in newspaper. American citizen now. Read American newspaper. Better than *Pravda*. Can believe what read. Say Vladik choke on vomit. Girls come in. I say, 'Why you no tell me?' They say not hear till that day."

"And you were doing what the night he was killed?" The man talked a lot and said very little. Typical criminal. Maybe he killed the other Russian because he wanted the free Russian dancers for himself.

"I here all night. Open till four, five in morning. I here. I have apartment." He gestured behind him. "Sleep after close. Wake up at noon. You think I kill Vladik? Ha! Vladik my friend. Not so many Russians Boris can be friends with. Talk about mother country." His laughter boomed again. "Hard mother, Russia. America better to us. Don't draft me, send me to shit-pile Afghanistan. Probably be in Chechnya now; get shot at if I didn't desert. But I immigrate and get nice business."

"Really nice," I agreed sarcastically.

"We were hoping, Mr. Ignatenko," said Carolyn, "that

you, being Vladik's friend, could give us a name. Other friends. Or enemies. No one seems to know with whom he associated, besides you."

"Ha! You think I give him something make him sick. He don't come here at all Saturday night of opera."

"So who do you think killed him?" I snapped.

He kept his eye on Carolyn, ignoring me. "So you like opera? What Russian opera you like?"

"*Eugene Onegin,*" she said promptly. "The duel scene with Lenski's aria and the beautiful duet. Prince Gremin's aria. Did you know Caruso once sang it when the bass lost his voice?"

Obviously you only had to mention opera to get her to forget about the subject at hand.

"And the end when Onegin realizes he's lost Tatiana forever." She beamed.

Jesus Christ! Did she really think that Boris cared about opera? He was just stalling. Pulling my chain maybe. "Ignatenko, do I have to call friends in Vice and have them toss your place and hassle your customers to get a name out of you? If you didn't kill him, and don't think I won't check that out, then who do you think did?"

"Why you care if you no more cop, now running around with an opera lady. Very rude, Vallejo. Interrupting we have opera conversation."

"Bullshit. You wouldn't know opera from rap."

Boris sighed dramatically, as if anyone would feel sorry for a ghoul like him. "Excuse this woman, Mrs." This was to Carolyn and about me. I could have kicked him. Then to me he said, "Vladik liking three things best: women, opera, and gambling. He is doing very good with women and opera. With gambling, he is losing pants."

"Shirt," said Carolyn. "The English idiom is Losing one's shirt."

"So shirt," said Boris agreeably. "You want a name, used-to-be-lieutenant. Salvador Barrientos. Is called

Palomino. Lives in Juarez. Vladik owe him maybe forty, fifty thousand. Could be Barrientos get tired waiting for money."

"Your friend Vladik have other business across the river besides gambling?" I asked.

"Why? You know Barrientos?"

I shrugged.

"Me, I don't know this Barrientos. Only what Vladik tell me. Go bother him. I am not killing my friend. I am sleeping. With—Carmen, maybe. You ask her. Maybe she remember she warm my bed Saturday." Then he turned back to Carolyn. "Nice to meet you, lady. Better you find other friends. Lieutenant here is mean woman. No one like her in my world."

20

"Who's Prissy?"

Carolyn

Once we were safely back in the car, I breathed a sigh of relief and turned the key in the ignition. I couldn't get away from Brazen Babes fast enough. And I *had* to rescue those two poor girls. "Did you recognize the name he gave us?" I asked Luz. "Salvador . . ." I couldn't remember the rest.

"Barrientos," she supplied. "Yeah, I know the name. I just didn't know he was into gambling, but if your Russian opera guy owed the Palomino money and wasn't paying off, well, Barrientos might have killed him and never given it a second thought."

"So what do we do now?" I pulled out of the lot and turned left.

"Turn back," she said. "You're going the wrong way."

I had to drive a half mile before I found a place where it was safe to turn around. "You could have stopped me *before* I turned the wrong way," I said, peeved.

"Hey, I got you out here. I figured you'd remember the way back."

"I don't know why you'd think that. It's dark. Everything looks the same," I muttered. "Now, tell me the next time I have to turn, and please do it in plenty of time."

"You're only driving about twenty miles an hour. Speed up a little, will you? At this rate, I won't be able to walk without a cane by the time you get me home."

I wondered exactly what she meant by that. Maybe that she'd be old by the time we got home. But I had noticed that sometimes she limped. I wanted to ask about the limp, but that wouldn't be very polite. My mother wouldn't have approved.

Luz broke into my thoughts. "I have to hand it to you. You may be prissy, but you've got the courage of your convictions."

"Who's prissy?" I demanded angrily. Here I'd come out to this disgusting place, got out alive while she was threatening everyone in sight and scaring me to death, and now she was calling me names.

"*You* are. Every time you hear a word you don't approve of, you wince. Makes me want to swear just to see you do it."

"How charming!" I snapped. She was really very rude. Boris Ignatenko had that right.

"I was paying you a compliment. When you slapped that guy who put his hand on your friend's leg—well, that was pretty cool. I'll bet he won't forget that any time soon. Comes to a skin bar looking for a hard-on, and some prissy woman walks up, says 'Shame on you,' and slaps his hand. Bastard probably thought his mother had caught up with him."

"I am not prissy," I mumbled, but still I was pleased. She'd said I was *cool*. Of course it had been a foolhardy thing to do, which I'd realized when the dreadful doorman came over, but still, it was *cool*. I'd have enjoyed telling Jason about my compliment from the grudging, tough-talking Luz Vallejo, but of course that would mean telling him about the visit to Brazen Babes. The chances that he'd think *that* was cool were minimal. Then I wondered if Luz was really carrying a gun. If so, where? In the pocket of her jacket? Could you just drop a firearm into your pocket? What if your pocket were picked. She probably had a permit to carry a concealed weapon. Texas issues those. Or maybe she didn't need a permit since she'd been a police person.

"As for Barrientos, I'm going to make a few calls. See what he's up to these days. Used to be drugs. Signal for a left. You gotta turn at the next light."

I was so shocked at the mention of narcotics that I missed the turn. She swore, but under her breath. I turned around as soon as I could and went back to make the turn. "What did you mean about needing a cane before we get back?" I asked. That wasn't as bad mannered as asking about her limp.

"My knee is aching like a son of a bitch, and it's not getting any better. I need to rub some chile glop on it and go to bed," she replied, her tone rancorous.

"Is it an injury from your days as a police person?" I asked.

"You mean did I get shot in the knee? Or kicked? Well, I did get kicked. More than once. But this is arthritis. Rheumatoid arthritis."

"Oh dear," I said, remembering Connie French, a friend at our last school. "I knew a woman who got it in her thirties. She had a terrible time. But I've read that the medications are much better now."

"They are, and they're much more expensive."

"Is that why you retired?" I asked, unable to suppress my curiosity.

"That's why I retired, and no one was more pissed off than me. I thought I was on the fast track to being the first woman chief in El Paso. Instead I was on the fast track to being a cripple. Of all the crappy luck!"

"No one in your family had rheumatoid arthritis?" I asked matter-of-factly. I doubted that she'd appreciate any overt sympathy for her plight.

"Not a soul. Diabetes, sure. Heart disease. Hepatitis."

"Good grief!" I couldn't help exclaiming. "At least the arthritis won't kill you.'

"No, but the meds may. Turn at the next light. Left. There's an arrow."

"Thank you." I made the turn. I was beginning to recognize the area and felt relieved. Now if I could just find my way up the mountain to the gates of her condo community. The streets twist around because of the arroyos that run down the mountain. They carry off the water when it rains farther up. If there isn't an arroyo handy for that purpose, the water rushes down the streets, sometimes in torrents, sometimes carrying cars away and drowning people. Not that any such thing had happened since we'd been here. The whole Southwest was suffering a drought with tighter water rationing and a good deal of public grumbling about it. Fortunately, since our house is fairly new, we have desert vegetation and underground drip irrigation in the yard.

"You want to go right, left, right," she ordered after we got off the main street and headed up.

I managed it.

"About Barrientos, like I said, I'll ask around. Be interesting if your Russian was in the drug trade as well as the white-slave trade."

"He's not my Russian," I protested. "My husband just served on a committee with him. And Mr. Ignatenko said the connection was a gambling debt."

"Maybe. Or maybe it was a drug debt. Barrientos supplied the product, and Gubenko saw that it got onto the streets."

I started to protest, but she said, "I don't mean he was out on street corner peddling coke. I just mean maybe he had students selling for him."

What a horrible idea. If it turned out to be true, I'd have to tell Dr. Tigranian, who would have a temper tantrum, shouting the news so everyone in Fine Arts heard.

"Turn right," said Luz. "You can pull into my driveway."

I insisted, against her wishes, on walking her to the door, and as much as she protested, she did lean on my shoulder, which meant her knee must have, indeed, been painful. And she thanked me for the help. *Maybe we're becoming friends,* I thought as I drove home.

Once in bed, and thinking back over the evening, I had to admit that it had been interesting. An adventure. Had Jason ever been to a place like that? He certainly hadn't wanted to take me into the New Orleans club with the tassel-twirler from New Jersey. The tassels had been on surprising parts of her body, and the fact that she could make them twirl was truly amazing. Obviously some women are able to develop muscles that rest of us never even know we have. Not that I'd want to do that.

I drifted into sleep and dreamed that I was teaching Polya and Irina to tassel-twirl. They said they were learning so many new things in America and thanked me for the lesson and asked if we could go out to lunch afterward and if I had any more pretty glass fish for them. They cried when I didn't. What a silly dream.

21
Calling Around

Luz

It must have been the tequila. I woke up that morning
with no pain at all. What a great feeling! Euphoria. I made
myself an egg and chorizo burrito while I thought about
who to call for recent info on Salvador Barrientos. He used
to be muscle for the drug cartel. Both sides of the border.
His friends called him Palomino because he liked to bleach
a blond streak in his hair, but in the department we called
him Piss-for-Brains Barrientos.

He was picked up by a cop from the Downtown Regional Command for pissing on a wall in Segundo Barrio.
The kid was going to issue him a citation for public nui-
sance or something, when Barrientos said, "You know who
I am? I got big-time friends," and so forth. So the beat cop
called him in and found out he had a warrant on him for assault. Barrientos had a good lawyer who got him pled
down to a misdemeanor; in those days we didn't have
room in the jail for all the people we arrested. But on the
job we called him Piss-for-Brains after that.

By my second cup of coffee, I'd decided on a narc sergeant named Chuy, Chuy Mendoza. We went to the academy together back in the old days. Chuy was glad to hear
from me and said, "¿Qué pasa, Vallejo?" which means
what's going on?

"Having a good day," I told him."Turns out tequila is
better for what ails me than all that damn medication."

"Well, hell, I coulda told you that. So what's up? Wanna go out boozin'? My old lady wouldn't approve, you being such a hot *chica*, but what's a marriage when it comes to getting drunk with an old partner. Hell, I knew you before I knew her."

"Yeah, Chuy. Say hi to Angie for me. As for being a hot chica, that's only if women with gray streaks and a limp turn you on. I think Angie can rest easy."

"Angie's gonna say hi back. So what can I do for you?"

"Tell me about Salvador Barrientos. What's he up to these days? Still taking his knife to enemies of the drug culture? And where's he living? Whatever you know would help."

"He's come up in the world. I hear he has a house across the river in the country-club district, and he's a lieutenant now in charge of sneakin' product across the river. You can tell that because we're bustin' so many mules. Still Piss-for-Brains. You hear about the two guys with bulgin' crotches who got caught at the border. Now who'd wanna buy an ecstasy pill that had been hangin' off some sweaty dumbfuck's balls?"

I had to laugh. "Yeah, I read about that. Should put a dent in the drug market at raves around town—or was it headed north?"

"Who knows, but we don't like to see it comin' over from Mexico. Just one more thing to worry about. But for sure the idea was Barrientos's."

"He hang out over here anywhere particular?" I asked.

"Ain't been across the border in three, four months that I heard. Got some heavy warrants on him these days. We get our hands on him, no one's gonna let him plead down on nothin'."

"You hear he's taking bets on sports? Anything like that?" I asked.

"Not my thing, but I haven't heard. Did hear he may be doin' some people smugglin'. Got some coyotes in his stable maybe. Just gossip so far. If he is, his bosses ain't gonna like him branchin' out."

"Maybe he's a lieutenant in that too." People smuggling? That sent a little tingle up my spine. Could Gubenko have been smuggling girls in through Mexico to dance in the clubs and service the local johns?

"What's your interest in Barrientos, Vallejo? You thinkin' about another bounty-huntin' run?"

"Is there a bounty on him?" I asked. Now that would be an added incentive.

"Damn if I know. If there is, it would be through the feds. Nothin' from Crime Stoppers."

"Well, it's no big deal," I said. "A neighbor of mine died. I found the body, and I think he was murdered. Art Guevara, that lazy prick, caught the case and thinks it's food poisoning."

"So you're gonna make an ass of Guevara? Sounds good to me, Vallejo. Need any inside help, let me know."

"Yeah, thanks, Chuy."

"*De nada.*"

Carolyn

I woke up with the telephone ringing in my ear. It was Jason from Austin—and at seven o'clock in the morning— after I'd been up way past my bedtime at Brazen Babes, a consideration that kept me from complaining about the early morning call. Of course the first question my husband asked was, "Where were you last night? I called three times. The last at midnight."

"Well, that was only eleven o'clock here," I protested sleepily. "I was out with a new friend I met through Opera at the Pass," which was sort of true. "I'm working on getting those two Russian girls out of that club. I did go to see Dr. Tigranian and, Jason, I have to say, *volatile* hardly describes him. All that shouting. And his vocabulary! My goodness. But he *is* the great nephew of the composer Armen Tigranian. Do you remember listening to *Anoush?* It was years ago."

A moment of silence while my husband processed that information. "I don't know why I never thought to ask him," Jason replied. "Is he going to do anything about the students?"

"He's going to try, and we have an ad hoc committee of women trying to get them clothes, food, and jobs, so they can leave the place they're now working." I mentioned neither that I'd actually visited Brazen Babes, nor that my "new friend" was not on the committee.

"If you manage to get the university through this without a scandal, they should give you one of the *Amigo* prizes," said Jason.

"What would they say it was for?" I asked, laughing, imagining the speech that would go with the award. "And to Carolyn Blue, friend of the university, for rescuing two music students from careers in exotic dancing, prostitution, and other nonacademic pursuits, not to mention saving our beloved institution from participation in white slavery, we grant this award . . ."

"By the way, Jason, when will you be home?" I didn't want him to return to his question about my activities the night before.

"Well, I'm not sure, Carolyn. I've put Mercedes in touch with a research group here and—"

"Who's Mercedes?" I asked.

"My graduate student from Mexico City. Mercedes Lizarreta."

"You didn't mention her to me."

"I'm sure I did. She started this fall. Very promising student, and God knows Mexico City has pollution problems that make ours look mild."

"And you took her to Austin? You didn't mention that either."

"Hmmm. Thought I had. We're talking to an environmental toxicologist at UT Austin, and now she's working with his group for a few days. I may not be back until Saturday or Sunday."

I can't say that I liked that much. Jason and some young woman from Mexico. Was she as pretty as Adela Mariscal, also Mexican, who had slept with Vladik? Of course, that had been at Vladik's instigation. But could my sensible husband be entering a midlife crisis? He'd just turned forty-eight last month. Probably a vulnerable age with fifty looming on his horizon. I didn't know what to say to him.

"So who is your new friend's husband?" he asked.

"Really, Jason. I'm surprised at you. Does a woman interested in opera have to be somebody's wife? Your mother wouldn't approve of an attitude like that."

"For Pete's sake, Carolyn, you never used to say that kind of stuff. I'm going to have to keep you away from her. She's a bad influence."

Jason's mother is a radical feminist and women's studies scholar in Chicago. We're on better terms than we used to be, although I'd have no objection to being kept away from her. She still hadn't replaced that dowdy size-sixteen dress she sent me for my birthday. I can't think of when I've been more insulted. I may be in my forties, but I still wear a size ten, even if I am a food columnist and duty bound to eat all sorts of wonderful meals in restaurants.

"Maybe you should introduce me to Mercedes," I suggested.

"Where did that come from?" He sounded aggrieved. "You'll meet her at the ACS picnic."

"That's next spring," I pointed out.

22

The Ad Hoc Committee at Work

Carolyn

I **punched my** pillow and tried to get back to sleep, but my mind wouldn't let go of Jason and Mercedes, his graduate student, and Professor Collins saying to give him a call if Jason got interested in some cute, young student. *Mercedes probably knows all about poisonous chemicals, while all I know about is history and food, and I don't even like to cook anymore.* My thoughts were interrupted by a second telephone call. What was wrong with people, calling before eight in the morning? Or maybe it was Jason calling back to say he'd changed his mind and was coming home today and leaving Mercedes in Austin.

No such luck. It was Barbara Escobar, who said she hoped she hadn't called too early; she wanted to tell me that, according to Frank, the bank couldn't hire the two Russian girls, no matter how much they needed jobs, but that she and Frank would be happy to make a donation to the cause, and she'd ask her friends if they needed babysitters. Barbara herself didn't because her mother was always available to take her children and loved to have them at her house, even Frank, Jr., who wasn't yet two, but adored his *abuelita.*

"That means *little grandmother.* No matter what Vivian says, I am teaching my children Spanish," she added defensively, "and I don't know why she thinks my Spanish isn't fluent. I've even read books in Spanish."

I thanked Barbara nicely, hung up, and closed my eyes again.

Not five minutes later Vivian Brockman called. Peter, she said, had been so touched by the plight of the two foreign-student sopranos that he offered, if they could type and do math, to hire them as billing clerks several afternoons a week. Now *that* was a good offer. I thanked Vivian enthusiastically and told her that I was pushing the Music Department to provide them with tuition and part-time jobs, not that anyone thought the university had any jobs, or money for that matter.

"I don't see why they shouldn't help," said Vivian. "There's always some extra money to be found for a good cause."

Especially when a scandal might ensue if the Russian girls weren't taken care of, I thought. I didn't mention that aspect of my conversation with Dr. Tigranian. He'd probably call next.

"And I had another idea," said Vivian. "Barbara Escobar has two daughters who love to sing. Not that I think they have a future in it, but the Escobars are always attending some school performance and signing the children up for classes in something. Why shouldn't they hire the Russian girls to give their daughters music lessons?"

I agreed. Why shouldn't they?

"I'll call her," said Vivian, "and get back to you."

Well, everything was moving along except for my need to sleep a few more hours after my late night. I dragged myself out of bed and took a shower. Naturally, the phone rang again while I was covered with soap. I didn't rush to answer it. After all, what were answering machines for if not to let you finish your shower? I did check the messages once I'd dressed. Dolly Montgomery. I'd call her after breakfast— yogurt, toast, and a sliced apple. I planned to remain a size ten forever, or at least until they buried me in a size-ten dress. *So there Vera*, I thought. Vera's my mother-in-law.

After sticking my nose out the sliding glass doors to check the temperature—which was still nice—donning a sweater; and tucking the telephone under my arm, I carried my breakfast outside onto the patio, where the sky was as blue overhead as my slacks and sweater set, and the mountains stood out clear and stark to the south and west. No smog. I arrowed through the caller ID screens to Dolly's number, pressed the Talk button, and waited for her to answer, remembering the plain black telephone in my father's house that did nothing but facilitate telephone calls. I had nagged him for almost a year before he agreed to get rid of the dial phone and replace it with a button-pad model. "Hi, Dolly, it's Carolyn. I was in the shower when you called."

"Oh, it wasn't that important, Carolyn, but I know you're hoping for calls about Polya and Irina. Unfortunately, I have no employment leads, but I do have lots of canned food around the house. Would that help?"

I was disappointed, but said it surely would. At least I'd have something to take out to the trailer.

"Howard was so envious to think that there are people available who can translate from the Russian and he has no money to hire them. The poor dear was in a blue funk when he left for the university. Or maybe it was that he has a freshman English class to teach today. The new chairman thinks everyone in the department should teach at least one, and Howard is always depressed at the literacy, if you can call it that, of the students."

Dolly got back to her bulbs—she must have had hundreds of them, or else she only dug up a few at a time, which made sense to me—and I drank the last of my coffee with a last bite of apple and mouthful of toast. I'd spread some of the jalapeno-peach preserves on the toast—very tasty. While putting my breakfast dishes into the dishwasher, my doorbell rang. What a morning! I hadn't even put on shoes yet. Maria-Reposa Hernandez

stood at my door, arms full of clothes, bags of food around
her feet.

"Martin can't hire them," she announced, "but the
church sent all this over." We carried the donations straight
to the trunk of my car, while she told me about a dawn
prayer breakfast for women. I hadn't realized Catholics did
that sort of thing, although I did know about early masses.
Anything at dawn was not a function I'd have wanted to attend.

Then Maria-Reposa came in for coffee and to hear what
other responses I'd had to our charitable endeavor. She
loved our patio and the view of the city and the mountains
beyond. I didn't even know what those mountains were
called. The one on which my house stood was named
Franklin, possibly the middle name of a pioneer whose last
name was peculiar, Coons or something. Maria-Reposa
pointed out Mount Cristo Rey and told me tales of the pilgrims who climbed to the top, where the figure of Christ
dominated the sky, and of the bandits who attacked them
and stole from them. "Poor dears, some have to come
down the mountain barefooted because even their shoes
and socks have been stolen. Of course, some make the pil-
grimage barefooted to begin with, so their shoes and socks
aren't available. I'm sure God takes note of their sacrifice
and devotion, as well as the evil deeds of the bandits."

"Bandits and armies weren't allowed to attack pilgrims
in the Middle Ages," I murmured. "It was called the Peace
of God, I think, or was it the Truce of God? Certain days
and people were protected by the Pope."

"Oh, there are always sinners who pay no attention,"
she replied. "No doubt pilgrims in the old days were as
much at risk as they are here and now."

I was enjoying the conversation until my phone rang
again—Dr. Tigranian ordering me to his office at one-
thirty. We were going to see his dean. That's all he'd tell
me, but I was hopeful that the university planned to meet

its obligations, not to mention avoiding a scandal because they'd hired a man who had preyed on their students. Who *had* hired Vladik? I wondered. Dr. Tigranian certainly didn't think much of him.

Maria-Reposa and I were speculating on what the university might have in mind for Polya and Irina when my telephone shrilled again. How many calls was that? Some days it never rings. That day, when a nap would have made me very happy, it wouldn't stop. My caller was Olive Cleveland, who had once mentioned that her husband was a relative of the late President Grover Cleveland. Hadn't the president been fat? Olive certainly wasn't. She was downright skinny. Maybe her husband was fat. I'd never met him.

"Which do you want to hear first?" she asked. "The good news or the bad?"

I didn't much care but said *bad* and learned that Ray Lee Cleveland didn't have any work for our protégés. "But the good news is," she continued, "that he knows someone at a maquila who does business with Russia and could probably use a translator. Or two."

"But aren't the maquilas in Juarez?" I asked. "I don't know if their immigration status would allow Polya and Irina to work in Mexico, not to mention their car. What if it broke down over there? They'd never get back, and it would take so much time waiting at the bridges, not to mention the fact that hundreds of girls working at the maquilas have been murdered and dumped in the desert in recent years. And they probably don't speak Spanish.The Russian girls, not the murdered girls."

"All true," Olive agreed. "But our friend has an office over here. They just do the manufacturin' over there an' then send goods off under bond to avoid the tariffs or whatever. Now, this is not a sure thing, honey. The friend is thinkin' about it. He'll probably want to interview them, but he's definitely interested. The local job market isn't crowded with Russian speakers, now is it? I'm not sure they even teach it at the university. And then there's the car. Hmmm. I'll have to talk to Ray Lee about that. He does own a used-car lot. Maybe he could find them something."

"Oh, my goodness Olive, you're a lifesaver!" I cried. "A car and jobs!"

"It is not a done deal, honey. We'll have to see. Any other offers?"

"Vivian said maybe Peter could provide them with part-time work typing bills, and she's going to suggest to Barbara that they teach the Escobar daughters singing."

"Oh, Lord yes. Those girls need lessons. Ray Lee an' I got roped into a middle-school production of *Oklahoma*. It was awful! Not that you can say that to the proud parents. Frank thinks his girls are headed for La Scala."

"Barbara offered money, and Maria-Reposa is here right now," I added. "We just packed my car with clothes and food from her church, and Dolly offered canned goods, and I'm going to the university this afternoon to see what they can do. Dr. Tigranian—"

"Oh, mah dear. See if you can't find someone else to talk to. That man is stark, ravin' mad. He threw a whole plate of little bitty tacos at Ray Lee durin' one of those alumni receptions. It had a bowl of salsa in the middle. And all because Ray Lee, who is, after all, a good ole Texas boy, said he'd rather give his money to the athletic program than to any ole dinner-theater fund.

"You know how he always manages to be out of town when the opera performances come up? He swore to me that he'd be here for the Friday night *Macbeth*, and sure enough Friday morning he had business in Cincinnati he just couldn't postpone. Or was it Chicago? Anyway, you don't want to get mixed up with Professor Tigranian. It was all I could do to keep Ray Lee from suin' the university, and God knows he loves the place dearly an' gives them tons of money. I have to nag him forever to get our yearly contributions to the opera and the symphony. Oops, my masseuse is knockin' at the door. Keep in touch, honey."

She was off the line before I could say thank you, and Maria-Reposa was getting ready to leave. Maybe I'd have time for a nap, after all. I didn't have another obligation until one-thirty, and if we were going to see the dean, surely Dr. Tigranian would mind his manners, so I could sleep easy.

23
How to Catch Salvador Barrientos

Luz

So Barrientos had moved up the drug ladder and was maybe mixed up in the smuggling of illegal immigrants. Boris had said the connection to Vladik was gambling debts, but that didn't sound right. Drugs and smuggling should be enough to keep a mid-level guy like Barrientos busy, unless it was a personal gambling debt. But the smuggling could sure connect the two. I needed more information. After considering my sources, I called a longtime connection in the DEA, Hector Parko, a guy who could go undercover and pass for anyone. Word was that he'd been assigned to a desk for a few months after getting hurt on the job in Colombia.

Hector was glad to hear from me. Once I told him I was doing pretty well with my illness, he wanted me to come out of retirement and join the DEA. "You an' me, babe— not a drug-dealing scumbag in the world the two of us working together couldn't put the screws to. We could pass for a nice middle-aged, dope-head couple, or dealers with a soul for romance. Or—"

"Hector, sexy as you are, I'm not into the idea of being the object of your lust. Anyway, we'd never know when my knee would start in and leave me limping."

"Plenty of crips among the folks I'm after. You'd fit right in."

I made a rude noise in his ear because, even when it's so, I don't appreciate being called a crip.

"Okay, babe, if you don't want to come back to work, what do you want from Hector?"

"Information. What else?" I retorted. "You keeping your eye on Salvador Barrientos? Palomino. I hear he's doing real good for himself."

"Temporary. Only temporary," Hector assured me. "That pendejo couldn't keep from fuckin' up if his mother's life depended on it."

"You ever hear he was taking bets?"

"Nah. He likes to gamble, but he's always on the wrong side of it. Puttin' his money down, not taking other people's bets."

"Smuggling? People?"

"That I've heard. Yeah. He may be runnin' some coyotes. If he is, and it's not a deal his cartel put him into, he's gonna get his ass kicked from here to Guatemala. *La dopa*—that's his main thing. I wish the bastard would come across the river. I'd put him out of business."

"Any dead-or-alive money out on him?" I asked.

"Oh, so that's your interest." Hector laughed. "There's twenty-five thousand. Not big bucks, but if you bring him back to me, babe, the money's yours, and I'll take you out on the town and dance that fucker arthritis right outa your bones. Count on it."

"That's a better offer than my doctors are making. Thanks, Hector. I don't suppose you've got a Juarez address on him. Another source said he had a place in—"

"Campestre—that fancy country club area with the golf course. Think he plays golf? I'd like to see that. He'd probably keep coke in them golf socks and heroin dissolved in his water bottle." Hector gave me the address.

Not likely I could get in there, but I could try. Now I needed to know where he hung out. Barrientos wasn't smart enough to be careful about stuff like that. I called a couple of Juarez numbers until I hit pay dirt. I should have remembered about the singing. Barrientos liked to sing with mariachi bands. Not so many of those places left these days, or so I've heard. His favorite was called Mariachi Caliente, and he showed up there a couple of times a week, according to my source.

Okay. There was the line I'd use to reel Barrientos in. With Carolyn as bait. Barrientos knew me, or used to. But I wasn't on the job anymore, and if I showed up at Mariachi Caliente with a respectable music lover like Carolyn Blue, he just might bite. He even liked blondes. He used to say he bleached that skunk streak in his hair to lure in blonde *chicas.* They'd be about the same age—Barrientos and the very nice Mrs. Blue, opera lover. If she told him his singing reminded her of some tenor—Caruso or someone—Barrientos would fall all over himself making up to her.

Perfect. I bent and stretched my knee. No pain. I was up to it. We could find out if he killed Gubenko, and if I brought him back, the twenty-five thousand wouldn't hurt. I punched in Carolyn's number, wondering if she'd want her share of the money. Well, if she hung in there with me and did a good job, she'd deserve it. I pictured her lighting into that scuzzball at Brazen Babes and thought the whole deal just might work.

"This is Luz. Vallejo . . . What the hell. Were you asleep? . . . Well, wake up and listen. I got a lead on Barrientos. So we're going to dinner in Juarez tonight. Great restaurant. You'll like it." I'd like it too. Best margaritas on the continent. Should do my joints a world of good. "You can write a column about it. That's what you do, isn't it? . . .

"Say, are the meals you eat out tax deductible? . . . Great. That should save us some money . . . No, we're not meeting him at the restaurant. We just want to get across the bridge without causing any notice. Two women going to dinner at a fairly early hour. No sweat. We'll look for Barrientos after dinner at a mariachi club. . . . So if he's not there, we go back tomorrow night, or is your husband coming home and he won't let you go? . . . So what's the problem? . . .

"You drive . . . Of course you can drive in Juarez. There aren't any more assholes on the roads over there than there are here in El Paso, and believe me, if we have an accident, no one wants to call the police. . . . All right. So you don't like the word asshole, and you don't want to drive in Juarez. How do you think we're going to corner this guy? By riding the tourist trolley? . . . Yeah, there is one, and no, it won't help us.

"Pick me up at seven. Wear something moderately sexy but still in good taste. We want Barrientos to be taken with you without trying to screw you under the table . . . Just kidding, Carolyn. See you at seven."

I hung up before she could raise any more objections. Of course she could fail to show up, but I'd have to take that chance.

Carolyn

Surely, she doesn't expect me to go over there with her, I thought. *And why does she think Jason controls where I go?* I was really irritated about that, especially since Jason was acting so peculiarly and making me uneasy in a way I'd never been before. *All right,* I thought defiantly. *I'll do it. In fact, it sounds exciting, chasing down a drug dealer or bookie or whatever he is. We'll be in a club, after all. What can he do to us? And there's the restaurant. But does Luz really know a good restaurant from a bad one? Well, I'd be finding out. In the meantime, I'll simply ignore the problem of driving in Juarez, which is truly terrifying.*

I looked at the bedside clock. Twelve-fifteen. Hopping out of bed, I rushed to change my clothes, comb my hair, put on lipstick, and fix some lunch. There were leftover enchiladas in the refrigerator. I zapped two in the microwave and ate them, keeping my mind on the afternoon's tasks. Once I'd met with Dr. Tigranian and the dean, I'd look up the Russian girls. After all, l had a trunk full of donations for them, not to mention the possibilities of part-time work, maybe even a used car, one that would start and keep running. I imagined how happy they'd be. Maybe I'd follow them out to the trailer with my presents.

Moderately sexy but still in good taste? What did that mean? No, I wouldn't think about the mission Luz had proposed. Time enough to worry about that when it was too late to back out. Maybe my car would break down, and I wouldn't have to go.

24

Protecting Academia

Carolyn

As Dr. Tigranian walked me at a very rapid pace from the Fine Arts Building to the Liberal Arts Building, I wondered irritably why I couldn't have of simply met him at the dean's office. He hadn't said a word to me in his own office other than, "Hurry. I don't want to keep the dean waiting." Well, I wasn't keeping the dean waiting. I'd been exactly on time. Tigranian had kept *me* waiting outside with his secretary while he shouted at someone on the telephone about the care of tubas.

The dean's secretary showed us right in, and there stood a short, plump man with fuzzy gray hair on head and chin; small, round spectacles; and a vested suit with the jacket removed. "Why you're the Middle Eastern history professor," I exclaimed. I'd had a fascinating conversation with him at a presidential reception. He and Jason are both chaired professors.

"And you're Mrs. Blue, who likes medieval European history." He shook my hand. "I'm also the dean. I don't think you know my name. Lester Latimer Britten, spelled like the English composer of ugly operas, as Tigranian can tell you."

"I never said 'ugly operas,'" the music chairman declared. "I love Benjamin Britten."

"I like the Italian composers better myself," I said, always happy to discuss opera. "Verdi, Puccini, Bellini, Donizetti."

"I quite agree. Much more pleasant," said the dean. "Except for that performance of *Macbeth* staged by Gubenko, with whom, I hear, we're having problems."

"Postmortem," I agreed. "You did know he's dead?"

"Small wonder," said the dean. "It's a miracle the audience didn't accomplish that. I personally like *Macbeth*, both play and opera, in period costume. I wonder who hired that man."

"I didn't hire him," shouted Dr. Tigranian, as if he'd been accused. "That Russian Don Juan, that seamy, long-haired . . ."

Oh dear, I thought. *Dr. Tigranian's working himself into a rage again.*

"*You* must have hired him," Tigranian roared at the dean.

"I did *not* hire him, and if you insist on having a childish temper tantrum in my office, Tigranian, I shall call security and have you locked in the men's room until you cool down," said the dean, without ever raising his voice. Then to me, "Now, tell me, my dear, did you read *Desert Queen* as I suggested?"

"I did," I replied enthusiastically. "And it gave me the shivers. So many things she talked about are happening all over again in the news."

"He who doesn't read history is doomed to relive it," said Dean Britten. "I'll be discussing *What Went Wrong* at your book club next spring."

"I'll look forward to it."

"What is this?" demanded Tigranian, who had been sulking over the threat of being locked in the men's room. "Gubenko leaves us with an ugly mess, which could explode in our faces and get us sued, and you are talking about romance books."

"Hardly a romance," said the dean. "A very timely biography that teaches us about the unfortunate parallels between Arab-English relations in the period of the first world war and American-Arab relations now. But you're quite right; we need to address this unsavory situation with the two Russian music students. It's not the first time we've had a similar problem, you know, but it wasn't in our college, and the young women, although they had student visas, weren't actually our students. That sort of thing couldn't happen now. The government is keeping close track of foreign students these days. Still, there's no question that we have to remove these young women from their present situation and see that they receive their degrees, in due time, without being sexually exploited." He patted his fuzzy beard as if hoping to rearrange it into a tidier configuration.

"Tuition is not a problem. Gubenko arranged for that, and I can see that the grant continues next year. However, I understand that their housing accommodations are unacceptable."

"Disgusting," I agreed. "I've visited their trailer. It's not fit for human habitation, but no one seems to know who owns the trailer, whether Vladik rented it for them, or owned it, or—"

"Yes. Well, we always have people dropping out of school and leaving the dormitory—for the most part athletes who haven't made and will never make their grades. Therefore, I can provide the young women with a double room and board in university housing that, happily, has already been paid for by the athletic department. Do you think that will suffice to solve the housing problem, Mrs. Blue?"

"I'm sure they will be terribly grateful and relieved. When can they move in?"

"As soon as they like."

"Maybe we can do it this afternoon." I glanced at my watch. "They can call the dreadful man who is making them work for free now that Vladik is dead, quit on the telephone, and refuse to tell him where they're going, if he should ask. That should take care of that problem."

"I can't provide them with jobs, however," cautioned the dean, "and Dr. Tigranian tells me there's no money in his budget to hire any student help."

"No money?" said Tigranian. "Worse than no money. We're—"

"Shhh," I cautioned, putting my finger to my lips.

"Stop doing that," he retorted, voice quieter.

"Maybe I should try the *shhh* option," said the dean dryly. "I'm sure, Mrs. Blue, that you know the state legislature is cutting our budget to the bone."

I smiled. "I hear about it all the time; however, I'm hopeful that members of Opera at the Pass, and, incidentally, they don't know about the strip club, just that Vladik was supporting the girls—"

"Thank goodness for that. Does anyone else know?" the dean interrupted.

"Jason, and Mr. Boris Ignatenko, whose club it is, and the girls, of course. Anyway, my committee is collecting clothes, food, and job offers. I may even be able to get them a car that actually runs."

"And you will explain to the young ladies that their present circumstances are not to be mentioned. By the way, you should not call them *girls;* it's politically incorrect. I'd rather not see them myself to explain things. The university cannot entirely divorce itself from this unfortunate situation, but the farther away I stay from it, the better. Which applies to you, as well, Dr. Tigranian. I do not want you yelling at these students about their late sponsor or the jobs he provided for them or anything else."

"I hope never to see them," said the music chairman, as dignified as if he hadn't just shouted at his dean.

"Well, I hope they'll receive parts in university productions," I hastened to add. "They have lovely voices."

"No more productions. We may even have to charge admission to the student degree recitals," said Tigranian, scowling.

Which should insure that no one shows up but relatives, I thought. *And maybe not even relatives.*

I went back immediately to ask the music secretary where I could find Polya and Irina and was sent to the practice rooms. There I discovered them trilling away, but without direction since their professor had vomited himself to death, probably with some help from an unknown murderer. In the remaining three hours of the afternoon, the excited girls—students—and I carried cans and clothes into their new room, which they thought was wonderful—so clean, such nice furniture, a nice bathroom; what more could they ask? Then we drove to the trailer, after I pushed their car from a student parking lot to a hill.

While they collected their pitiful cache of possessions, I presented myself to the woman who ran the park to give notice that her tenants were leaving. She said whatever Mr. Gubenko wanted, but the November rent was late. I told her to call the professor. She asked if I wanted to leave a forwarding address for girls. I didn't.

What a strange-looking woman she was—squat, with a light mustache. And what a strange trailer park! I had always imagined them as being places full of children and people sitting outside in lawn chairs drinking beer. This one might have occupants, other than Polya and Irina, but I didn't see any—just the twitch of a curtain as I passed, but no visible people. After collecting the young women and giving their car another push, we drove back, in separate cars, to the university and recruited some large young men from the lobby to help carry things upstairs. Polya and Irina might have been exotic dancers and lesbians, but they could giggle like any American college girl in the presence of young men.

My last duty was to shoo the football players out of the room and have a serious talk about never discussing Brazen Babes or their housing or association with Vladik and his seamy associates. They assured me that they would be very happy to forget that part of their lives immediately and, instead, look forward to jobs and a viable car and all the good things that might be coming their way. In the meantime they had rooms, meals, classes, different clothes, and cans of soup that they could warm up in the microwave down the hall. They were ecstatic. I warned them to remove the soup from the cans before microwaving it.

I received more hugs and kisses from my new protégés than I deemed necessary. Such gratitude can be embarrassing. After all, my motives were not entirely charitable.

With one last goodbye, I headed for home and the choice of a moderately sexy, but tasteful outfit for my venture into Juarez. God help me! Jason would be very angry if I wrecked my car in a foreign country and ended up in a foreign jail, one that has a very dubious reputation, according to the newspaper.

25

Parallel Parking and
World-Class Margaritas

Luz

I made her come in so I could take a look at her. Not bad. Long black dress with a high Chinese collar but open enough to hint at a bit of cleavage and a red stone pendant hanging around her throat with earrings to match. Low heeled boots. That was good in case we had to run. "You'll do. In fact, Barrientos likely never saw anyone like you." She gave my compliment the evil eye. My outfit was what I had—dark blue silk pants and blouse, silver and turquoise jewelry that came from my grandmother. "Come here, Smack." I clipped the leash to the dog's collar.

"We're taking the dog?" she asked. Now she really looked nervous.

"Right. When we get to Mexican customs, you tell them I'm blind." I slipped on dark glasses and grabbed my cane. The rest of my protective gear was in my purse—a roll of duct tape. "Say I never go anywhere without the dog, and Martino's is expecting the three of us. People coming over for dinner are good for the economy. They'll let us pass. Then we'll give the same story to American customs. It should work."

"Won't the dog have to go into quarantine after being in a foreign country?"

"It's just Mexico, for God's sake. As long as we get in the right lane, the customs agent should be a cousin of mine. So stop worrying."

"But why are we taking him?"

"Her. Because if we get in a tight spot, Smack will attack the attackers. Otherwise, we leave her in the car, and she keeps car thieves from stealing it."

Obviously Carolyn liked that part of the deal, but the attack business didn't go over well. "Are you expecting anyone to attack us?" she asked as she started the car.

"Nope. Just playing it safe." And from there on I gave her specific, long-term directions so we wouldn't have to keep turning back to make the turns she'd missed. She did okay, for a woman who was scared to death. But she did think we should park and walk across the bridge. I pointed out that the bridge arched up over the river so much that it was steep walking up and steep walking down, not the kind of exercise that did my knees any good, especially in a cold wind. It was pretty obvious that she didn't want to drive in Juarez and was still hoping to get out of it. She then remarked that it wasn't much of a river when its banks were encased in cement. I said the cement kept it from changing course and dumping part of the U.S. in Mexico or part of Mexico in the U.S.

While we were circling San Jacinto Plaza, something we'd have avoided if she'd been listening more carefully to my instructions, she told me that the plaza had once been a manure dump until someone named Satterthwaite in the 1880s put in bushes and trees, built a fountain, and then filled a pool for a couple of alligators. She thought having alligators in the town square was pretty weird and very dangerous.

I told her that the city finally had to get rid of them because the citizens picked on them. "Now we have the plastic alligator sculpture, and the climate is doing that in. A local guy sculpted it."

When we got to the Santa Fe Bridge, the one-way traffic to Juarez was pretty slow and my driver pretty jittery. While we were inching across, she rambled on about the

swinging footbridge they'd had from Smeltertown to
Juarez during Pancho Villa's time, so people could go
across and have their pictures taken with him and so the
revolutionaries could come across to buy clothes and boots
and plot against the Mexican government in the Sheldon
Hotel. "Madero stayed there," she confided, as if I didn't
know. I had family on both sides of the border back then—
still do, for that matter.

The footbridge story only got us halfway across, so she
told me that people used to shout good wishes and throw
food and money across the river to the rebels when they
weren't going across to take revolution pictures for the
family photo album. Carolyn had seen a lot of those pictures in books and at a library collection. "The river wasn't
cemented then," she said. "I imagine it was a good deal
more impressive."

"Right. It was still flooding all over the place," I replied.
Which brought us to Mexican customs, where they didn't
make any fuss about the dog, not when it accompanied a
blind woman, who looked like one of their own, and an
Anglo woman, who wouldn't shut her mouth and didn't
speak Spanish. After she got through with poor blind me and
my faithful Seeing Eye dog, who was faithfully asleep in the
back seat, she just had to mention that the first customs col-
lector on the American side of the river was appointed in
1849, and he formed patrols to stop smuggling. She wanted
to know when Mexico first set up customs and patrols. She
evidently thought these guys were the perfect people to ask.
Of course, they had no idea what she was talking about.
Meanwhile, like the blind woman I was supposed to be, I was
smiling at them, but not quite in the right direction. One guy,
who was about two sizes too big for his uniform, reached behind Carolyn to pat Smack, who woke up and growled.

"Now, now. Be a good doggie." I cooed. Poor Smack
didn't know what to make of that. She nosed over the back
seat to be sure it was really me.

The customs guy jumped back and waved us on, so we got the dog across.

The problem came when we were driving along beside the railroad tracks looking for a place to park. "There, "I said. "There's one."

"I don't know how to parallel park," Carolyn admitted.

"You're kidding, right? How did you get a license if you don't—"

"That was over twenty years ago, and I did everything else right. Can't we find a slanted parking place that I can pull straight into?"

"No, we can't. You'll have to try this one."

"The street's full of cars, and it's getting dark. I don't want to. I'll hit something."

Christ! "Okay, get out," I muttered. She could have mentioned this *before* we got to Juarez. But then she probably never parked anywhere but in mall and grocery store lots.

"Get out *here?* By myself? On this street? I don't know how to get to the restaurant, and we can't leave the car in the middle of the road."

"Get out, and I'll move over and park it."

"You're supposed to be blind," she grumbled, but she did get out and stood apprehensively on the sidewalk. I parked, after yelling at a guy who pulled up too close for me to back in. Probably figured on stealing my spot. I pressed the buttons to roll down both windows on my side, yelled at the guy again, and Smack stuck her head out, growling and barking. She's one dog who knows an enemy when she sees one. The guy backed up, causing the guy behind him to honk wildly.

Carolyn had her hand over her mouth, obviously figuring a terrible accident, involving her car, was about to occur, but it worked out. I backed her Camry right into the spot, and we set off for Juarez Avenue and Martino's, Carolyn bitching all the way.

A pitcher of their world-class margaritas calmed her down considerably. She even got comfortable enough to tell me, amazed, that children's funerals in Spanish colonial days had been merry affairs, the dead kid dressed up in white with flowers and ribbons and the mourners dancing and chatting. "Can you imagine?" she asked, taking another slug of her margarita. I suppose she'd been anticipating her own funeral on the way over, and this story came to mind. "Most parents are distraught when they lose a child," she pointed out. "I was astonished when I read about some of the customs. For instance, a bride changed her clothes and jewelry repeatedly during the wedding reception because—"

"A child is an innocent and goes straight to heaven," I interrupted before she could list every Spanish colonial wedding custom she'd read about. "The parents probably figured dying and going to heaven was a much better deal than getting kidnapped and tortured by raiding Apaches or dying of smallpox or even living long enough to earn a place in hell." And if I didn't get to confession pretty soon and put in for forgiveness for blasphemy, which seems to be a consequence of cop friends and painful arthritis, I'd have my name on Satan's list of good prospects.

Carolyn nodded thoughtfully. "I've always found Catholicism very interesting. Would you pass the margarita pitcher? These are delicious."

I reminded her that she was driving. Jesus! Drunk and terrified, she'd be a real menace. And what woman her age can't parallel park?

"Do you think I could get the recipe for these—what are they? Nachos?"

We were eating the little goodies Martino's serves while you're trying to work your way through the longest menu I've ever seen. "Forget it," I said. "Just enjoy them."

She took another sip of her drink and wondered whether margaritas would be even better if you floated some rasp-

berry liqueur on top. "That's disgusting," I said. "It's probably a criminal offense to change Martino's margarita
recipe."

"I don't have their recipe," she retorted. The waiter arrived to take our orders, and Carolyn said, "I can't decide
what to order."

"We'll have the mushrooms in sherry and filets stuffed
with crab and shrimp," I told him.

Carolyn wanted lamb and said, "Did you know that the
local Spanish settlers used to think they could tell when it
was going to rain because the lambs could smell it and
started to bleat and shake themselves as if they were already sopping wet?"

"I didn't, and you can't order lamb. You only get to
choose how you want your steak cooked." Sulking, she
said "medium-rare." I said "rare." The waiter asked what
soup we wanted. "Gazpacho," I said.

"I make better gazpacho than anyone," Carolyn objected. "I want to try something else."

"Okay, she'll have the avocado soup."

"But—"

"It's great. We'll both have house salad with Roquefort,
and be sure we get some *jicama* slices."

"What's jicama?" she asked. The waiter had hustled off
before she could raise any more objections.

"Like raw potato, only better. Harder to peel too. Imagine a mango with all that stringy stuff you gotta cut off.
Then imagine the mango with a dirty, stringy skin like a
potato and no mango inside. You got a jicama."

"That sounds dreadful," she complained. "And I don't
appreciate having my dinner ordered for me."

"There are three thousand things on their menu. We
want to be at Mariachi Caliente before ten. I'm just helping the process along. Have another nacho." That was a
sacrifice on my part. I love them too. They've got nacho
ingredients, but somehow they're different. Like they bake

them or something. And they're all the same shape, instead of a bunch of tostados piled on a plate with refried beans, cheese, and jalapeno peppers dumped over them. I guess you'd say they're a real canapé.

She ate the last one and then dug into her avocado soup, saying stuff like, "Ummmm." Guessing at what was in the soup. Glaring when I warned her off asking for recipes. "*The New York Times Cookbook* has recipes for avocado soup," I said, "so knock it off."

"I'll bet you don't even own a *New York Times Cookbook,*" she retorted, scooping up the last crouton with the last drops of soup.

"Don't be a snob, Carolyn. Man, is that a prissy name."

"All right. Call me Caro. Jason does. What do I call you?"

"How about Vallejo?" I suggested. "My friends do. Not that I'm saying we're—"

"Ha! This is the jicama, isn't it?" She had been turning over leaves in her salad when she spotted it and took a bite. "It's delicious. So crispy. And juicy. Where can you buy it?"

"Your supermarket," I replied. "Look for a blobby mutant potato, extra dirty."

Over our steaks, I prepped her for the second leg of our journey. I wasn't telling her about the third, if I decided on one. "This guy, Barrientos, thinks he's got a great voice. You ever heard mariachis?" She had—on the car radio. "He's not bad, actually, but when I get him over to the table, you act like he's got a great voice, operatic quality. Lay it on thick. He'll believe you. We want him to stay at our table for drinks so we can tell him he knows a friend of ours, Gubenko. Bring up the gambling. Like that. I know you're new to all this stuff. You just follow my lead, okay?"

"Actually," she said in that snippy voice, "I happen to know my way around a murder investigation."

"Uh huh."

"No, I really do," she insisted. "Let's order another pitcher."

"No," I said. "I'm not sure I should let you drive as it is."

"It's *my* car."

Walking along Juarez Avenue after dinner, I had a hard time because she wanted to look in windows. She thought she'd buy some stone bookends. I discouraged it. Then she saw the tequila in the window of a liquor store. "Can you believe that price?" she exclaimed. "I have to buy some. I want to experiment with margarita recipes. That's what we drank at the après-opera party, you know. Margaritas. A few people drank the champagne, but it was awful."

I tried to dissuade her from buying tequila, but she was adamant. Why pay so much in El Paso when she could get it cheap here? What was the best brand in my opinion?

"Why don't you get a bottle of mezcal," I suggested when I couldn't talk her out of tequila. "It's sort of tequila with a worm in it. The real fancy mezcal has a scorpion in it."

Carolyn turned away from the window and gave me a look. "That's disgusting. A scorpion? However, the worms from the agave were very popular with the Aztecs. They ate them with guacamole. In fact, I think people still eat them. Not that I would. And I don't want a bottle with a nasty creature in it. How many bottles can I bring back?"

When I told her one, she said I could bring one back too, and she'd pay me for it. I refused. She squinted at me and went in to buy her bottle. That whole deal took about twenty minutes because she had to ask about every brand she saw.

Then she wanted to know why there were so many dentists' offices in a tourist area. "You can't get your teeth fixed," I said. "We don't have time."

Finally, on the back streets, heading for the car, she tripped twice, but the sidewalks and streets are all broken up, so I couldn't be sure whether it was the tequila she'd drunk or the unrepaired public paving of Ciudad Juarez that was causing her problems. She damn near dropped her bottle of tequila. Then she insisted on driving. Just to prove she was sober, I suppose. Maybe bringing her along had been a bad idea.

26
Mariachi Caliente

Carolyn

It had truly been a delicious dinner, and I felt uncomfortably stuffed. I should have saved some of my steak for Smack, as Luz suggested. I just couldn't call her by her last name, as if we were two males in a locker room. And Smack probably wouldn't have liked the shellfish stuffing in the steak.

"Now listen, Carolyn, you have to knock off all this history crap when we get to the mariachi place. Barrientos will think you're some kind of nut."

"I don't see why," I protested. "What am I supposed to talk to him about? I don't know anything about the drug trade, but if he's a smuggler, I know some very interesting smuggling stories. For instance, during Prohibition when illegal alcohol was coming across the river from Mexico, there was a young woman who pushed a baby carriage along the levee every day, picked up a package containing bottles of mezcal, and slipped the package under her baby. Can you imagine putting smuggled goods under a baby? That's terrible."

"I can't imagine having a baby," Luz replied, "and that is absolutely your last historical anecdote until we get back across the border."

I suppose it seemed very silly to her that I kept telling her about the history of her own area, but I was so nervous. I tend to do that when I'm nervous. And I suppose she thought I was drunk and shouldn't be driving, but I did just fine. We arrived at the nightclub with no problems whatever, except that she had to park the car. Maybe I *should* learn to parallel park.

On the other hand, what were the chances that I'd be driving over here again? I read the papers. Every time a car pulled up beside us at a light or corner, I kept my eye on the passengers. People are shot in their own cars in Juarez. By mistake. Of course some are drug dealers, shot by rival drug dealers. Still, I was ready to shout, "Down!" if I saw a gun in a car window. She was lucky to have a driver as alert as I was. *She* just slouched in the seat and gave directions occasionally.

Mariachi Caliente looked rather run down, but then the whole city did. No wonder Jason seldom brought me over here. The sidewalks were in terrible shape. A long, vertical neon sign announced our destination, but enough letters had burned out that I'd never have known if Luz hadn't said that we'd arrived. I asked if she was sure the dog would be safe in the car in this neighborhood, and she said Smack would be safer than the car or us because she had big teeth. Fortunately, I was feeling much more relaxed and didn't take that too seriously. Really, driving in Juarez, now that I was used to it, wasn't that bad.

Inside, the place was dark and smoky, reminding me of a flamenco club I'd visited in Barcelona, not to mention several less reputable places in that city. I asked if they had flamenco here, but Luz said only if I felt like getting up and dancing. We walked down the long bar, lined with stools and customers, some of them in cowboy hats. I asked her if they were really cowboys, but she didn't know—or didn't care. On the other side were tables full of people drinking, mostly beer, busty women in low-cut blouses and men in ranch attire, some with those string ties.

We found a table by the wall at the end of the bar with

an obstructed view of a small stage where men in tight
suits with gaudy trimming down the trouser sides and
jacket sleeves strummed a variety of stringed instruments
and sang. Just as I was taking my seat, two trumpets
blasted into the song and frightened me half to death. Beyond us were more tables filling the back of the club. I was
quite interested and wished that I'd brought my camera
along.

Luz ordered cans of Tecate with salt and cut limes and
instructed me on sprinkling the can tops with the salt and
squeezing lime juice over that. The next time we ordered,
I intended to ask for club soda. We must have sat there an
hour, nursing our drinks and listening to the music, which
was very lively and *very* loud, especially those trumpets.
She explained that the word *mariachi* referred to the marriage bands that serenaded lovers and newlyweds in the
Mexican reign of Maximilian and Carlota. I nodded and
said their costumes reminded me of a description of bridegroom's clothing at hacienda weddings. Then I remembered that I wasn't supposed to provide her or anyone with
historical tidbits.

So there we sat—silent. She didn't say anything more
until she sat up, alert, and hissed, "Here we go. Check out
the guy talking to the leader. See, he's handing him
money."

I resisted the urge to comment on her confusing pro-
noun usage—two masculine pronouns referring, presumably, to two different people with antecedents in the
previous sentence.

"That's Barrientos. See if you can stay awake long
enough to listen. You'll need to say something about his
singing."

I resented the implication that I'd been falling asleep.
I'd been thinking about Adela Mariscal and what would
happen when the toxicology tests arrived in the hands of
Sergeant Guevara.

The object of our trip was a broad man, rather short for his weight but not fat at all. He had on tight jeans held up by a belt and a huge silver belt buckle decorated with a gold scorpion, fancy tooled cowboy boots, a cowboy shirt with gold scorpion studs and embroidery, and a cowboy hat, which, when removed, revealed the telltale bleached streak in his black hair. I thought he'd have looked much better without the streak, but then what did I know about drug-dealer fashion? Obviously it involved a lot of gold—and scorpions. He was also wearing a heavy gold cross on a chain, a gold watch that looked like a Rolex, and several large gold rings. Good grief! Didn't he realize that so much gold jewelry was in poor taste? As he began to sing, I slipped a notebook and pen out of my handbag.

"What are you doing?" Luz hissed.

"I'm going to take notes. You said I'd need to critique his—"

"Oh, for Christ's sake. Put that stuff away. You're supposed to be here enjoying the music, not writing a damned newspaper column. I'm convincing you that opera isn't the only game in town. Remember? Now will you act like a normal person?"

"I am a normal person," I protested. "And that man has a good voice. Not well trained, but powerful, nice tone, even some vibrato."

"Great. Save it for him. He's singing 'Granada' now. It's a big favorite. That's the one you should really listen to."

"I've already heard Placido Domingo sing it. Mr. Barrientos isn't as good by any means."

"Shit, Carolyn. We're running a scam here. You need to get with it. Now, this song is about a burro."

"Really. Why would a bride want to hear a song about a burro?" I asked.

"How the hell do I know?"

We listened to that song and then a third that had people smirking at each other and shouting encouragement. "Scumbag," Luz muttered under her breath.

"What's the matter?" I whispered. "This one is very dramatic."

"Right," she snarled. "It's a *corrida*. About some scumbag drug dealer who supposedly helped the poor and the Church and was shot up by the badass *federales*. Robin Hood in the coke trade."

Her expression was really ferocious, and I could only hope that Mr. Barrientos didn't notice her reaction to his singing. If he did, he certainly wouldn't want to join us. In fact, he might tell someone to shoot us, or do it himself. Then suddenly she was smiling and clapping.

"Here we go," she said to me, and waved the waiter over as Mr. Barrientos finished what was evidently to be his last number. He bowed to enthusiastic applause, in which I joined since I was supposed to be a new fan. My partner, if you could call her that, was telling the waiter we'd like to buy the singer a drink. But what were we to do if he refused? I wondered. He looked our way, stared rather too closely at my hair, and strode through the tables in our direction. "What did I tell you? The blonde hair did it," Luz murmured.

Suddenly a thought occurred to me. "Are we traveling incognito?" I asked in a whisper.

She snapped, "Just shut up. Follow my lead, and we'll be fine."

"Hey, Salvador," she greeted him. "Long time no see. What can we order for you?"

He stared at her and then frowned. "*Jesus i Maria!* Vallejo? Aren't you a narc? What are *you* doin' here?"

"I was in Vice," she replied, "not narcotics, but I'm retired. Meet Carolyn Blue. She's a friend of mine who likes opera. I told her she hasn't heard real music till she's heard a good mariachi singer. Right, Caro?"

Now I was Caro. "Right, Luz. Won't you sit down?" I

smiled at Mr. Barrientos. He certainly was muscular, but he didn't look exactly like "muscle" in the violent sense. The way that bouncer at Brazen Babes had looked.

"Caro, meet Salvador Barrientos. We're lucky he was here tonight. Wasn't the singing as good as I told you?"

Mr. Barrientos was smiling back at me, taking a seat, ordering a straight shot of tequila evidently, since that's what the waiter brought him. Well, it was my turn now. "You do, indeed, have an excellent voice, Mr. Barrientos."

"Yeah? *Gracias, senora.*" He actually made a sweeping motion with his hat, like someone in the movies. Old movies.

"Yes, I've heard Placido Domino sing 'Granada,' and I wasn't a bit more moved by him than by your rendition. Your voice has extraordinary power."

"Yeah? Real loud, huh?" He moved his chair closer.

I scooted to the other side of mine and buried my nose over my beer can.

"Hey, lemme fix that for you," he said and went into the salt-sprinkling, lime-squeezing routine. "I can tell you're a classy Anglo lady who don't know much about Tecate. How come you got her drinkin' that horse piss, Lieutenant? Yeah, I remember you. Lieutenant. Vice." He turned back to me. "How about a shot of this?" He held up his tequila. Luz shook her head ever so slightly.

"That's very kind of you," I replied, "but I'm afraid I don't have a head for more than one tequila drink, and we had dinner at Martino's."

"Sure, Martino's. Good place. Me, I like the *sesos.*"

"I'm sorry. I don't speak Spanish."

"Sesos. Brains. *Muy sabroso.* You oughta try 'em. And hey, I'm an American citizen. You don't have to speak Spanish to me. So you like my singing, huh?"

"Very much," I replied. He was leaning my way again. "Excellent tonal quality, and you have a good range."

"Nah. I ain't got a ranch. But my yard's pretty big. Over

near the golf course. Big yard. Maybe you want to come see it."

Did I? I looked toward Luz, and she replied for me. "Say, that would be great. Now that I'm not a cop anymore, I can associate with whoever I want."

"They kick you out? Catch you takin' the *mordida?*" He grinned, rubbing his thumb and forefinger together suggestively.

"Nothing so sexy," she replied. "Medical retirement." She picked her cane up from beside the chair and displayed it.

"Got shot, huh? It happens. I been shot myself."

I'd decided that I didn't want to go to his house, so I didn't wait for Luz to bring up the subject of our quest. I did it myself. "I think you may know a friend of mine, Mr. Barrientos. Another opera lover," I said. Luz frowned. Barrientos denied knowing any opera lovers, although he said that he'd like to get to know *me* better. I tried to simper, but I'm afraid it wasn't very successful. "Your name sounds so familiar," I murmured.

"Well, I got a reputation." He nodded, looking tough and proud of it. "But I don' know that a lady like you would have heard about me."

"No," I insisted. "I'm sure Vladik Gubenko mentioned your name."

"Who?" He looked puzzled, but I assumed that he was acting.

"Aren't you connected with gambling?"

"Well, I lay a bet now and then. An' I know where to put my money too. You don't see Palomino—that's what my friends call me—Palomino—you don't see me making or taking sucker bets."

I nodded admiringly. "I know that's so. Vladik said you were too lucky for him, and he owed you money."

"Yeah? What kinda name's that? Va-dik? He got a big one?"

"Debt you mean? Well, forty thousand dollars sounds big to me."

My new friend Palomino roared with laughter. "No, chica, a big dick. Well, I guess that ain't no conversation for a nice lady, huh? Sorry. But I don't know nobody with a name like that."

"He's Russian," I persisted. "The artistic director of Opera at the Pass."

"Don't know him. Sorry. Hey, there's someone waving at me. I'll get back to you ladies."

"Well, you really screwed that up," said Luz angrily. "You should have let me handle the questioning."

"He doesn't know Vladik. He doesn't even seem to know that Vladik's dead."

"Right. Or he's not gonna admit to knowing a dead guy, especially if he killed him. Now we'll have to go out to his house and wait for him. Could be half the night. If you hadn't screwed up, we could have gone with him and got on with it."

"Got on with what?" I asked, bemused. She'd done it again—*he killed him*. Two male pronouns with only one instead of two antecedents. Should I mention it to her?

27
Stake Out

Luz

Well that's what I *get for teaming up with an amateur,* I thought as we drove toward Campestre, where everyone said Barrientos lived. Luck was with us when we got to the guard station. I ordered Smack down out of sight and told the guard that we had been invited by Mr. Barrientos to visit him at home. The guard and I leered at each other knowingly, and he opened the gate, even told us how to get there. Of course, the two of us were speaking Spanish, so the directions passed right over Carolyn's head. We found the place, a big, sprawling adobe house with a three-car garage and a lawn, for Christ's sake. No wonder Juarez was running out of water.

I found us a good stakeout spot under a tree with a straight line of sight to the house. "Why don't we park in the driveway?" Carolyn asked.

"Because we need to find out if there's anyone in the house, and if there isn't, we don't want to look too eager when he gets home. I told her to keep the motor running, and I took out a gadget I had for opening other people's garage doors and began trying different wavelengths. Of course she wanted to know what I was doing, but just about then one of his garage doors zipped up. The space inside was empty, and it looked like the middle space was too. While Carolyn gaped, I closed the one door and kept trying frequencies until I got the middle door open. I'd been right. I noted the two frequencies, figuring he'd put his car in one of the spots. There was a monster pickup in the far one, a big black number with dark tinted windows, a chrome roll bar, and spotlights. The steel looked heavy enough that you wouldn't be able to shoot through it, which was a nice feature if you were a drug dealer. Since no one came out to check the garage doors going up and down, I figured the house was empty, but I didn't count on it.

Of course, I'd rather Barrientos came home and let us in himself. Then we wouldn't have to mess with security alarms, but if that didn't work, then we'd drive right into his garage after he was asleep, kick the door in if I couldn't open it with picks, and drag him out to the car. Whatever worked. When she asked again what we were doing, I told her we were on a stakeout and to keep her eyes open for lights and movement in the house.

"A stakeout?" She actually sounded intrigued. Didn't take much to entertain the woman. Nothing in the world more frigging boring than a stakeout, but she didn't know that.

"You want to go to sleep, feel free. We could be here a while."

"What? And miss my first stakeout?" she exclaimed indignantly. "I wouldn't dream of it."

"Okay. So what are these murder investigations you've been involved in?" Might as well do something to pass the time, and I sure as hell didn't want to be subjected to any more history lessons. I wished now that I'd had her use the john before we left the mariachi place. She wasn't going to want to pee behind someone's bush if she needed to go before he got home.

"Well, a friend of mine went missing in New Orleans, and the police wouldn't do a thing."

Her voice sounded kind of weepy. Must have been a good friend.

"So I found the murderer myself."

"No shit?" I didn't believe a word of it.

"And a colleague of Jason's was murdered in New York. We solved that one together. And my mother-in-law was accused of murdering someone in San Francisco, and again the police weren't helpful, so a private detective and I saw to her exoneration. And then there was the corpse I found in a Barcelona art exhibit—"

"Jesus, you seem to run into a lot of corpses. Maybe I better take you home before you get me killed."

"I'm driving," she pointed out. "Are we doing something dangerous? Besides visiting Juarez?"

"It depends. Just follow my lead."

"Your knee seems to be feeling better tonight," she remarked. "I noticed that you didn't seem to limp at all."

"Yeah, I figure it was the tequila."

There was silence for a while, and then she said, "Your condo is very nice, and all on one floor. That must be a blessing."

She was obviously one of these people who feel obligated to keep the conversation going. So all right. I'd entertain her and maybe set her mind at rest about my ability to take care of us if the situation got sticky. "Well, the house that I got in my divorce settlement and still owned when I had to retire was two-story and a real pain in the ass for someone in a wheelchair, which I was after a while. That was before I started taking the expensive meds and got better."

"Does the police medical insurance pay for them?" she asked. "Our medication insurance at the university has co-pays up to eighty dollars for three months for some prescriptions, or so a friend told us. Neither Jason nor I have had to use it for any long-term treatments."

"Eighty for three months would look good to me," I said bitterly. "I got insurance, but it doesn't cover the eighteen thousand they charge every year. I had to mortgage my house to pay for the first couple of years, so I could get mobile enough to earn some money."

"I didn't realize you had a job."

"I don't. I do a little bounty hunting now and then. For instance, the first time I heard about a guy with a big reward on his head, the scuzzball was over here in Juarez. Bounty hunters don't like to come over here. They don't want to end up in jail. But I figured I didn't have anything to lose, and I knew where he went to visit a lady friend—without body guards—so I came on over, caught the two of them fucking—you're wincing, right? Well, what they were doing couldn't be called making love, if you know what I mean."

I gathered that she didn't and still objected to my choice of words, which made it damn hard to tell the woman a story. "Anyway, I made the guy tie up the woman. Then, I stuck the pistol up his nose—"

"Are you carrying a gun tonight?" she asked. "We could go to jail if you are. I've read in the newspaper that the Mexican authorities don't allow people to transport guns across the border. They throw visitors right in prison if there are weapons in the car, even if the people just forgot—"

"I'm not carrying," I interrupted. "I was more desperate in those days. Say, do you want me to finish this story?" She did. "So I made him shoot himself full of his own product." I had to laugh just thinking about it. The guy was a dealer who was smart enough not to use, so the heroin he'd brought for his true love was enough to send him right into the nodding-off stage.

"Then I strapped him into my car and told the agent at customs he was a boyfriend who was drunk. Since I'd declared American and didn't have an accent, Immigration took my word for it, and I hauled my prisoner off to the feds. The reward paid for the new condo and a lot of meds."

All and all, Carolyn thought that was pretty neat and wanted to hear more bounty-hunter stories. Since I only had one more, which I didn't want to talk about because it had gotten pretty messy, I told her about busting whores and johns in the downtown area when I was a beat cop and later working the stash-house detail. That one got her all upset. She thought maybe she'd need to keep her eyes open for stash houses in her neighborhood. I assured her that she should. So that's the way it went.

Next she said, "I didn't realize you'd been married."

"Yeah. Right out of college. Big wedding, white dress, the whole enchilada. My parents were pretty pissed off when we got divorced. Dad had to come back from a prospecting trip in Mexico to catch the wedding, they spent a fortune to give away their number-two daughter, and then the bridegroom gave her back. I'm not saying Francisco was a bad guy. He wasn't. Probably the nicest banker you ever met."

"You married a *banker?*" Carolyn exclaimed.

I was kind of insulted at how surprised she was. "Right. He graduated in business from the university here, then went on to the Wharton School of Business for his master's, which is a big deal, fancy Ivy League university. Then he came home and married me. Is that so hard to believe? I told you he was a good guy. We loved each other, and he didn't even mind a wife on the job, but he wanted kids in the worst way. Frankly, I wasn't crazy about the idea, but I wanted him to be happy, so we tried. When normal screwing around didn't do it, we both went to doctors. He was fine. I was going need all that hormone stuff and getting it on at just the right time, maybe some test-tube deal. That was where I drew the line. I told him he'd better get an annulment because I wasn't going for the hormone stuff. No way. Imagine me on the streets chasing some criminal type and all of a sudden I'm having PMS to end all PMS. So we split. The Church gave us an annulment. The state gave us a divorce. It was too bad, but that's the way it had to be."

"And you never remarried?" Carolyn asked, sounding kind of sad.

"No reason to. Frank did. After we split, he moved to L.A. Came back about ten years later to take a job as VP of a bank here and married some nice little Maid-of-Cotton type. I hear they have some kids, so maybe he's happy. I hope so."

She sat silent for a while. Then she said, "His name isn't Escobar, is it?"

I was surprised. "Yeah, Francisco Escobar. You know him?"

"He's on the opera board."

I had to laugh. "Poor Frank. The new wife must have dragged him into that."

"I wouldn't be surprised," Carolyn answered. "She strikes me as sort of snobbish. They have two girls and a baby boy. He's evidently crazy about them and goes to all the school productions the girls are in."

"Better them than me," I said, glancing at my watch. Thank the Holy Virgin, Carolyn hadn't asked to pee. Smack was snoring happily in the back seat, minding her own business, when Carolyn changed the subject and asked why I'd given my dog such a strange name. Maybe she thought I smacked the dog around. Anyway I told her it was slang for heroin, Smack heard her name and woke up, sticking her nose in my ear, and Barrientos pulled into his driveway in a red sports car that he'd screwed up with a lot of fancy detailing.

Guy was as dumb as ever. You'd think with a record like his and a reward on his head in the States, he'd want to make a stab at anonymity. No way. Asshole had that skunk streak and a loud, expensive car. Piss for brains. No question. "Quit it, Smack," I told the dog. I like her, I trust her, but I'm not crazy about dog drool in my ear.

"Let's go." I wanted the three of us to get to him before he pulled into the garage or went into the house. Hadn't seemed to be anyone there. I'd got out once and walked the perimeter. No lights. No TV. No noise. If there'd been bodyguards, even after all the garage-door racket, we'd have been up shit creek. And nobody followed him home, thank the Lord. My luck was holding. "Call out to him," I told her. "Tell him we're accepting his invitation."

28

The Capture

Carolyn

The stakeout had been fascinating, but I really didn't want to talk to Mr. Barrientos again. I personally thought he hadn't killed Vladik, so why take the risk? However, Luz insisted, so I got out of the car and called, "Hello there, Salvador. I hope it isn't too late to accept your invitation."

He whirled, hand stabbing toward the back of his trousers, scaring me half to death because I thought he might have a gun tucked into his heavy belt. When he recognized us under his own safety lights, he squinted suspiciously, not at me, but at Luz and the dog, which had clambered out of the back seat at her mistress's command. "What's with the dog?" he demanded, hand still behind his back.

"I'm blind half the time," said Luz. "My sight comes and goes. The dog's doesn't."

I'd never heard of anyone whose sight came and went. Surely he didn't believe that. But I guess he did because he said, "Man, that's tough. No wonder you had to retire. Does the dog bite?"

"She's a Seeing Eye dog, leads me around when I need it. Seeing Eye dogs don't bite," Luz responded, as if anyone with half a brain would know that. "Her name's Smack. How about that?"

Barrientos laughed and opened his front door, without

taking his eyes off us, which made me very anxious. Then
he insisted that we go in first, acting as if he was being polite. Luz and the dog went right in. I followed less will-
ingly. Didn't she see the danger in this? I wondered.
Maybe the drugs she took for arthritis affected her judg-
ment. For a moment the room was dark, but I hadn't heard
the door close. I wanted to scream and run for my life, but
I knew that Luz would be even angrier about that than my
taking over the conversation at the mariachi bar. Before I
could act on my fears, he snapped the lights on.

"Cool place, Barrientos," said Luz, walking from the
entry hall into the living room and dragging me along with
her. The dog led, its nose in the air.

Heaven help us, I thought. *This is a drug dealer's
house. Obviously he has drugs in it, and Smack has
smelled them.* Any minute now the dog would howl and
head for the drugs, and—well, I didn't want to think of
what would happen next. And why had she said this was a
cool place? It was the ultimate tasteless room—all fake
zebra and leopard skin and naked women painted on velvet. I was gaping at one picture that had a naked man as
well, the depiction positively pornographic. I hadn't seen
anything that shocking since a Japanese lady showed me a
prized antique scroll when Jason and I were invited to visit
a professor's home in Tokyo.

Then suddenly everything happened at once. Everything horrible. Mr. Barrientos grabbed me from behind,
dragged me backward toward the entry hall, and said to
Luz, "Okay, Vallejo, what's up here, and you keep your
hands away from whatever you're carryin' or I'll blow this
pretty gringa's head off." He could have done it too. I felt
what I took to be the barrel of a gun pressing against my
ear. But worse than that, his hand was clamped onto my
right breast. Not only was it shocking and embarrassing,
but it hurt.

Luz remained perfectly calm and said, "If this is what

you call hospitality, Palomino, it sucks. You invited us over. We came. And here you—"

Given my position, I wasn't about to wait for negotiations. I placed my hand over his, the one on my breast, not the one that held the gun to my ear and said, "You're hurting me, Mr. Barrientos."

"Tough shit," he snarled.

So I got hold of one of his fingers, a strategy I'd read about in an article on protecting oneself against rape and other assaults. He laughed and said, "Knock it off!" I yanked the finger back as hard as I could, so angry that I completely forgot about the gun at my ear. The finger cracked loudly, he screamed, and the pressure on my ear eased. Luz murmured, "Get the gun, Smack," and the dog lunged, mouth wide and snarling, and clamped its teeth onto Mr. Barrientos. I was still clinging to his hand and— I don't know what got into me—I bit his broken finger. The gun fell to the floor and discharged, sending a bullet into a pornographic pillow on his zebra couch, I—feeling dizzy—removed my teeth from Mr. Barrientos' hand, and he fell down with the dog on top of him.

While I was staving off a nervous breakdown, Luz walked over to him and placed her cane carefully against the left side of his groin. "If you move, my piss-for-brains friend," she said, "I press the button on the cane, and the blade goes right into your crotch. Then if you don't die from arterial bleeding, I might consider cutting off your balls in the course of the little talk we're about to have."

I leaned against the wall, breathing deeply.

"Now, don't pass out on me, Carolyn," Luz said.

Mr. Barrientos stirred. Maybe he was considering a counterattack, but there were tears on his face—it probably hurts to have your finger broken and your wrist bitten by a huge dog that still has its teeth in your flesh, although Smack was now stretched out comfortably beside her prisoner.

"And you, Palomino, don't move a muscle. Caro, go get his gun. It's under the magazine rack with all the girlie magazines." Then, when Mr. Barrientos stirred again, she snapped, "Watch it, Palomino. You make me mad, and looking at magazines is all the sex you'll ever get."

I wobbled over to the wrought-iron magazine rack, studiously avoiding the sight of the naked women on the covers while I fished the gun out. Then, without taking my eyes off Luz and Mr. Barrientos, I returned and handed the gun to Luz, who went to the other side of the prisoner and squatted, gritting her teeth, to stick the muzzle against his ear. "How's that feel, you frigging bastard?" she asked.

I must say, in that instance, I could forgive her language because she was paying him back for what he'd done to me.

"Now Carolyn," she ordered, "I want you to look in my bag. There's a big roll of duct tape and some scissors. Tape his feet together. Don't spare the tape, and make it real tight."

It wasn't easy to do. I dragged over a footstool with a tapestry picture of two lions having sexual intercourse. Maybe his mother made it for him. I giggled at the thought, and Luz said, "Don't fall apart on me, Caro." I didn't. I sat down and wound the tape around and around his ankles. Some experimentation led me to the discovery that it was easier to shove the footstool under his calves and sit on the floor to finish the taping. While I was at work, Luz stood up. I heard her sharp indrawn breath and assumed that she'd been in pain, although she looked less stressed when I looked up.

"Done," I said, pleased with myself. I started to put the tape and scissors back into her handbag, but she said we needed to save them for his hands, so I settled for returning the footstool to its place. No need to make a mess. His finger and wrist were already bleeding on the tiles. It occurred to me that blood might be very hard to get out of the grout.

"Smack, bite." Luz pointed to Mr. Barrientos's thigh and leaned over to press the gun against his ear in case he had any idea of resisting. The dog scrambled up, shook Barrientos' wrist while looking for the next bite site—*bite site—that rhymes,* I thought giddily. Smack dropped the wrist and sank her teeth in the selected thigh. Barrientos groaned again.

"Shut up," said Luz. "She's not biting hard, but she will if you make a fuss. Carolyn, go look out the windows and see if any lights are coming on in the neighborhood."

Obediently, I went to look. In fact, I circled the house looking out windows and satisfying my curiosity about drug-dealer accommodations and taste in decorating. Except for security lights, the neighborhood was dark, and the other rooms were just as tastelessly furnished as the living room. He had a bed, in what I took to be the master bedroom, with a mirror on the ceiling, not to mention a mirrored bath. I took the opportunity to use the toilet. When Luz shouted, "You okay?" I hurried my rounds and returned to report.

"There are no lights in the neighborhood, but I found several bathrooms if you need to go."

She shook her head.

"You really should," I urged. "You'll never see another like his. I can hold the gun on him."

"Have you ever shot a gun?" she asked.

"No, but it's just a matter of pulling on the trigger, isn't it? Not only does he have mirrors in his bathroom and over his bed, but he also has overhead lights in his shower and tub and pornographic tiles. It's amazing." Not that I approve of pornography, but I got the giggles when I told her about the décor.

Luz grinned at me. "Well, I'm glad you're having fun, but you've got to settle down now and tape up his hands."

Mr. Barrientos had been glaring at us, particularly during my description of his bathroom "Hey, that bitch broke my finger, and then she bit it. You can't—"

Luz hit him in the temple with the barrel of the gun and said, "Watch who you're calling bitch, you ass wipe." His forehead developed a blood trickle that headed for the tiles. This house was going to be very hard to sell when he went to jail or died. His poor mother, who'd gone to the trouble of embroidering the amorous lions for him—how would she explain the red stains to prospective buyers? And was she able to buy kits for those footstool covers? I started to giggle again, thinking of what a stir such a kit would cause among respectable customers in a craft shop.

"Are you drunk, Caro?" Luz asked me.

"No," I replied. "It's just the nasty embroidery his mother did. No wonder he's a drug dealer."

There was an angry reaction from Mr. Barrientos about what he took to be a slur on his mother. Luz put her knee on his broken finger, and Smack shook her head, teeth still attached to his thigh. That put an end to Mr. Barrientos's latest protest, but I worried about how much pain kneeling might cause my partner. What if she fainted?

"Up you go." Luz yanked him into a sitting position. "Hands behind your back. Caro, get the tape."

In no time at all I had Mr. Barrientos's hands crossed and taped up. I was getting good at this, not that it was a skill likely to prove useful in later life. Once our prisoner was immobilized—and groaning, although I'd been as gentle as I could with respect to his broken finger and gnawed wrist—Luz shoved a heavy, upholstered chair behind his back. *There goes the upholstery,* I thought. *He'll bleed on that too.* Then she stood in front of him and demonstrated her cane. When she pressed a button, a thin, wicked-looking blade about nine inches in length shot out with a soft *snick*.

"So," said Barrientos, trying to look unafraid, "you got a fancy switch blade. Big deal."

Luz nodded, retracted the blade, and placed the tip of the cane against his crotch again, the gun still aimed at his head. "Conversation time, amigo. The name Caro mentioned at Mariachi Caliente, Vladik Gubenko, also known as Vladislav Gubenko. A source told us you know him. Said he owed you gambling money." She put pressure on the cane. Barrientos tried to squirm away, but the chair at his back held him.

"No one named that owes me no money," he cried, looking as earnest as he could.

"Unzip his fly, Caro." Luz ordered.

"*What?*" I didn't want to unzip his fly.

"That way we'll *see* what happens when I push the button. Bet you've never seen an artery let go. Lotta force there. Sends up a real fountain of blood."

"*Jesus i Maria,*" cried Barrientos. "The El Paso police don't do this kinda stuff."

"I'm not in the police department any more. And I'm not in El Paso," she said with a really scary smile. It frightened me, so I can imagine how he felt. "Caro."

Before I had to refuse, Barrientos said, "So I know him. Okay? But he don't owe me no money."

"Go on," she ordered, pressing harder on the cane. He was sweating.

"Quit it, will you? We have a little deal going, okay? I ship people across the river for a price. Vladik puts them in this trailer park in West El Paso. Then my cousin, who runs the park and ain't got any warrants on her, puts them on tractor trailers, a few at a time, an' sends them up to Chicago. I don' know why the hell you'd care. Smuggling illegals was never your—"

"So why did you kill him?" Luz snarled.

"What d'ya mean? Who killed him? If he's dead, I

never heard it. I got more people comin' across this week-end. I never heard nothin' about—"

"What's the name of the park?" she asked.

"Piñon Park. It's on the Westside."

"That's where Polya and Irina live," I said, astonished.

"So you believe him?" Luz asked.

"I don't know." Did I? "They did say they never got to know their neighbors, who spoke Spanish and were always changing."

"See! It's the truth. They was comin' an' goin' all the time because they're my illegals. But they din' all speak Spanish. We took anyone wanted to cross an' had the *dinero*."

"Well, I got it on tape," said Luz, tapping his gun against one of the two patch pockets of her blue silk blouse, but keeping the cane in place. "We'll see how your story goes over with the feds."

"Ah, come on, Vallejo. What feds? What'd I ever do to you? Anyways, the federales, they're gonna nod their heads, let me go, and lock you up. What d'ya think? We ain't got them bought? 'Course we do."

"I believe it, amigo," said Luz. "but we're taking you home with us. Caro, dial this thing to eleven and push the button. That opens the garage door on the left so you can drive in. We'll put him in the trunk."

"In *my* trunk? He's bleeding. And he—well, you may not have noticed but he had an—an accident."

"Right. He pissed his pants. So what?"

"I don't want him bleeding all over my trunk. And it will smell like urine in there. Why don't we take one of *his* cars? You drive him over, and I'll follow. People in the neighborhood are much less likely to notice if—"

"Damn it, Caro, will you just go get your car. You are the most—what word do I want?—fastidious woman I've ever seen. Picking up after yourself when we've got a dangerous prisoner to watch, checking out the bathrooms, worrying about the upholstery in your trunk. You can take the damn car to El Paso Car Wash and get it cleaned. Have lunch and write about it in your column."

An interesting idea—column-wise—but how was I supposed to explain what had happened in my trunk to the attendants?

29

Bounty Hunters

Luz

It took some doing to talk Carolyn into bringing her car into the garage, especially since Barrientos kept taking her side of the argument. "You try kidnappin' me, my people are gonna kill you," he said to me. "Her too. You want to end up in a shallow grave outside town in the desert, lady?" he asked Carolyn. She didn't of course.

"When *your people* find out you were running a smuggling business on the side, they won't care what we did to you, Palomino. And they'll find out. There'll be big headlines tomorrow: 'Wanted Drug Dealer/Smuggler Brought in by Female Bounty Hunters.' Gonna look bad. You know? Two women kidnapping a tough guy like you and turning him over to the feds."

"Are we bounty hunters?" Carolyn asked, wide eyed.

"Yup. He's wanted by the DEA, the FBI, the EPPD, and now the Border Patrol will want their share of him too. Only person who's gonna get killed here is Piss-for-Brains if he rats out the drug cartel. They may have him whacked in the county jail just to be on the safe side." I don't think Carolyn heard anything beyond her own role as a bounty hunter. She stopped arguing and went out for the car. But Barrientos heard. He started struggling, so Smack clamped down on his thigh, and I tapped him on top of the head. More blood. Carolyn was going to be pissed off about that.

She got her car safely in the garage. Got the garage door closed, and even found a paint-spattered, plastic drop cloth to protect her trunk, but then there was the problem of getting him into the trunk. I said we'd carry him. She said one woman with arthritis and one with no athletic ability or pastimes weren't going to be able to carry a man as stocky as he was.

"Wha' d'ya weigh, Barrientos?" I asked.

"Three hundred pounds," he said, real fast.

"See," said Carolyn. "We'll never—"

"He's lying. Tape his mouth shut."

"I don't want to," she said.

"Come on. Smack's got her teeth into him. He moves, she bites down. I got a gun on him. What are you afraid of?"

"I'll bite her," said Barrientos.

"Cut off a strip of tape," I told her. "I'll tape him." She cut. I squatted behind him, which was hell on my knee, put the gun muzzle against his forehead, and slapped the tape on his mouth. I thought that was that, but she had a new idea.

"There's a dolly out in his garage. One of those things on wheels you carry heavy packages on. We can put him on that."

"The hell we can. You can't wheel a person around on a dolly."

"We'll tie him on." She looked around the room, grimaced at the sight of his velvet pictures, and tore down some drapery cords. Then she went out for the dolly.

Barrientos mumbled desperately under his tape. Carolyn rolled the dolly in, pulled the chair away from his back, and lowered him to the floor by clutching his hair. His head still clunked, and he passed out, which was okay with me. He'd be less trouble at the border if he was unconscious. Smack woke up, thinking her prisoner was causing trouble again. You had to feel sorry for the dog.

She was a little old for this sort of thing and deserved a nap when she could catch one.

Interested to see what would happen next, I called the dog off Barrientos when Carolyn asked, and she laid the dolly down beside him. With a lot of puffing on Carolyn's part and some help from me, we shoved his lower body onto it. Then she tied him on with the drapery cords and said, looking pretty pleased with herself, "See. Now when we get him upright, we can bend him over from the waist and roll him out."

Frankly, I think it would have been easier if each of us had taken a foot and dragged him into the garage, but whatever baked her cake. She decided the scientific thing to do would be to lever him up by shoving a dining room chair under the dolly, so we tried that. The back broke off the chair. Then we tried with a heavy Spanish chair she found in the entry hall. That worked. By then the dog had dozed off again, so we left her there, rolled him out, got his upper body partly into the trunk, untied the drapery cords, and shoved the rest of him in.

"Jesus," I groaned. "I ache all over. You drive."

"I can't. I hurt too, and I'm having a nervous breakdown."

Great, I thought. I could feel the damn knee swelling. I'd probably have an accident before we ever got to the bridge. *Which is worse?* I wondered. *The pain like it is, or driving drunk from killing it with tequila?* I chose the pain because I figured it was gonna be just one more hassle with Carolyn if I had a couple of shots of tequila before we left, so I limped back into the house, woke Smack up, and turned out the lights. In the garage I took a last look at Barrientos, but he wasn't moving, so I slammed the trunk shut, climbed into the driver's side of the car, and took the keys from Carolyn. She was right about the nervous breakdown. Her hands were shaking.

"Calm down," I told her. "You don't have to do a thing

from here on except say 'American' when they ask for your citizenship at the bridge. I'll call in the guys who want him as soon as we get into El Paso and dump him off at the jail. Hell, I'll even drive you home if you don't feel up to it." I had the car backed out into the driveway and the garage door closed by then.

"You can sleep at my house," she offered, looking relieved.

"Whatever." I debated whether I should wipe off the garage door thingy and throw it into Barrientos's bushes, but what the hell. It was a neat gadget, something you never knew when you might need it. So I put it in my purse and told Smack to go to sleep. If she stayed lying down in the back seat, they might not even notice her at the border. Otherwise, Carolyn was going to have to play the blind woman, since obviously it wasn't me. I was driving, and there was only so much I could expect of my cousin at the bridge.

I explained that to her, and she said, "Fine."

"Get the dark glasses out of my bag," I suggested. "Unless you've got some of your own."

She didn't and fumbled around in my bag. "Oh, you remembered the tape. That's good. Our fingerprints are probably on it. Goodness, I never thought about leaving prints in the bathroom and everywhere. I'll never be able to come back to Juarez, not after taking part in a kidnapping."

"I wouldn't worry about it. Your prints probably aren't on file anywhere."

"I suppose not." She was silent for a long time. Then she said, "Are we really bounty hunters?"

"Sure. There's a reward on his head. You're entitled to half."

"Is it a lot?" she asked.

"Twenty-five thousand, and I think there may be money for catching a smuggler, if they can make that case against him."

"My goodness," she marveled. "And if we're bounty hunters, it's all right for us to bring him back, isn't it?"

"Nah. The Mexican government frowns on scooping up thugs in their territory. They'd throw us in jail. But then we'd bail out and head for the States. *That's* when we couldn't go back."

"Hmmm. I'm so glad I got the two Russian girls into the dorms. They could have been deported when the trailer park is raided."

If they were legally in the States, they wouldn't have been, but I didn't bring that up because we were almost to the other side of the bridge. Not much traffic this late. The Mexicans had just waved us through, didn't even notice the dog. Of course, I had to pull up on the American side.

Shit. It wasn't my cousin. He must have gone off shift. What time was it?

"Citizenship?" asked the immigration agent in the booth. He peered out at us as we both said American. "You can't bring a dog in from Mexico," he said.

Damn. He's noticed Smack.

"I'm blind," said Carolyn. She held up my cane, scaring me half to death. If she pushed the button by mistake, we were in deep trouble. "He's my Seeing Eye dog."

That's when the shit hit the fan. Pounding started up in the trunk. Smack woke up and licked my ear instead of Carolyn's, which screwed up that story. "What's that sound?" demanded the agent.

"What sound?" Carolyn asked, looking very innocent behind my dark glasses.

"That pounding. Sounds like it's coming from the trunk."

"Well, if you'd ask me what I have to declare, I'd tell you," I said.

"Oh, my goodness. Declarations. I have a bottle of tequila," said Carolyn.

"Screw your tequila," snapped the agent.

"Well, that was rude," she snapped right back.

"I got a wanted drug dealer in the trunk," I said before the two of them got into it.

"Don't be a smart-ass," he retorted. "Pull over. I'm going to search the car."

30

A Night at the Jail

Carolyn

I couldn't believe that a federal official had spoken to me in such a rude way, and why was Luz admitting that we had Mr. Barrientos in the trunk? It was sure to lead to misunderstandings.

"Fine," Luz agreed when the Immigration agent directed her to drive to an area of pavement evidently set aside for searches. I couldn't imagine why she was being so good-natured with him. To me she said, after glancing at my expression, "Now keep your mouth shut about his language. He's probably been breathing too much carbon monoxide. They usually go for the stern but courteous attitude."

The agent waved someone into his booth and followed us on foot.

"We're bounty hunters," I told him.

"I thought you said you were blind," he retorted.

Oh dear. I'd forgotten about that.

Luz got out of the car, and he pulled a gun on her. She didn't even have her cane to defend herself. I had it, but she seemed perfectly calm and said. "Boy, am I glad to see a gun. But look, before we take a chance of him getting away when you open the trunk, I'd appreciate you calling a couple of people to come and take charge of him." She handed the agent her cell phone. "Hector Parko at the DEA and Chuy Mendoza. He's a sergeant in the EPPD. Narc squad. I've got the numbers. And you might want to get hold of the Border Patrol. I have a tape of this guy saying he's smuggling illegals into a trailer park on the Westside and from there to Chicago."

By then the man from the booth was looking confused, and the pounding in the trunk had grown louder. Putting her paws on the window ledge in the back seat, Smack started to bark.

"Narc dog," said Luz. "She probably smells coke on him."

"You said it was a Seeing Eye dog," said the befuddled agent.

"I've got the ownership papers and shot records on the dog if you want to look, and she's got tags. I have to tell you, we've had one hell of an evening. Bastard grabbed my partner and put a gun to her head. Dog jumped him, and when we finally got him under control, we had to get him into the car. Sucker weighs a ton. You're looking at two ladies with lots of aches and pains. Lemme give you the first number."

"You dial it," said the INS agent. He obviously wanted to keep his gun on Luz until he could be sure that her strange story was true.

I didn't even leave the car because I was feeling jittery again. Had Barrientos gotten loose? I was so sure I'd taped him up thoroughly enough that he could hardly move, much less escape from his bonds. Maybe one had to take classes in that sort of thing. I imagined him bursting from the trunk and attacking us all. Could a man from a border booth with one little gun protect us?

"Hector, this is Luz," she said into the cell phone. "I got Barrientos in my trunk, and we're at the border crossing. Bridge of the Americas. Could you talk to the agent here and then come down and pick up the prisoner? He's kicking the hell out of my friend's trunk."

That was nice. She'd called me her friend. I felt a bit better about the situation. Maybe she'd like to go to lunch

someday. From the bridge to the jail, things went reasonably well. Agent Hector Parko came to the bridge and
looked in on Mr. Barrientos, who hadn't gotten loose. He
was lying on his back, kicking the trunk lid. Agent Parko
suggested that we leave our prisoner there until we got to
the jail, which didn't please me very much. The smell of
urine was permeating the car, that and something even less
desirable. Twenty or thirty more minutes and my trunk
might never be deodorizable—if there is such a word.

Meanwhile, the INS agent summoned someone from
the Border Patrol. Luz gave the tape in her pocket to the
Border Patrol agent. After he'd listened to it on her
recorder, he went off to set up a raid on the Pinon Trailer
Park. All this would have been very exciting if I hadn't
been so tired.

Sergeant Chuy Mendoza met us in an underground entrance to the jail, into which Luz drove my car with Agent
Parko following in his. Sheriff's deputies came down and
extracted the struggling Mr. Barrientos from my trunk, and
everyone incoming who had a weapon put it into a locker.
Luz even offered her cane, demonstrating its unusual features. Sergeant Mendoza said something to her in Spanish
about it, and they both laughed.

I thought that rather impolite, since I don't understand
Spanish. I ought to ask for my money back on that Castilian Spanish course; it hadn't done me a bit of good. For instance, the professor never mentioned the word pendejo,
which kept coming up in their conversation. I asked what
it meant, and Luz said it referred to someone who was stupid. Then all three of them, plus the uniformed officers,
laughed. Obviously there was more to it.

With many unkind comments on the state of his
trousers, the officers carried Mr. Barrientos off to be
checked into jail and cleaned up, while Luz and I were escorted elsewhere to give statements. "Couldn't we do that
tomorrow?" I asked. "I'm exhausted. It's way past my bed-

time." They all thought that was very funny, so I added that I'd been up late the night before interviewing the owner of Brazen Babes with Luz.

"Geez," said the oh-so-amusing Agent Parko. "You two looking for a job? I'd pay to see that."

"Knock it off, Hector. Carolyn's a civilian. She doesn't appreciate cop humor."

"Geez, Vallejo, ex-*cuse* me," said Agent Parko.

After that we were interviewed separately. Frankly, I don't know what I said to the man who talked to me. Someone else from the DEA. I dozed off right in the middle of a question at one point, and he sent out for coffee. I suppose I told him the whole story, hoping I could go home and fall into bed.

No such luck. We were then taken to an observation room, where we watched Mr. Barrientos being interviewed. The idea was that every time we heard him tell a lie, we would notify the man who had interviewed me, who would then go into the interrogation room and whisper to Agent Parko, who would threaten Mr. Barrientos for lying to him. This went on forever because Mr. Barrientos told so many lies. Probably everything he said was a lie, but we couldn't identify all of them.

The things he said about us were certainly lies, particularly about me. I *never* responded sexually to his hand on my breast or fondled his genitalia once I had him taped up. Luz thought it was hilarious when I turned red and started to sputter. Some friend she was. I was so angry with Mr. Barrientos that I hoped they'd give him the death penalty. I even offered to testify at the death penalty hearing as to the emotional anguish he'd caused me by the nasty things he said. Luz didn't think the prosecutor would ask for capital punishment. She said they'd try to "flip" him for a lighter sentence and testimony against his colleagues, unless, of course, he admitted to killing Vladik. It was all very disheartening.

When we finally left the jail, we were met by a newspaper reporter, a photographer, and representatives of three TV stations. Luz said something or other to them. I suppose she was used to such unpleasant and embarrassing scenes. I refused comment, and we made our way to the car, which had been brought around for us.

We didn't get home until seven-thirty. I provided Luz with a bed, a nightgown, a toothbrush, and a tube of ointment for her knee, something Jason uses when he becomes over enthusiastic about his athletic pursuits and strains his muscles and joints. I'd have felt much more sympathetic to her pain if she hadn't laughed during Mr. Barrientos's slanderous testimony about me.

31

Targeting Boris

Carolyn

Imagine not getting to bed until seven forty-five in the morning. I was still in deep sleep at twelve-thirty when Luz woke me up. "Get dressed," she said. "I've made coffee."

I peered blearily at the clock, calculated how much sleep I'd had—less than five hours—and told her to go away.

"We need to talk," she insisted, and threw off my covers. I snatched them right back.

"What do I have to do? Turn the shower on for you? Draw a bath? Pour cold water on your head?"

I sighed because it was obvious that she wasn't going away. When I sat up, I had that dizzy, half nauseated feeling induced by rising when seriously sleep deprived. "I'm sick."

"Nothing coffee won't fix." She went into the master bath and grabbed a toweling robe off the hook, Jason's as it happened, and insisted that I put it on, then kicked some fuzzy slippers out from under the bed. "Cute," she commented. "Do I have to put them on your feet?" I was still fumbling with the tie belt of the robe. "I warn you, kneeling hurts, which makes me real grumpy. So get into your own slippers."

No matter what I wanted—and that was to crawl back into bed—I ended up in the kitchen drinking coffee that was strong enough to remove the enamel from my teeth.

Did she carry her own brand, or had she boiled some of mine for several hours? It did wake me up.

"So, Boris Stepanovich. The SOB obviously lied to us about Barrientos killing Vladik. I didn't hear anything in that interrogation to indicate that there was bad blood between Vladik and Barrientos, did you?"

"I missed a lot of what he said. Didn't you notice? I kept falling asleep."

"Well, Barrientos claimed that he was at Mariachi Caliente singing for half the night when Vladik died. And when a man won't confess to me when he thinks he's going to get a blade in his—"

"Yes," I interrupted quickly. "And I noticed, when I happened to be awake, that the agents and detectives at the jail were throwing so many questions that he got his lies confused, but he still didn't admit to anything but the— what are *mojados*, anyway?"

"Wetbacks."

"Ah. Isn't that term politically incorrect? Well, he never admitted to anything having to do with Vladik except illegal-alien smuggling."

"Oh, hey, let's be really politically correct—undocumented-immigrant smuggling."

I giggled. "How about poor-folks-looking-for-a-home smuggling? Or—"

Luz grinned. "Knock it off. My ancestors waded across the river."

"And mine were probably unpleasant Protestants whom nobody liked in their country of origin," I said, still giddy from too little sleep.

"Sounds right to me," she said. "Now can we get back to the point, which is Palomino didn't kill Vladik. Which makes you wonder why Boris told us that." Luz was wearing her scary look.

"Because Boris killed Vladik himself!" I guessed, having caught the drift of her reasoning.

"It's sure worth investigating. Want more coffee?"

"I think I'll make some breakfast. Your coffee is—ah—strong. Very strong."

"Wimp," Luz said laughing. "Boris claimed he was at Brazen Babes when Vladik died. We should check that out."

"We could ask the Russian girls—women." I had no idea whether Luz was interested in feminist, politically correct designations for women. She probably was. "They're in the university dormitory now, and I'm sure they'd be glad to help."

"Okay. And I think we should look up that bouncer. Then when we get some information, we'll head for Brazen Babes, later tonight. First, we talk to the dancer Boris claimed to have slept with—Carmen, he said. Then we ask him why he lied to us."

"I'd really rather not have to talk to him again." That preference didn't do me much good, nor did the statement that I needed more sleep. Luz said we wouldn't be hitting Brazen Babes until late, so I could catch some sleep before we went. Then she offered to make breakfast while I called the Russian sopranos.

I had the telephone number for their floor at the dormitory, but another student answered. She said Polya and Irina were out in their new car with a couple of "jocks" from the dorm. That did not sound good to me. New car? Jocks? Perhaps those huge young men who had helped carry in their belongings? Perhaps I needed to have a talk with the girls about preserving one's good name—wait. Had they decided that they weren't lesbians? I asked the student when they might be back and was given a cell phone number. They had cell phones? I'd been soliciting help from the ad hoc opera committee, and the objects of our charity had already acquired cell phones and a new car?

I was somewhat reassured to find that the cell phone belonged to one of the athletes, who promptly put on Irina, who was so excited that she could hardly talk. Evidently Ray Lee Cleveland had arrived that afternoon in person with a 1985 convertible of some sort. The girls were stunned by the fact that it was a convertible, which they evidently considered the ultimate in American chic. I thought nothing could be more dangerous to one's skin than daily exposure to El Paso's continuous and powerful sunshine.

Even more exciting than the fold-down top, according to Irina, was the fact that the car started every time they turned the key. They had tried it ten times already, and the ignition had never disappointed them. They could have gone out by themselves, without their large neighbors on hand to push when necessary, had they realized what a treasure the car was.

Irina thanked me. Polya thanked me, and she was driving so I cut that short. Irina said that as soon as they had jobs—and they had an interview on Monday with the maquila person who needed translations from and to Russian—they planned to buy the ingredients to bake something (the name was Russian and the description was not promising) for the Clevelands and for me.

Evidently my earlier worries, except for those concerning skin cancer, were unfounded. I no longer felt it incumbent upon myself to warn the girls of the sexual dangers of association with brawny athletes. I finally managed to break into "Car Talk—Russian Style" to ask at what times, if any, they had seen Boris Stepanovich on the night Vladik died.

"He is being very angry with us that we do not dance for him anymore," said Irina, sounding much less exuberant than before. "He threaten to turn us in to immigration peoples, but we say we have friend, Mrs. Blue, who is protecting us and seeing we have food and car and nice place to live."

Wonderful, I thought. *Now he's probably very angry with me.* "Can you remember if he was in the club that night?" I asked again.

Irina and Polya conferred. I could tell that they had restarted the car several times since our conversation began. If they weren't careful, they'd burn out the ignition. Even I knew that. "Boris Stepanovich is there when we come to work because he complains how late we are, but he knows why we are coming late. Because of opera party," said Irina.

"And after that?" I asked.

"He send for Carmen after she dance, and we are not seeing them again before we are going home to trailer."

After hanging up, I passed this information on to Luz, who said, "We need to talk to the stripper before we go into Boris's office."

"But I don't want to go into his office. He's mad at me because I lured his dancers into respectability. He's threatening to turn them into the INS."

"Yeah, right. Like he's going to tell INS he's got two girls working without green cards and not getting paid." She set plates of toast down on the table and picked up the Sunday paper. "Take a look at this. We hit the front page."

My heart sank when I saw the picture right in the center—in color. Luz and I, leaving the jail. "Look at my hair," I cried. "There should be a law against photographing a woman who looks that bad."

"Hey, I think it's cute. All those pieces sticking up every which way. Makes you look younger. Except for the circles under your eyes. But don't worry about the picture. Get a load of the copy. We're both quoted."

The headline said, "Ex-Cop and Food Writer Kidnap Wanted Drug Dealer in Juarez." I sighed and skimmed the copy. Luz was quoted as saying, "It's always a pleasure to see evil people brought to justice." I was quoted as saying, "I'm tired, and I want to go home. If you and your microphone don't get out of my way, I'm going to box your ears with it."

"I couldn't have said that," I groaned.

"Oh, but you did. I heard it. You scared that TV guy half to death. He fell over a camera cord trying to get away from you."

32

The I-Got-Kids Excuse

Luz

Carolyn didn't think much of the breakfast I produced: two slices of toast each, spread with some jelly I found in the refrigerator, and another cup of coffee. She said the *preserves* were for canapés. Like I cared. Then she apologized, admitting that she was just grumpy and that she'd used the preserves on toast herself.

We tracked down the bouncer by calling the Russian girls again and asking for his name, which was Marcus Finnegan, aka Fats. Finnegan was listed in the phone book, so we got his address and visited his house across the mountain off Copia without telling him we were on our way. So much for elaborate detective work.

We found Finnegan in his front yard, a patch of yellow, scraggily grass in front of an adobe house that needed paint everywhere paint could be applied. He had a defunct refrigerator and some discarded furniture decorating the front porch, and he himself was sitting in a sagging lawn chair set in the middle of dead grass, sunning himself and his tattoos and protruding belly in his undershirt and grease-stained pants. A pretty sight.

"Hey, Marcus," I called, climbing the cracked cement steps to his yard. "We came to ask you a couple of questions."

"Piss off," he replied, but with no particular animus. He was drinking beer from a can and promptly laid a newspaper over his face when I spoke to him.

I removed the paper, which had a story I hadn't seen that morning. I hadn't read much beyond the piece about us on the front page and our picture. On page two, section B, I learned that the Border Patrol had raided the Pinon Trailer Park on the Westside and caught fifteen illegal aliens, presumably in transit away from the border, and Ramona Islas-Barrientos, who was arrested for smuggling illegal aliens. Handing the article to Carolyn, I leaned over Fats and poked him in the chest. The man might have impressive arm muscles, but he also has tits that are bigger than mine.

"Let's start again, Mar-cus. You being an important employee at Brazen Babes, which is to say their bouncer, and tight with your boss Boris, that asswipe Russian entrepreneur and purveyor of naked—"

"Hey, shut up, will you? I got kids. They're right there in the house."

I could hear them, galumphing around and shrieking. "Like I care, Mar-cus. You don't want your kids to hear the questions, get your fat ass outa that chair. The three of us can take a stroll down the street and have our chat in private."

Carolyn cleared her throat and discreetly nodded toward the porch where the noise had shut down, and two kids were peeking out the screen door. Obviously she thought I should watch my language in front of the children. How did she think he talked at home? Like he suddenly changed from a dirty-mouth bouncer to a clean-spoken daddy. Marcus saw them too. His beady little, fat-encased eyes jumped back and forth between us and the offspring, one of whom was yelling, "Hey, Ma. There's two ladies out . . ."

Before Mrs. Marcus could respond, we were all crowding down the cement steps and heading away from the house with Marcus in the lead. We got as far as a stone-and-weed-choked arroyo at the end of the street, where

Marcus sat down on a rock and said, "So what d'ya want? I'm a family man. I don't take my work home. Ain't the kinda thing a man tells his wife and kids about."

"How old are your children, Mr. Finnegan?" Carolyn asked, ever the polite conversationalist. Pretty soon she'd have him discussing the weather.

"That's touching, Mar-cus," I cut in, "and we got no designs on screwing up your happy family. Just answer a few questions, and you can go home and finish your beer."

"Shit." He looked at his hand and realized that the can wasn't in it.

"Our questions have to do with Mr. Ignatenko and his whereabouts last Saturday night and Sunday morning," said Carolyn. "Did you see him that night?"

Marcus gave her a *duh* look and said he saw his boss every night. "I work an eight-to-four shift. That's when we're open, so that's when we're there, me an' Boris, the girls, waitresses, bartenders. Everyone."

"Right, but was Boris there the whole time?" I asked.

"Where else would he be?" Marcus looked confused. "It's his place."

"Answering a question with a question is not helpful to us, Mr. Finnegan," said Carolyn sternly.

"Right. Maybe we should go back to your house," I put in. "Your wife might have heard you say—"

Marcus belched. "He was there, okay? In his office. On the floor if there was any trouble, not that I ain't up to takin' care of anything them guys can dish out."

"Would you have known if Mr. Ignatenko chose to leave the building for, say, an hour or more?" Carolyn inquired.

Damn. The woman had a notebook out.

"Yeah. Sure. I stick my head in every half hour to report. Unless he's got company."

"What company?" I asked. "What company did he have that particular night?"

"Well, he called Carmen in about two, and they was going at it—you know what I mean. She come back in when we closed, so I guess they had another—uh—" He glanced at Carolyn. "Meetin'."

"Who else?" I asked.

"Just them two. Boris don't usually go for threesomes."

I noticed that Carolyn was embarrassed at talk of threesomes, but if she wanted to investigate scumbags, what did she expect? Those other murders she said she'd looked into—they must have been classier than this one. "Anyone but Carmen go in to see him when Carmen wasn't in there for their *meeting?*"

Marcus scratched his bald head, puzzling over the question. "Manny. Manny come in around midnight."

"Who's Manny?"

"He does hits, an'—like that. Muscle. You know? Only he don't necessarily use his fists like me, not that I don't use a bat if I gotta. But I just work in the club. Manny works outside. Like a freelancer."

Now, Manny was of interest to me. If he came in at midnight before Vladik was killed, maybe Boris *had* hired a hit. "How long was he there? Did Boris give him a job?"

"How the hell would I know? Boris don't tell me about his business with Manny. I just work inside, like I said."

"How—long—was—Manny—in—there?"

Marcus shifted uncomfortably on his rock, evidently catching on that I was getting pissed with the lack of information. "Fifteen minutes?"

I kept staring at him.

"Whyn't you ask Manny. He went in right after I did my twelve o'clock check with Boris, an' he was gone by twelve-thirty."

"Fine, I'll ask Manny. Where do I find him? What's his last name?"

Marcus scratched his head again. Many more questions and he'd have a scab there. "Diaz? I heard he got a place over a pool hall downtown, but I ain't never been there. Listen, can I go back now? The kids an' me is gonna watch *1001 Dalmatians*. It's on cable. They'll be pissed off if I ain't there when it starts."

I let Marcus go, and when he was out of earshot, Carolyn said, "Poor man. I think he's retarded."

"Or maybe that's what he wants us to think." I watched Marcus shamble down the street. Looked like he couldn't hurt anyone unless he fell on them, but I knew he had fast fists and a mean temper.

"You're thinking that Mr. Ignatenko hired a hit man to kill Vladik, aren't you?"

"I don't know. Maybe. Smothering someone with a pillow isn't your usual hired-hit weapon of choice. More like a weapon of opportunity."

"I think we should investigate this Manny," said Carolyn, as if that idea wasn't obvious.

"Did I say we weren't?"

"You don't have to be sarcastic about it," she retorted as we walked the half block between the arroyo and the car.

"Ever been in a pool hall?" I asked, feeling kinda mean.

"Yes, I have. In San Francisco. I helped question a tattooed criminal named Arana. It was a life-enhancing experience."

"Now who's being sarcastic?" I asked as she started the car.

33

The Hit Man's Ex

Carolyn

We found the pool hall, but there was no Manny Diaz in an apartment above it. The proprietor downstairs and, evidently, the owner of the building said Manny had moved in with his wife and three children several months ago. He gave us an address in the Lower Valley. We found that too, although I feared for my car's suspension on the pot-holed and, ultimately, unpaved road.

"Cold front coming in," Luz remarked as we opened an iron gate and walked up to the door. She was right; the temperature had dropped perceptibly, and sunshine was intermittent rather than continuous, as I'd come to expect during 99 percent of the daylight hours. Mr. Diaz's house was painted a deep blue green and had bars on every window and door. No doubt hit men needed extra security. I could hear the sound of children's voices behind the house and had to wonder how much danger they were in because of their father's profession.

"We're looking for Manny Diaz," Luz said to the woman who answered the door and peered at us suspiciously from between the intervening bars.

"What for?" she replied.

"Business," Luz answered.

"Need someone to take out your old man?" asked the wife cynically.

"Exactly. My friend here wants to hire your husband."

I was horrified, not only to be identified as a woman who wanted her husband killed, but at the wife's easy admission of her husband's business. Didn't she realize that we might be the police? Luz *had* been the police.

"Well, you're out of luck. Manny took off for Mexico Monday. Thought the cops was after him. And I'll tell you, if he figures he's coming back here when the heat's off, he's wrong. I'll kick his ass right off the doorstep. I don't need his customers and the cops showing up at my door. I got kids, an' only one of 'em's Manny's. An' he ain't my husband. I never married him in church or nothin'. I'm too smart for that. I'm takin' a computer course at the community college, an' I got my eye on a new man. Me an' my kids will do just fine without that pendejo."

There was that word again. "Tell me, Mrs.—ah—" If she wasn't Mrs. Diaz, what was her name?

"Tell you what? You want the name of some other pendejo to kill off your old man, you gonna hafta ask someone else. I'm out of the hits-for-hire business."

"No, I wanted to ask what *pendejo* means. My Spanish is minimal, but I keep hearing that word."

"It means *stupid prick. Pendejo* means *stupid prick.* Spanish or English, don't matter. That's what it means, and that's what Manny was, a stupid prick."

"Thank you," I murmured.

"Probably you old man is too."

"Not at all," I protested, forgetting that I was supposed to be a customer in search of a hit man.

"Okay, if we're through with the language lesson," said Luz, "I got a question for you. Manny had a talk with Boris Ignatenko Saturday night. You know what that was about?"

"Sure," said the non-wife. "Boris wanted to hire him."

"And did Manny accept?"

"Hell, yes. Offer him five hundred, he'd shoot me an' the kids. He is one real mean bastard."

"So who did he kill?" Luz asked.

"He didn't kill no one. There was a guy makin' book and sellin' dope at Brazen Babes. Which wouldn't make no difference to Boris. I know Boris. I used to dance there before I had the third kid, Manny Junior. But the guy wasn't kickin' back Boris's share of the profits. So Manny beat the crap out of him. It was a lesson. Know what I mean? Don't fuck with Boris. That was the message."

"Was this Saturday night or Sunday morning early that Manny earned his five hundred?" Luz asked.

I was too bemused to join in the questioning.

"Nah, Manny caught him comin' out of the can in some bar on Texas Sunday night, dragged him into an alley, an' broke all his ribs an' whatever. Guy recognized Manny and swore he'd set the cops on him, so Manny left him there, hopin' he'd die. Then he thought about it all night. Woke up the damn kids about three times bitching about his bad luck the guy had made him and Boris didn't want the guy killed. So he took off Monday morning. Good riddance, I say."

"You're sure it was Sunday night?" Luz asked.

"What do you care, anyway? You act like a cop, but *she* don't look like no cop." Manny's ex pointed at me. "Since when are cops helpin' gringo women hire hits. Some new battered-wife protection deal? If it is, gimme your card. I had a few guys beat me up. Manny included."

"I'm not a cop," said Luz.

"And I don't want my husband murdered," I added. What if Jason ever heard about this? I glared at Luz.

"So you're both liars. You want any more information, go find Manny. He's probably shacked up with some *puta* in Ciudad Chihuahua."

"Do you think she was misleading us?" I asked shortly thereafter as I started the car.

Luz shrugged. "Hard to tell. Probably not. He must have had a car, and I didn't see one in the yard. But then he could have gone straight out of Brazen Babes Saturday night, walked into Gubenko's house, and taken him out. Be nice if we had a witness. For sure, we gotta go see Boris tonight."

"For sure, I've got to go home and get some sleep," I said wearily. "What time do you want me to pick you up? Definitely not before ten."

"What we need," said Luz, who didn't seem to care about my state of sleep deprivation, "is a new suspect, or someone to break Boris's alibi." I drove, and she grumbled to herself. "You notice anything in the paper about some guy beat up in an alley downtown?"

I didn't remember. There were so many stories of violence in the paper and on TV then; it wasn't likely I would. In Africa and the Middle East people were killing each other off by the thousands. A few broken bones in an El Paso alley wouldn't be a big story. Which is a sad comment on our time. We're becoming desensitized. I wondered about people in the Middle Ages. Those had certainly been violent times. But, with no newspapers and TV, they wouldn't have known what was happening forty miles away, and by the time they realized what was happening in their own areas, they were either dead or running for their lives. Medieval people probably didn't live long enough to become desensitized.

"Hey, you're not asleep at the wheel, are you?" Luz asked.

"No, I was comparing violence and the public perception of it in our time to what it must have been in the Middle Ages."

"Terrific. That's going to be a big help in finding out who killed the Russian opera guy. Not that I miss him. He was a real noisy SOB. Say, maybe those two students of his killed him. With one on either side of the pillow, that would work."

"They were taking their clothes off in public when it

happened," I replied. "They worked until four. Didn't you hear what Marcus said?"

"If you believe what Marcus said. Or any of these upright citizens we've been talking to."

"They are a distasteful lot, aren't they?" We were quiet for a moment, thinking about the people we'd interviewed just lately. "Since we're in the Lower Valley, we could visit one of the missions. That might be uplifting," I suggested.

"You're kidding, right? Uplifting? The Spaniards and their priests just about killed off the Indians—took their land, turned them into slaves, made 'em wear clothes in hot weather, worked 'em to death or killed them with smallpox, cut off their hands when they rebelled. You didn't know that with all your history reading? Now we want to put up the world's biggest statue of Don Juan de Onate and his horse. Figure that out."

I sighed. "I do know about Spanish treatment of the Indians, but *you* evidently don't know that Onate was born in Mexico—Zacatecas. His father was a Spaniard, but his mother·was a direct descendant of Montezuma. What could be more Mexican? As for violence, both the sides were violent. The Aztecs ate their victims after cutting their hearts out."

"Okay. Truce. But I don't want to visit a mission."

"Fine," I agreed. "Let's go back to El Paso and get some sleep."

There was silence for a mile or so as I bumped over the unpaved road, and then the pot-holed road, toward I-10. "By the way, did you know that Ysleta used to be the county seat?" I couldn't help asking. We were passing a sign directing us to the Ysleta Mission. "The people from El Paso hired Mexicans to cross the river and vote, so El Paso won the county seat by fraud."

"Right. Ysleta was where the Mexican Americans lived. They got screwed by the Anglos. Again."

"Why, Luz," I exclaimed. "You're an activist."

"Nah," she said. "Just a woman short on sleep and long on bum knees. That smelly goop of your husband's isn't half as good at killing pain as my hot-chile salve, and don't, for Christ's sake, start telling me about the Aztecs and chile."

I grinned at her. "They did have some interesting uses for it in the old days, but I'll save that information for later."

Luz groaned and closed her eyes.

34
Boris Loses It

Luz

Of course she didn't show up on time. I had to call her and roust her out of bed. *How much sleep can one woman need?* I wondered as I waited. She was probably showering, dressing, and eating. By the time we got to Brazen Babes, Ignatenko would have picked his Friday night lay, and we'd be locked out until he came up for air. It wasn't that I thought he'd killed Vladik. His alibi seemed pretty solid. I just wanted to know why he sent us after Salvador Barrientos, who'd ended up in jail. Maybe that was just what Boris wanted. Maybe Vladik and Barrientos wouldn't cut him in on the border smuggling route, so he got even. Like he got even with the poor slob who had been taking bets and selling dope at Brazen Babes without giving Boris his cut. Nice guy.

Well, finally. She pulled up in front, and I headed out. Tonight I was carrying a gun. The cane was good, and I had that too. The dog was good, and I put her on the leash and took her with me. You couldn't have too much back up when your partner thought biting a drug dealer's finger was a big deal. Of course, she'd broken it first. Poor Barrientos. If he ever got out of jail, he'd be the laughing stock of the trade, kidnapped by two women in his own house. Of course, if he ratted out his bosses, he'd be a dead laughing stock. His future didn't look rosy. Maybe we could do the same for Boris, although I didn't see how at the mo-

ment. Unless this Carmen said, "Hey, you think I did the
dirty with Boris. No way. Why would I?" Or something
helpful like that.

"Hey, Caro. Think you can find your way to the strip
club without directions?"

"Maybe," she replied. "I feel much better after a decent
night's sleep, even if I got it at the wrong time. Why is
Smack going with us?"

"Backup," I replied, closing the door behind the dog,
which settled down for a nice snooze. When I first got her,
she used to want to stick her head out the window, and she
liked it when I drove fast. Now she'd rather take a nap.
Wouldn't you know old age would catch up with her when
I was finally starting to get back on my feet. Smack wasn't
going to be up to much bounty hunting in the future. Last
night had been hard on her. I think her jaw was hurting
after staying clamped on Barrientos for so long.

"Well, you're quiet tonight," Carolyn said to me. She was
actually taking the right turns on her own. So far, anyway.
Feeling pretty frisky after all that sleep. I don't sleep that
much myself, so my time drags most days. I have to say,
since Carolyn showed up at my door, with her improbable
take on crime, things had been looking up. She was a pain in
the ass, but she provided a few laughs and a lot of surprises.

"We'll talk to Carmen first," I said.

"I wonder if that's her real name. And if she knows
she's named for the heroine of a fabulous opera. Have you
ever seen it?"

I hadn't, so she hummed some music, which, for a wonder, sounded kind of familiar. Then she wanted to tell me
the story. Jesus, that was a lot of fun.

"Doesn't sound like good stripping music to me," I remarked.

"Oh, you're wrong. It's very sexy music. Maybe I'll
recommend it to Mr. Ignatenko. Some music by Bizet
might add a little class to his establishment."

"Class isn't what he's after. Take my word for it. And I doubt if she thinks of herself as named after an opera character she's probably never heard of. In fact, most of those girls use fake names."

"I can understand that," said Carolyn. "One wouldn't want one's mother to see her daughter's name in the paper and say, 'I can't believe it. Could that be my Dora advertised as an exotic dancer?' "

"Dora?" I had to laugh. We pulled into the parking lot, which was packed with the cars of randy Friday-night guys, and whisked right by Marcus, who said we couldn't bring the dog in.

"We're just going to see Boris, man," I replied. "We're not going to sic the dog on your customers."

"What about Carmen?" Carolyn whispered.

"Right. Carmen. We want to talk to Carmen first, Marcus." Smack had been sniffing him, and the poor guy looked terrified. "Sit, Smack," I ordered. "Our friend here has to bring Carmen out."

Marcus pointed a finger with deformed knuckles over at a woman with purple-red hair and big boobs. She was waggling them at a leathery-looking dude in a three-sizes-too-big polyester jacket with string tie hung under the gaping neck of his shirt. "Carmen," Marcus croaked.

Carolyn, Smack, and I went over to interrupt Carmen's chat with her admirer. Of course, she told us to get lost. Carolyn looked the john straight in the eye and said, "You're HIV positive, aren't you?" The poor guy tried to deny it, but Carolyn said, "Oh yes, you are. I've seen you at the Tillman Clinic on AIDS day. Are you trying to seduce this young woman without telling her the risks? Shame on you!"

Carmen got up so fast, she knocked her chair over. Carolyn then took her arm and said, "Come along, my dear. You can't be too careful about sexual partners. I'm so glad I was here to rescue you," all the time dragging Carmen toward the side of the room.

The stripper finally dug in her heels and said, "Hey, all my johns gotta use a rubber."

"One in ten AIDS cases occur even after the use of a condom," Carolyn told her. "Did you know that there's a city in France, in Gascony, I believe, named Condom? You have to wonder whether the place was named after the prophylactic or vice versa."

Carmen was gaping at her. I may have been doing a bit of gaping myself. Had Carolyn really seen that guy at the Tillman Clinic, and if so, what had she been doing there? And what about the city in France? Condom, for God's sake? Someone asks you where you're from and you have to say Condom?

"We did have a question for you, my dear," said Carolyn. "Were you in Boris's office last Saturday night and Sunday morning?"

"Jesus, you gonna tell me *he*'s got AIDS too?" asked Carmen, looking seriously alarmed.

"Can I take that as a yes?"

"Yeah. Yeah, me and Boris got it on Saturday. I dunno. Three or four times. That SOB! He claims his dong—"

"Dong?"

"Penis," I translated.

"Yeah. He says it's too long for a rubber," said the indignant Carmen. "If he—"

"I have no information on Boris's health," said Carolyn, "but it wouldn't hurt to get tested as a precaution. Ladies of the evening can't be too careful in these perilous times."

Carmen was still trying to decipher Carolyn's last remarks while we sailed toward Boris's office, Smack in tow, Marcus lumbering after us, but not too close. My guess was that he's terrified of dogs—and him the guy who watched *1001 Dalmatians* with his kids. Go figure. "What were you doing in the Tillman Clinic?" I asked Carolyn.

"I've never been there in my life, but I do read the newspapers." Then she stopped dead to study the lighting, after which she said to Marcus, "Those lights are dangerous."

He looked perplexed. I barged right into the office without knocking. "How come you sent me after Barrientos?" I asked. I sounded mean, so Smack growled.

"Get that damn dog outa here," Boris shouted. "Marcus, get hold of that dog." Instead of obeying, Marcus backed up.

"Barrientos didn't kill your pal Vladik," I said. "They had a nice alien-smuggling deal set up together. And Barrientos was singing mariachi and ranchero numbers in Juarez while Vladik was taking his last gasp, which was probably more puke than air."

"Barrientos lying," said Boris. "Why you bothering me again? I not inviting you." Then he caught sight of Carolyn. "You. Why you taking my dancers away?" he shouted. "Giving ideas about being good girls."

"Slave labor is against the law in this country, Mr. Ignatenko," she said calmly.

"My girls is none of your business."

"Did you realize that those pulsing lights you have on the stage could cause seizures? Epileptics, people prone to migraines—you could find yourself fighting an expensive lawsuit if one of your customers is affected."

"Shut up. No one getting sick my club."

"What if an epileptic swallowed his tongue and died? And in such a sleazy situation. The family would be furious."

"Trouble-making bitch," he snarled.

Now this is fun, I thought, not quite sure whether she was being dumb or gutsy. Boris looked like *he* was about to have a seizure.

"I imagine they'd call the police and write to the newspaper, not to mention hiring a lawyer to sue your socks off."

"Get out my place," he said, taking a threatening step in her direction.

"I would certainly try to get even if I were in their shoes," said Carolyn. "You should change the lighting as soon as possible."

I should have seen it coming, but I didn't.

"I show you getting even," said Boris, and he hit her right in the eye with a round-house punch.

Without a word, Carolyn collapsed on the floor, which was none too clean. She'd be upset when she came to. I drew my gun and assumed a two-handed stance, aiming for his nose.

"Get gun, Fats," said Boris to his bouncer, who had been watching the drama with an anxious look on his face.

"You make a move, Marcus, and I'll sic the dog on you." I didn't need to deal with two guys at once, one extra tall ghoul and his extra fat bouncer. Marcus swallowed hard and nodded his head. The dog, having been directed to do so, was looking at him. Marcus started to sweat.

"I fire you," Boris threatened.

"You didn't say nothing about fightin' dogs, Boris. I'm afraid of dogs."

I'd fished my cell phone out, one handed, and called 911. "I'm at Brazen Babes," I told the operator. "It's a strip club off . . . Good, I'm glad you've heard of it. I got a woman who's had her lights punched out." Since I couldn't hold both phone and gun in the same hand, I couldn't check to see that Carolyn was breathing, but her color was okay, except for the eye. That was going to be something else. "I want the police here to pick up the guy who punched her. They'll need backup. This isn't the YMCA. This place got an address, Marcus?"

Marcus didn't know, and Boris wouldn't say, so we stood around until we heard the sirens. Boris then muttered, "You're being real sorry you do this."

"Not as sorry as you, Boris. You shouldn't have sent me on that wild goose chase, not that I mind putting Barrientos in jail, but he got real fresh with my friend there. And you sure shouldn't have hit her. She's a food columnist, a professor's wife, and a member of Opera at the Pass. You don't go around hitting women like that."

"If she so good lady, what she doing my club?" he responded sullenly. He'd started to sweat too.

"And then there's the deal you made with Manny. Remember? The guy you had him kick half to death in an alley downtown? The cops are going to look into that. Hell, Boris, you'll be lucky if they deport you. Or maybe that won't be so lucky. Didn't you say you deserted from the Russian army? What do they do to deserters? Shoot 'em?"

Boris's fists were clenching. He was probably mad enough to jump me, and I was being a dumb shit for baiting him, but it was fun. Fortunately, reinforcements showed up before I had to shoot the sucker. Having a grand jury asking me questions about a shooting would have been a royal pain. I'd been there.

35

First Black Eye

Carolyn

I regained consciousness quite rapidly—at least I think so. What I didn't do was move a muscle or open my eyes. My whole head ached dreadfully, and I had to wonder if he'd given me a concussion or fractured my skull. What an amazing thing. That a man would punch me in the eye. Even if I *had* been making irritating remarks. Occasionally I make irritating remarks to Jason. He never punches me. And of course, I should have risen to lend assistance to Luz. I could tell by the conversation that she was holding two large, unfriendly men at bay with one gun and a dog. And she was baiting Mr. Ignatenko. Obviously neither one of us had an ounce of sense. Look what baiting him had gotten me.

Once the sirens wailed into our area and then fell silent, once I could hear the voices of the policemen who had responded to Luz's call, once someone laid fingers on my neck to determine whether or not I had died, I did open my eyes. "I thought you were playing possum," said Luz. She was the person taking my pulse. "Thank God you had enough sense to stay that way. A couple more remarks from you and Boris would have killed us both."

"You should talk," I retorted. I tried to raise myself on one elbow, but immediately felt dizzy and edged back down.

"That's right, ma'am," said a young policeman, who

was standing beside Luz. "You just stay right where you are. You're gonna have some shiner there. You wanna press assault charges against the man who hit you?"

"I do, and I want to testify at his trial and see him led away in handcuffs."

"Well, you'll get to see that last in just a few minutes. What about the fat guy? Did he hurt you too?"

"No. Mr. Finnegan was, in his own fashion, quite placid. He's afraid of the dog."

"You want me to pick you up and put you on the sofa, ma'am. That carpet's kind of dirty."

"I'm sure any sofa belonging to Mr. Ignatenko would be equally dirty, and I'd rather not move for a minute or so." While we were waiting for the paramedics, I gave my statement from a prone position. Luz pulled the desk chair over and sat beside me to give her statement. We both insisted that the drug dealer in the alley and his assailant, Manny, who was hired by Mr. Ignatenko, be found, one for medical treatment, both for arrest.

More sirens wailed, long blasts sounded, and several firemen arrived, suited out for fighting fires. They clumped in, turned me on my back, took my pulse and blood pressure, shined flashlights in my eyes, waved fingers in front of my face, and pronounced me concussion-free but entitled to a ride to the hospital where x-rays would determine if any skull or facial bones had been broken. I said that Luz would drive me in my own car. Since she'd gotten me into this mess and had thought it hilarious that I had complained about sleep deprivation, I fully intended to see that she didn't get to bed until I did. The young policeman carried me to the car through a group of gaping perverts and staring, scantily clad dancers. The performance had stopped when the police arrived. Boris was being held outside in the club and snarled at me as I was taken away.

With Smack in the front seat and me curled up in back, beset by dog hair and the lingering odor of Mr. Barrientos, not to mention the air freshener that I had used liberally before leaving home this evening, Luz drove to the hospital. I must say, she didn't allow the people in the emergency room to put me at the end of the treatment list. I was rolled right into the back, then examined and x-rayed from all angles by curious technicians, nurses, and interns. Each new purveyor of care wanted to hear about Brazen Babes, why I had been there, and the assault on me. Didn't they know that I felt horrible and had no desire to describe my experiences? Evidently not. Since I had neither a fracture nor a concussion, they all felt quite free to bombard me with questions.

Finally, I was left with one nurse, a very kind lady who let me have some Seven-Up, although she freely admitted that they wanted to know if I could keep it down. "You must have been having a boring evening if my little misadventure caused so much interest," I remarked.

"Oh, no. We've been busy. Friday night/Saturday morning and Saturday night/Sunday morning are always a circus. Everything from knifings and car pileups to barfing kids who ate too many hot dogs at the ball game." She held out the cup with its bent straw, encouraging me to take another experimental sip. "Now if you feel like vomiting, honey, let me know right off. Then we won't have to change the sheets."

"I've stopped feeling queasy," I assured her. "And I should have remembered that weekends bring lots of emergencies. Dr. Peter Brockman, an acquaintance of mine, was called out in the middle of the night for emergency surgery just last weekend."

"The neurosurgeon? Not here, he wasn't. I'd have remembered that. He's ultrapicky about everything."

"I'm sure it was here. Maybe you were off duty. According to his wife, the call came after midnight."

"I had that shift. Both Friday and Saturday. I promise you he wasn't here."

Now that's strange, I thought. *Vivian definitely told me that he was home with her after the opera party, until the hospital called him in to perform surgery on an auto accident victim.*

"You cold, honey? Want me to get you a blanket?"

I said that I wasn't. That shiver, those goose bumps running up my arms were caused by a very disturbing thought.

"Another half hour and we'll let you go home. Anyone waiting for you in Admitting?"

"Yes, a friend," I replied. A friend that I wanted to talk to right away. I didn't get to of course.

We were in the car heading for my house before I had the opportunity to tell Luz about Dr. Brockman, who had said to his friend Frank Escobar, Luz's ex, that they needed to get rid of Vladik—Dr. Brockman, who had told his wife he had to go to the hospital to perform emergency surgery on someone's head, when there wasn't any such surgery. So where *had* he gone?

"Sounds thin to me," said Luz, ignoring the mention of her ex-husband. "Who goes over to someone's house and kills them over a weird opera production. But, hey, we can worry about that tomorrow. You want me to stay with you tonight?"

I did. For the second night. We were having a weekend sleepover, only more violent than the ones I'd given and attended as a child, and there hadn't been any more at my house after my mother died. My father didn't like giggling. Or noise of any kind if it involved children.

36

A Butt Print Remembered

Luz

Even considering the strange bed, I should have slept right through because I'd been pushing myself too hard and needed the rest. Instead I kept waking up and checking on Carolyn—like my subconscious thought she was going to die on me. The woman never stirred all night. Once the hospital staff satisfied themselves that she didn't have a concussion or fracture, she was given a prescription for pain pills, which she couldn't wait to get home and take. The only thing that changed with her that night was her eye, which had puffed up and turned multicolored by morning. She was not going to be a happy camper the first time she looked in the mirror.

At dawn I'd wrapped up in a blanket on her patio to watch the sunrise creep over the Franklins, but then I dozed off in one of her loungers and woke up with my knee aching, so I rubbed on some of her husband's pain cream, thinking that my chile-pepper stuff would have done me more good. Maybe that's because I've got Indian blood. My ancestors probably used chiles to doctor all their ills. Then I made myself some coffee and toast and ate it in the warm kitchen while I waited impatiently for Sleeping Beauty to wake up; I needed to get home, change clothes, and give myself a shot— it was that day—but I didn't want to do it until she woke up. It was a bitch, being tied to a medication schedule when I actually had something interesting to do with my time.

Carolyn staggered out around ten-thirty. "Have you seen my eye?" she groaned.

"It'll clear up in a week or so," I said.

"A week," she cried, and dropped into a chair, aghast.

I told her she was lucky to come out of last night with just a black eye. I'd been reading the paper. Ignatenko was in jail, and the cops had found the alley victim at Thomason Hospital. The guy talked his head off, identified Manny Diaz as the attacker, said Ignatenko had threatened him because of the drugs and bookmaking at the club. So the guy was arrested, him and his broken bones: collar bone, six ribs, and three leg bones, plus some cracks in his arms and a bleeding kidney. There was a warrant out on Manny and more charges on Ignatenko. INS was talking deportation hearings, so Boris was, as I'd told him, thoroughly screwed. "We did good work last night," I told Carolyn, and read her choice bits of the story.

That brightened her up a little bit, but not much, so I said she should get a black eye patch for her eye, sew some beads or sequins on it, and set a fashion trend in El Paso.

"That's a ridiculous idea," she said sternly, and then started to giggle.

I was on a roll, having cheered Caro up without even knowing I had any talent in that area. My mother once told me she'd rather be sick on her own than have me around looking glum and botching up the nursing chores. Once Caro stopped giggling, I told her what I'd been thinking about her doctor friend. While I talked, I poured her a cup of coffee; from the look on her face, you'd think she didn't like my coffee, even though I was known at Central Regional Command for my great coffee during my days on patrol. I fixed her some toast too, and even poured her a glass of juice since I figured she needed healthy stuff.

"Tell me about his butt," I said, plunking the juice down in front of her.

Her expression was amazed and offended. Carolyn

would make a crappy poker player. Everything shows on her face. If she got a good hand, she'd probably light up the room. "The doctor's butt," I added, just to be sure she understood what I wanted. "How wide would you say it is?"

"I don't go around measuring men's bottoms," she replied stiffly.

I took a deep breath. "Look, you think he might have killed Vladik. It's a long shot, but what have we got to lose? We need to think about him, this doctor. One thing I noticed in Vladik's house was his sofa. He's got this microwave upholstery on it. Feels like suede."

"Microfiber," she corrected.

"Whatever. Anyway, you sit down on it; your butt leaves a print. Lean your hand on it. Handprint. One of each on the Russian's sofa. I had the crime-scene guys take a picture. Of course, that dumb Guevara thought it was a waste of time, but then he thought Gubenko died of natural causes. Probably still does."

"If he's so sure of that, why is he harassing those of us who provided food for the party?" Carolyn asked sharply.

"Because it's easier than doing a real investigation," I told her. "So how wide is the doctor's butt?"

"I have no idea," she said. "He's had trousers over it every time I've seen him."

"This wide?" I spread my hands to about two feet.

"Luz, he's a thin person, but quite tall, and I don't how wide his rear end is."

"What about his hands?"

She thought about it. "Large, but then they would be. As I said, he's tall. You wouldn't expect little bitty hands or feet on a tall man. And his fingers are long and thin with short, manicured nails."

I nodded. My recollection of the prints on the sofa was pretty vague, but it seems to me that the hand did have long fingers; of course so do Boris Ignatenko's hands.

Now Manny Diaz—he'd be more likely to have short, broad hands, but since I'd never seen the man, that was a guess.

"What we need to do is knock on my neighbors' doors and ask if anyone saw or heard anything that night. If we can get a description of someone going in or leaving—"

"We? You expect me to go out looking like *this?*" She covered her eye with her hand.

"You planning to hide out for the next week or so?"

"I've heard of putting steak on a black eye," she said. "But I'd have to go to the store to get some, and that would be so embarrassing."

"Right. I get the idea. I have to do the canvassing by myself. Only problem is, you know what the doctor looks like. I don't. And steak never did me any good. Course I used cube steak. Maybe you need a more expensive cut— sirloin or T-bone. Or a filet. That would be about the right size."

"You're making fun of me," she said.

"Instead of a steak, why don't we get you an eye patch? The decoration is up to you. Go for plain if you want. You could wear a hat too, a big, wide one. My neighbors won't even notice you got a black eye. They'll think you're a gardener in your big hat."

"What a wonderful idea. The pirate-gardener. Maybe I should bring along gardening gloves. And a trowel."

I grinned at her. "So are you in?"

"I suppose so," she grumbled. "If we can find an eye patch. But you'll have to drive. I'm taking pain pills."

37

Canvassing in Black and Blue

Carolyn

There were various minutiae to take care of before we could actually begin canvassing Luz's neighborhood. I had to shower and dress, then find a suitable hat and a picture of Peter Brockman. There had been a photographer at the opera party, and we'd been sent a picture of the two of us standing with Peter and Vivian; I put that in an envelope. Luz had to purchase an eye patch for me at Walgreen's. Then she had to stop by her condo to change her clothes and give herself a shot of the very expensive medication that keeps her mobile. Finally it was necessary to console Smack, who wanted to accompany us but wasn't allowed. Luz said her neighbors might not appreciate a visit from the dog.

The security guard didn't remember the man on night shift mentioning any strangers wanting to come in after midnight the Sunday morning in question. We picked up that discouraging piece of information before we even started the canvass. Because it was Saturday, we found people at home, but all had been asleep a week ago after midnight. Luz grumbled that she'd hoped to find at least a few swingers among the group who might have seen something. Our last stop was across the street and several doors down from Luz's.

"Not much hope here," she muttered. "This woman's old. Probably goes to bed at nine." She rang the bell, and the householder answered after a rather long interval and several more rings.

"You don't have to lean on my doorbell," she said, thumping her cane irritably on the floor. "I have arthritis. It takes me a while to get to the front door, and having the bell ringing in my ear doesn't make me any faster, young lady," she said to Luz.

Mrs. Filbert was a tall, lean woman, somewhat humped, very wrinkled, with liver spots on her hands and face. The rest of her was covered by a long, baggy dress with purple flowered stripes and large pockets on the chest, stuffed with Kleenex. Over the dress she wore a heavy green sweater that looked hand knitted. A pair of well worn, New Balance tennis shoes completed the outfit.

"I've seen you from time to time," she growled at Luz. "You limp. Mine's arthritis. What's your problem?"

"Same," said Luz grumpily.

"You're too young for arthritis."

"Tell my rheumatologist."

"Oh, that kind of arthritis. Well, come in, both of you. Don't stand out there in the wind." She led us into her living room, where every chair and sofa was straight-backed and very firm. "You'll appreciate my furniture," she told Luz. "Easy to get out of. I'm not so crippled up yet that I have to have one of those chairs that shoot you onto your feet when you push a button, but I suppose that's coming. Do you have one of those?"

"No, ma'am," Luz replied. "My medication's working pretty well."

"Lucky you. Not that having a crippling illness at your age is lucky. I have a friend with the rheumatoid kind. It's always women. Have you noticed that? As if God didn't give us burdens enough—menstruation, childbirth, men. Either of you have children? Mine are a thankless lot. They think I should go into a nursing home. As if I'm likely to do that. I plan to stay right where I am. Maybe when I turn

a hundred and don't care any more, but for now I can take
care of myself. Can't drive anymore, but there's bus
pickup for seniors. You could probably use it too, young
lady. You being crippled and all."

"I still drive," Luz said.

"I have two children," I replied, in answer to the question
our hostess had asked and forgotten. "Both in college."

"You find you don't know what to do with yourself now
you don't have to pick up after them and wash their clothes
and all that?"

"Actually, I keep quite busy," I replied, smiling.

"So do I. I have no patience for women who sit around
their houses moaning about empty-nest syndrome, of all
the newfangled ideas. I'd offer you refreshments, but I
don't feel like getting up. When people lean on your doorbell and force you to hobble faster, you need a little rest afterward." She aimed a challenging glance at Luz, and then
turned to look out the front window, by which her chair
was placed. "What with TV and watching what's happening in the neighborhood, I keep busy. Used to do crewel
embroidery, but it makes my fingers hurt now. You have
trouble with your fingers, young lady?"

"No, ma'am. Mostly my knees, although at times it
jumps around," said Luz. "Those are the worst spells."

"Well, you have my sympathy. I know just how it is.
Can't sleep because you're aching so bad, can't garden
anymore. That's a nice hat you've got there," she said to
me. "Must be good for gardening. A good hat's a blessing
in this town. I always wore a big hat when I gardened. Of
course here in Casitas they do your gardening for you."

"You have trouble sleeping?" Luz asked. She'd become
quite alert when she heard that. I could see her chafing to
break into the neighbor's monologue.

"Sure do. Sleeplessness trouble you?"

"No, I'm used to it. You weren't by any chance awake
last Saturday night late, were you?"

"Yep. An interesting night, that was. That young man with the condo by yours—he came home drunk as a sailor. Staggering into the wrong yard. He fell into your bushes. Did you notice that? And he was throwing up from the bushes all the way to his own door. I reported him to the association. But I tell you, I had to laugh to see him trying to get out of those bushes. Men and alcohol are a bad combination. The fool didn't even close his door."

"Did you see anyone else go in his house that night, Mrs. Filbert?" I asked, now feeling that we were getting somewhere.

"Oh, yes. He must have called his doctor. Now most folks wouldn't bother to call a doctor when they're vomiting from too much alcohol, but sure enough a while later along comes this fellow with a doctor bag, finds the door open, goes on in, comes out maybe an hour later; no, probably a half hour. I was sorry I'd called the association on this young lady's next-door neighbor if he was that sick, but then I heard he died, so I guess they never reported the complaint to him."

I whipped out my picture and showed it to her. "Did the doctor look like any of these people?" I was thinking that this was the best we could do in the way of a lineup, not that Vivian, Jason, or I looked like Peter.

"Well, he wasn't a woman, and he wasn't the short fellow with the beard. Might have been the tall fellow in the tux, but the one in the picture isn't carrying a doctor bag. That's what I noticed. The bag. Why are you wearing a patch over your eye, young lady?" she asked me. "And don't I see bruising spreading out from under that patch? My eyesight's still good. My late husband always said I could spot the warts on a warthog from fifty yards away. Stupid thing to say. I never saw a warthog in my life."

"She got slugged last night in a strip club," said Luz, grinning.

Very funny, I thought. If she'd been closer, I'd have kicked her.

"My land!" exclaimed our hostess. "You're too old to be stripping, and you got that prissy look about you. Like you wouldn't approve of strip clubs. Now me. Walter and me took in a few strip clubs in Juarez when we were younger. Chunky, brown-skinned girls taking their clothes off. Didn't seem that much of a show to me, but one of the places had a fellow singing bullfight music. I liked that one."

"Can you remember anything else about the man who visited my neighbor last Saturday, ma'am?" Luz asked. "Like his car. What kind of car was he driving?"

"Oh, it was just an ordinary car. I never pay much attention to cars. That's a man's thing. Walter could have told you, but he's dead, more's the pity. It was a dark color, or maybe it just looked that way because it wasn't parked under a light. Doctor obviously didn't know what house he was going to, parking two houses away. Not even in front of a door. His car was pretty long. Not one of those runty little cars they got these days. Course, him being a tall fellow, he probably couldn't get into one of those runty cars."

After we'd thanked her for the information, she said, "Well, it was my pleasure. Nice to have company from time to time. Wouldn't like it every day, but now and then's nice."

"She's going to have more company," Luz said as she walked toward the street. "We'll have to give her name to the police." She sighed. "We need to get hold of Guevara. And what did I tell you? Prissy. She noticed it too."

"Am not," I retorted.

38

Going Behind Sergeant Guevara's Back

Luz

Carolyn didn't want to visit police headquarters at Five Points with a black eye and an eye patch. "They'll take one look and arrest me," she predicted. I pointed out that she was the person who discovered that Dr. Brockman had not been where he claimed while Vladik was being killed. Her testimony was important. "You could tell them about it," she insisted. I got her there by the simple expedient of refusing to drive her home or let her drive herself, but I had to listen to her debating on whether or not she should wear the hat into the police station.

Personally, it cheered me up to go inside. Previously, I hadn't wanted to. It would have been a reminder of what I'd lost to this damned disease, or so I thought. Guevara wasn't there, but Lieutenant Robert Matalisse, a man I'd broken in in Narcotics, was and running Crimes Against Persons these days. Who wouldn't rather talk to Rob, I thought, when the alternative was Art Guevara? I hustled Carolyn down the hall to Matalisse's office and stuck my head in. "Got a minute for a retired cripple?" I asked cheerfully.

He stood up and ushered us in, smiling. To my surprise there was gray showing in his hair. I'd always thought of him as a young man. "Making waves again, Luz?" he asked. "Lots of cop gossip making the rounds. You and Chuy and some DEA agent bringing in a Juarez cartel guy.

Heard you came across the border with the guy in the trunk of your car."

"Trunk of Carolyn's car," I corrected, and introduced her. "And the two of us brought him in. Chuy and Parko from DEA just got us out of the hands of INS and into the jail with our prisoner."

"And now you've got someone else in the trunk?" He motioned us to chairs and dropped into his own behind the desk.

"No, but we've got a suspect in a murder case. Of course, it could still be Ignatenko from Brazen Babes, but—"

"Hold on." He studied Carolyn, with her eye patch and huge, floppy denim hat. "You the lady got knocked out by Gubenko last night?" He nodded. "I saw the assault report this morning. What are you two? A ladies' detective agency?"

"Oh, that is a delightful series, isn't it?" Carolyn exclaimed. Up till then she'd been silent and sulky. "But it's called the First Ladies Detective Agency. Those books are so charming; they make you want to visit Botswana."

Rob looked blank, and I said, "He doesn't read books. Whatever you're talking about, it's not what he meant. Anyway, Rob, and before my friend here reviews the whole damn book for you, we've found a local doctor who told my ex the night it happened that they needed to get rid of Gubenko. Then he told his wife he had to go in for emergency surgery at Providence, only a night nurse who was on duty while Gubenko was being suffocated said the doctor wasn't there—at the hospital. Then this afternoon we found an old lady who saw a tall guy with a doctor's bag go into Gubenko's house. That was after Gubenko staggered in."

"Guevara's case." Rob squinted at me. "This wouldn't be you trying to get your ex in trouble, would it, Luz? What's his name?"

"Escobar. Francisco Escobar, and no, I don't think he had anything to do with the murder."

"He didn't," Carolyn chimed in. "Barbara, his present wife, said he was home in bed with her while Vladik was being killed."

"And how did she happen to tell you that?" Rob asked Carolyn.

"Because our ad hoc ladies' opera committee was trying to figure out who could have killed Vladik, and we started with our own husbands. That's how I know that Vivian Brockman thought her husband was at Providence Memorial for emergency surgery when he wasn't."

"Carolyn was another person who heard Brockman say he had to get rid of Vladik, but you'll want to talk to my ex as corroboration. Just don't tell Francisco I was behind it," I added. "I haven't seen him in years, but we parted on good terms, and I'd just as soon keep it that way."

Rob studied us thoughtfully, probably trying to decide whether we were both crazy or what. "Guevara says the guy died of food poisoning. In fact he got tox screens back today that say something bad was in the guacamole the victim ate."

I could see Carolyn tense at the mention of food poisoning and guacamole. *Damn! What if she made the guacamole? Here she'd had me running around looking for a murderer, when she—*

"He's out trying to get his hands on the guacamole maker right now."

Again I glanced at Carolyn, who was biting her lip. But then there was the pillow. I'm the one who said it had been used to smother a sick man. Was she just going along because she hoped it was true? I explained the pillow evidence to Rob, then the butt and handprints I'd had photographed. "Guevara knows about the pillow and the prints on the sofa. He just didn't want to bother following up."

Rob shrugged. "You and Art never did like each other."

"Doesn't mean the department shouldn't look into the lead," I retorted.

"I didn't say it did. What's the doctor's name?"

"Peter Brockman. The neurosurgeon," said Carolyn. "He's the current president of Opera at the Pass, which explains his association with Vladik Gubenko. He made the remark about getting rid of Vladik at the party where Vladik got sick and went home. If the guacamole made him sick, it was probably because he ate several pounds of it. As nice as guacamole is, and this was very good, it's not meant to be eaten in such large quantities."

Matalisse was frowning. "You couldn't have found a suspect who was less prominent in the community?"

Carolyn, who had the bit in her teeth at that point, said, "Most of the people at that party are prominent in the community. They may not all like opera—they certainly didn't like that particular performance—but supporting opera is seen in that group as a fashionable thing to do. Not Jason and I—we love opera—but—"

"Yeah, thanks. I'm getting the picture. We'll definitely look into Brockman."

"And don't forget the butt print," I reminded him.

Rob grinned. "We'll ink his ass and make him sit down."

Carolyn looked shocked. "I really need to get home now, Luz," she said plaintively.

"I can believe it," Rob agreed. "That's some shiner you've got there. I can see it spreading out under the patch. Me, I'd take that patch off. It's not like you need to wear it for us. We've all seen shiners before. Hell, a lot of us have had them."

"Thank you for your concern, Lieutenant," she replied. Prissy again. She probably felt like crap. I'd like to have stayed to be sure that they followed up on Brockman, but I figured I owed it to her to get her home.

"Okay, Caro. Let's hit the road," I agreed. "And Matalisse, don't let Guevara talk you out of the follow-up on Brockman. I guess if you piss an opera lover off enough by screwing around with a good opera, you might get killed."

"I wouldn't have thought so," said Carolyn. "Professor Gubenko presented *Macbeth* as a story about drug dealers, and it did offend a good many people, but surely killing someone over it is an extreme reaction. Perhaps the doctor is overworked and having a nervous breakdown."

"I read *Macbeth* in high school. Pretty violent. I can see the connection to drug dealing," said the lieutenant. "You might have got a few cops over to the performance if they'd known what Gubenko had in mind."

"If it's ever brought back, I'll certainly advise the publicity committee to send flyers to police stations," said Carolyn. She had risen and looked a little wobbly. *The woman is a wuss*, I thought. *A black eye isn't that big a deal.* But it turned out that she wasn't even wobbly. She insisted on dropping me at home and driving off on her own. Now what was that about? I'd pissed her off again? Or Matalisse had? She was a hard woman to please.

39

Anxious Relatives From Juarez

Carolyn

Swaying on my feet had been a good move. It was obvious that Luz hadn't wanted to leave, but she did when she thought I was ill. From the time I heard that the sergeant was after the guacamole provider, I couldn't wait to get out of there. I was probably too late to defend Adela from him, but I had to try. I drove straight home and checked my answering machine. Nothing—not even from Jason. He hadn't called in several days now, even to say for certain when he'd be back, which was very irritating, especially considering that he was in Austin with some young thing named Mercedes Lizarreta. Nothing from anyone else. I called the dormitory, but Adela wasn't there. Had she been arrested? I couldn't very well call Crimes Against Persons and ask. That wouldn't be very subtle.

I ducked into the "maid's bathroom" to examine my eye. My house has a room and bath for a live-in maid, which I don't have; mine comes once a week but not that week because she was visiting relatives somewhere in Mexico. My eye was truly dreadful, all puffy and a rich, dark purple with red streaks and black edging. Driving home had been a chore because my vision on that side was pretty much obscured. I discovered that one's depth perception is quite altered when only one eye is functioning. I had to start braking as soon as I saw a traffic light in order to avoid running into the back of the car ahead of me if the light turned red. I was standing sideways to the mirror over the little sink, trying to look at my injured eye from a side view, which, of course, wasn't possible, when the telephone rang. While rushing into the kitchen to answer, I bumped into the side of the door. Consequently, I was wincing when I picked up.

My caller was Adela, in need of my advice. Her aunt and uncle from Juarez had come to visit, so she had spent much of the afternoon giving them a walking tour of the campus. When she returned to her dormitory, the student on desk duty told her that the police had been looking for her. "That horrible sergeant is going to arrest me," she wailed.

I couldn't tell her that was unlikely. He probably did plan to arrest her. Instead I asked where she was at that time, and she replied that she was in her uncle's car, calling on her aunt's cell phone. Would that be Tia Julietta, who had given her the guacamole additive? I asked. It was, and Tio Javier, the lawyer. I suggested that they leave campus immediately and meet me at Casa Jurado, where we could have a nice dinner—I had to eat, so why not in company?—and decide what to do. Adela agreed immediately, whispering that her relatives from Juarez had been suggesting all sorts of peculiar strategies.

This should be interesting, I thought, *if I manage to drive there successfully.* I hung up, went back to the maid's bath, retrieved and donned my eye patch, and decided that a large denim garden hat might not be the proper headgear for dinner. After ruffling through the hatbox in the hall closet, I selected a wide-brimmed black hat that necessitated changing to a black outfit. Finally, I was ready and drove off to the restaurant, where I found Adela, looking distraught, while her aunt and uncle dipped chips in the excellent chile con queso, the large size, and conversed in Spanish. Introductions were made, the language switched to English for my sake, and Tia Julietta complimented me on my hat, remarking that she herself liked hats because they were dressier for evening and warded off evil spirits that might be lurking above one's head.

Tio Javier told me to pay no attention to his sister, who clung to all sorts of old-fashioned, supernatural ideas instilled in her at an early age by their *abuela,* a delightful but somewhat crazy old lady, now deceased. I felt as if I'd walked into a scene in a magic realist novel—Isabela Allende or Gabriel García Márquez, neither of whom is Mexican. We consulted our menus. The aunt ordered *Pescado al Mojo de Ajo,* a fish filet in garlic butter; the uncle ordered steak *Tampiqueno*; Adela ordered, at my suggestion, spinach enchiladas, which are *so* very good and have such a lovely, subtle sauce; I tried something new, *Enchiladas de Calebacitas*, Mexican-squash enchiladas. Then we gingerly approached the subject of Adela's fear of arrest.

"It may be about to happen," I admitted. "I was at police headquarters this afternoon, giving evidence on a man who may have smothered Adela's professor, when I heard that the toxicology reports had come in and revealed an unusual addition to the guacamole, which, as you know, Adela made."

"Why are the police pursuing my niece if her professor died from smothering?" asked the uncle.

"Unfortunately, the sergeant in charge of the investigation does not believe in the smothering theory because it is obvious that something made Professor Gubenko very sick before he died."

"But you convinced him, no?" said the aunt.

"He wasn't there. He was out looking for Adela."

Adela started to cry.

"There, there child," said Tia Julietta. "There is nothing in your horoscope to suggest that you will be arrested."

"Julietta, *mia hermana,* this is not a time for horoscopes," protested Tio Javier. "This is a time for logic. Do you not agree, Senora Azul?"

"Quite possibly," I agreed, assuming that I was the Senora Azul he had addressed. "A friend with police connections and I have been investigating this death. We talked to the sergeant's lieutenant, who has promised to look into our suggestions."

"Well, that is excellent," said Tio Javier.

Why was I thinking of him as *Tio?* I didn't speak Spanish, and he wasn't *my* uncle.

"No sergeant will ignore the wishes of his superior," said the uncle as he popped a bite of steak into his mouth. "The food here is excellent."

"It lacks something," said Aunt Julietta.

"Then don't add it. We have enough troubles for our poor niece because she listened to you."

"I do not blame Tia Julietta," said Adela, who was sniffling over her spinach enchiladas. "I asked for her help, and she gave it."

"And look what happened," said the uncle. They fell back into Spanish to argue the matter. I pretended not to notice and occupied myself by admiring the delightful window that decorates the front wall of the restaurant—thick chunks of colored glass set deep in a black, rough-surfaced, flaring frame, which is, in turn, inset in the thick adobe wall. It rather reminded me of the window in the Juarez Cathedral, one side of which has a very modern wall. On the other hand, part of the cathedral is definitely Spanish colonial style, the part that survived an earth tremor, which occurred soon after the structure was finished. I wonder if the parishioners considered that disaster a message from God or a simple misfortune. Whatever they thought, they redid the destroyed part behind the spires with cement blocks and the memorable modern window. Peculiar, but interesting. The old mission sits right beside the cathedral.

I savored my Enchiladas de Calebacitas, which were delicious, the yellow and Mexican squash, the corn niblets, the diced white onion and tomatoes all lightly cooked. The squash and onion were rather crunchy. This concoction was layered and topped with white cheddar cheese between corn tortillas and baked. Adela and her aunt and uncle continued to argue. Now Julietta was shedding tears.

I looked over the new art exhibit decorating the walls—paintings reminiscent of Frida Kahlo's work. Not only in Kahlo's style, but some that looked like Frida herself. As far as I know, Frida Kahlo never painted anything but self-portraits. The restaurant paintings, which are for sale and change from time to time, hang on white walls or walls paneled with slanting boards of dark wood. In a place of honor near the cash register, highlighted with an orange arch, is a framed, highly polished frying pan that was the first when the restaurant opened over thirty years ago. The pan has an engraving, thanking the owner's mother for her help in establishing the restaurant. What a delightful place!

Since the argument at our table was escalating, I said, "Have you noticed these paintings. Very like Frida Kahlo, don't you think?"

Enchiladas de Calebacitas

My favorite dish at Casa Jurado in El Paso is the spinach enchiladas, but those are a Jurado family secret. Second in my heart, and almost as good are the squash enchiladas, for which the owner dictated the recipe on the spot when I asked for it. After the dictation, we discussed the trip Henry and his wife are planning with their son. How envious I was. They plan to start in the mountains and walk the pilgrim trail to Santiago de Compostela. Not that I can imagine myself walking five hundred miles, but what an adventure it will be to follow in the footsteps of the thousands, maybe millions of pilgrims who have traveled to Santiago since the Middle Ages.

- Scrub skins, cut off ends, and slice off damaged portions of *2 or 3 yellow and/or Mexican squash*. Dice squash, *1 peeled white onion* and a *ripe tomato*, removing seeds and liquid. Add *corn niblets,* and cook the mixture lightly in *vegetable oil.* Squash should be al dente.

- Set oven at 350°F.

- Grate *white cheddar cheese* or *Monterey Jack*.

- On a greased cookie sheet, spread the vegetable mixture on *4 fresh corn tortillas* (including liquid), sprinkle with cheese, layer another corn tortilla on top of each serving; spread and sprinkle more vegetable mixture and cheese. (You may soften tortillas in hot oil by dipping on each side for no more than 20 seconds or use them as they are if they are quite fresh.)

- Bake in the oven until cheese melts.

- Serve with whole, not refried, pinto beans.

Serves 4.

Carolyn Blue, "Have Fork, Will Travel,"
Richmond Herald-Traveler.

40

Recipe Strategy

Carolyn

Evidently **Frida Kahlo** had not been a good subject with which to interrupt the family argument.

"Humph," said Uncle Javier. "*Comunista*. Her and her fat husband. Diego Rivera was a great artist, much admired in Mexico and all over the world, but his politics were quite unacceptable. I am myself a member of the PAN party, which, you may know, has a sensible philosophy on matters economic, which is what Mexico needs. More jobs, more industry, less mordida."

"PAN isn't going to keep me out of jail," said Adela. "I can't even go home to visit Mama."

"Of course, you can," said her uncle. "You just can't come back."

"Leaving the country would make Adela look guilty," said Aunt Julietta. "What is she guilty of? Making an excellent guacamole that did not turn black. I'm sure you noticed that, Senora Azul. By the way, this fish is very tasty. Perhaps you would like to sample it. Adela tells me that you write about food, and arguing with Javier has ruined my appetite." She transferred a small filet to my plate.

"Blue, Tia. Senora *Blue*," said Adela. "If your name were Blanco, would you want Americans calling you Senora White?"

"I did notice that the guacamole kept its color," I interjected and took a bite of the fish after thanking Adela's aunt. She was right. Very tasty, just slightly crisped, redolent of butter and garlic. "Even after several hours, the guacamole not only stayed green, but also it didn't get that nasty, rotten flavor. Was that the addition of lime juice? I didn't notice it in the flavoring."

"No *limon*," said Aunt Julietta. "Is my herbs. They keep the avocado fresh. If the professor had not eaten it all, he would not have been sick. Not very sick."

"So the herb is a preservative?" I asked, seeing a way out of the maze in which Adela found herself.

There was a discussion in Spanish over the meaning of preservative. Then Adela and her aunt agreed that one of the herb's qualities was the preservation of freshness.

"In that case, I think we should all go to the police station and explain the misunderstanding. We will say that we have heard the sergeant is looking for Adela because of a . . . compound discovered in the guacamole. Then Adela will give him the recipe."

"It is a family recipe. Mama would not be happy to think I gave it to the police."

"Your mother will be happier to know that you aren't going to be arrested."

"Her mother does not know of that problem, but your reasoning, Senora, is impeccable," said Uncle Javier.

"Thank you. Then, when he asks about whatever it is that Adela's aunt gave her, Adela will explain that ingredient is the preservative. If he does not accept that explanation, I will comment on the amazing freshness of the guacamole over such a long period of time. I will ask how to get some of the preservative. Tia Julietta will suggest sources. We will discuss what other preservative uses it might have—such as keeping apples from turning color after peeled and cut."

"It does not do that," said Tia Julietta.

"Well, it must do something besides keep guacamole green and cause people to vomit," I suggested.

"Of course it does," she agreed.

"Then you can tell me about that in front of the sergeant."

"Who by then will be very tired of cooking instructions and want us to go away," said Uncle Javier gleefully. "A splendid strategy, Senora—Blue."

"But what if he still puts me in jail?" asked the dubious Adela.

"Then I will provide bail and find you a good lawyer," said her uncle. "However, our family name will be tarnished if you escape to Juarez and the Americans ask for extradition."

Thus it was agreed, and I, having finished my squash enchiladas and Julietta's fish, ordered Mexican crepes.

Pescado al Mojo de Ajo

Our host, Henry Jurado, said, when I mentioned how much I liked the fish, that it was a very easy recipe to make. I pass it on to you.

- Mix *melted butter,* not too much, with *diced pimentos and garlic* and *chopped green onions (optional).*

- Sauté *thin filets of orange roughy or rockfish* in the garlic butter.

- Serve.

Recipe provided by the owners of Casa Jurado in El Paso, Texas

Mexican Crepes

This Mexican crepe dish is simple enough to make, or would be if you didn't have to make the crepes. I've always wondered why some company doesn't make frozen or refrigerated crepes that one can pop into the microwave before filling them with tasty things. I even called my favorite supermarket to ask if they had such an item. They informed me that there are no preprepared crepes on the market. What a disappointment.

Therefore, you'll have to make crepes if you want to try this recipe. Or go to Casa Jurado and order them. For home cooking, you may also have to order the caramel sauce. As for the pecans, many pecans come from our area. Stahmann Farms, in the upper Rio Grand valley, has the largest pecan orchard in the world, 96,000 trees, 5,000,000 pounds of nuts, probably more since the book I got these facts from was written. Whatever the current figure, that's a lot of pecans. And they use geese to keep the grass trimmed between the trees; then they sell the geese. I wonder, if you stuffed a goose with pecans, whether the pate would be wonderful. Or maybe geese don't like pecans. Personally, I think they'd be much tastier than grass.

- CREPES: In a blender or food processor combine in order *1 cup half-and-half, 2 eggs, 2 teaspoons sugar, 1 teaspoon vanilla extract, 1 cup unbleached all-purpose flour, 3 tablespoons yellow cornmeal (stone ground if possible),* and *2 tablespoons unsalted butter, melted.* Blend until smooth. Transfer to bowl, cover, and let stand at room temperature for 1 hour.

- Warm a 7-inch crepe pan, preferably nonstick, over medium-high heat. Brush it lightly with *corn oil.*

Briefly stir the batter to recombine. When pan is hot (oil should smoke slightly), spoon ¼ cup batter into the skillet, tilting to coat the bottom completely. Set pan over the heat, cook 20 seconds, turn the crepe, and cook another 10 seconds. Slide the crepe onto waxed paper. Repeat this with the remaining batter, stacking crepes when cool between pieces of waxed paper. (Crepes can be wrapped tightly and refrigerated for up to 2 days.)

- ASSEMBLY: Place a rack in upper third of oven and preheat the oven to 375°F.

- Spread ½ *cup pecans* in a layer on a metal pan (like a cake tin) and toast them, stirring once or twice, until crisp and fragrant (8 to 10 minutes). Remove from pan, cool, and chop coarsely.

- Fold crepes in quarters, most attractive side out. Spread on each *½ tablespoon out of 4 tablespoons unsalted butter, softened,* and wrap in foil. Warm crepes about 15 minutes or until hot and butter has melted.

- Meanwhile, in a small saucepan over low heat, warm, stirring often, *1⅓ cups cajeta.* (Available in specialty stores such as The El Paso Chile Company. *Cajeta de leche,* caramel based on goats' milk, is preferable.)

- Arrange two crepes on each of four plates, spoon the cajeta over and around them. Sprinkle the pecans over all, and serve immediately.

Recipe provided by W. Park Kerr and Norma Kerr from the *El Paso Chile Company's Texas Border Cookbook.*

Carolyn Blue, "Have Fork, Will Travel," *Nome News*

After dessert, we drove to the police station in Uncle Javier's car, a huge, beautifully maintained vehicle that was probably twenty years old. It was so comfortable that I could easily have gone to sleep in the back seat if Adela hadn't whispered an embarrassing question in my ear. She wanted to know if I had a black eye.

Her question was evidently heard in the front seat because she received a sharp reprimand in Spanish from her aunt. It had something to do with my *esposo*. Possibly Aunt Julietta was saying that my husband might have hit me and that it was impolite for Adela to embarrass me by asking.

In order to clear Jason's good name, I replied to Adela, but loudly enough to be heard by the relatives in the front seat, that during the investigation made by my friend and myself into the murder of Vladik, I had been assaulted by an evil man, who was now in jail. They were all sorry to hear of my misfortune but glad to hear that my attacker had been arrested. Uncle Javier, whose last name I can't remember, told me that I should try not to interfere in police business in the future for the sake of my own safety. He had a point, one that Jason would have made had he not been in Austin with his graduate student, Mercedes.

At Five Points we were told that Sergeant Guevara had gone home. I asked for Lieutenant Matalisse, who had, after all, mentioned that he had hours of paper work ahead of him. He scowled at me when we were escorted into his office. "I've set the wheels in motion on the doctor," he said.

"This is another matter. You'll remember you said Sergeant Guevara was looking for the guacamole maker. This is she—Adela Mariscal. She's a graduate student in music at the university. She sang one of the witches' parts in the *Macbeth* performance. Then I introduced her aunt and uncle, who, I explained, were visiting when they heard that the police were looking for Adela. Adela had then called me, so we'd all come over after dinner at Casa Jurado.

The lieutenant shook their hands and directed them to seats. He asked me if I ever ordered the chicken mole, a favorite of his. I said I didn't care for unsweetened chocolate and hot chiles on my meat, but I did love the wonderful spinach enchiladas, among other outstanding dinners. The lieutenant had never ordered the spinach enchiladas, which was no surprise to me. I hadn't talked Jason into trying them either. It must have been a male thing.

"So you think the family guacamole recipe killed this man?" Aunt Julietta asked, evidently tired of the polite conversation. I sympathized. Adela was looking more and more stressed as we talked. "Generations of our family have eaten that guacamole with no sickness."

"That may be so, ma'am, but there was something weird in that guacamole. Our toxicologists analyzed it along with the rest of the victim's stomach contents."

"That must be an unpleasant job. Who would wish to examine such things?" Aunt Julietta remarked.

"My niece is prepared to give you her recipe. In fact, she has written it out for you," said Uncle Javier. "Please examine it. There is nothing in it to be blamed for a man's death." He nodded to Adela, who, with a trembling hand, passed the recipe across to the lieutenant.

Lieutenant Matalisse studied the list of ingredients. "Looks innocent enough, but the recipe is no guarantee that she didn't put in something more she didn't mention to you folks—wait. What's this?" He pointed to the last ingredient.

"That is the preservative," said Aunt Julietta, as if preservation was its only role. "You will know that the avocados turn black and—untasteful—if they are allowed to sit out of their skins. That is my special herb for preventing this tragedy. Otherwise, a big guacamole could not be served. You understand?"

"Could it make someone sick?" asked the lieutenant, not to be bamboozled by talk of exotic herbs he'd never heard of.

"Perhaps. But one would have to eat very much guacamole for sickness to occur."

"He did, right?" The lieutenant turned to me.

"Yes, he tried to keep it all for himself."

"But my niece could not have known he would do this. It would not be gentlemanly to do so," said Uncle Javier. "Therefore, if he experienced illness, he brought that illness on himself. My niece cannot be held responsible for his gluttony, which is one of the seven deadly sins. He should have considered the *deadly* element in his sin."

"I'll have to ask the toxicologist about this stuff," said the lieutenant. "In the meantime, young lady, you stay at the university until we get this cleared up."

"My niece is a student. She will stay at the *universidad* until the end of the semester, traffic on the bridges being dangerous and time consuming. I, a lawyer, will see to it. American police are known to be reliable, so my niece, as you see, is cooperating."

"*Gringo estupido*," muttered Aunt Julietta as we left headquarters after friendly farewells to the lieutenant.

41

The Investigation Moves Elsewhere

Carolyn

Obviously things were going on Saturday night and
Sunday morning in which I was only peripherally involved, which was fine with me. Adela's uncle dropped me
at my car on the university campus, and I drove home, very
carefully, then fell into bed and read the fourth book in
First Ladies Detective Agency series: *The Kalahari Typing
School for Men.* It was quite as delightful as the first three
books, and I found the title wonderfully amusing, since I
pictured in my mind groups of small desert tribesman, vir-
tually naked, squatting in the sand, typing. That was not
the case, as I learned. The typing school in question was
held in a church in the capital of Botswana and served men
in Western clothing.

I had only one interruption Saturday night. Luz called
to say the lieutenant wanted the name of the nurse with
whom I had spoken at the hospital. "Irma," I said, remembering her name tag. That was the best I could do, other
than reminding Luz that the nurse had worked the night
shift on this weekend and the last. Glad as I was to realize
that my information was leading to a stirring of police interest, I went back to my book and was asleep by ten
o'clock, through no fault of the book. I fell asleep smiling,
and that was directly attributable to the book.

The next morning, thoroughly refreshed, I fixed myself
breakfast—including eggs, in which Luz evidently didn't

believe or which she didn't know how to cook, if her toast-only offerings the last two mornings were any indication. Then I settled down to read the Sunday paper. I was either getting used to reading one-eyed, or I was seeing more out of my black eye. I'd been careful *not* to look in the mirror when emerging from the shower.

"INS Considers Deporting Russian Strip-Club Owner," the Borderland section proclaimed. They included a picture of Boris Ignatenko, looking more ghoulish than ever in black and white, being escorted into a federal courtroom. His lawyer argued that for a Russian army deserter deportation was akin to the death penalty, which would be overly harsh, considering the crimes of which he was accused. It would seem that Boris preferred to be tried in this country. Since I had been one of his victims, I was less inclined to view his predicament sympathetically. Before I could talk myself into a more tolerant frame of mind, I was saved by my telephone.

When Vivian Brockman identified herself, I groaned inwardly, expecting that she intended to chastise me for focusing police suspicion on her husband. That was not the case, however. Vivian, sounding rather flustered, had called to ask if I knew what was going on with the investigation of Vladislav Gubenko's death. I replied that I hadn't heard anything lately, adding silently, *which is to say today.*

"Well," said Vivian, "this has been a very peculiar twelve hours. Last night we received a call from the police. They said they were checking the whereabouts afterward of everyone who had been at the opera party. I told them I had been at home asleep, and Peter had been called out for emergency surgery. Of course, I offered to put Peter on, but they said that wasn't necessary. Then Peter received a call early this morning from the hospital. I checked the caller ID after he left the house. He was very upset with the caller, so of course, I asked what it had been about. 'I have to go to Cincinnati,' he said. Naturally, I asked when, wondering if I'd have to iron shirts for him, since the maid doesn't come until Monday. To my amazement, he said, 'Right now.' Can you imagine? Why would the hospital be calling to send him to Cincinnati? He said he didn't have time to explain, threw some clothes in a carry-on bag, and left. That's quite unlike Peter.

"*Then*," she said dramatically, "well, actually a half hour may have passed, but the police arrived at my door. I was still in my dressing gown. They wanted to talk to Peter, so of course, I told them that he had left for Cincinnati. They had all sorts of questions for me: How long ago? Where in Cincinnati? For what reason? Traveling how? By plane I assumed, but I couldn't even say that for sure. And finally, they wanted a description of his car. At least I could give them that, but they wouldn't tell me why they were looking for Peter. The only thing I could think of was our artistic director's death, which they'd talked to me about, indirectly, the night before."

She sighed, a long-suffering sigh, and said, "I'd really like to know what's going on."

I thought I knew. Vivian had told the police that Peter was at the hospital. Luz had asked me for the nurse's name, and Irma had told them sometime last night that he hadn't been at the hospital. They'd probably also interviewed Luz's neighbor, and her ex-husband, who had heard Peter talking about getting rid of Vladik. Peter's call from the hospital might have been from Irma, telling him that people, namely, Carolyn Blue and the police, had been asking if he'd been at the hospital a week ago Saturday. Peter had put two and two together and fled. Then another question occurred to me: Was it my duty as a friend to forewarn Vivian, or my duty as a citizen to keep my mouth shut?

Since Peter had already fled with the police at his heels, I decided that nothing I said would either hinder or facilitate his capture. "Carolyn," said Vivian. "Are you listening to me?"

"Yes, Vivian. I'm afraid I have some rather frightening news for you."

"Frightening? Don't tell me another Opera at the Pass member has died."

"Not that I know of, but when Peter told you he was at the hospital performing surgery the night Vladik died, he wasn't telling the truth—or at least that's what one of the night nurses in Emergency says. Perhaps it was she who called this morning to warn him that the police were making inquiries about him."

"I wouldn't have thought any of the nurses liked Peter well enough to forewarn him of anything. They even complain to me about his domineering personality. As if I didn't know. I'm his wife, for goodness sake. I just tell them to ignore him."

"That's probably hard for a nurse to do—ignore a doctor."

"Still, he must have gone to a different hospital, and I misunderstood. I was, after all, half asleep when he said he'd been called in. Peter may be difficult, he may even have hated that opera, but that's hardly reason for him to—well, so the police think he killed Vladik? That's ridiculous. He's a doctor. It would be quite outside his area of expertise and his moral obligation as a doctor to deliberately kill someone."

"Hmmm," I said.

"They'd have to have some other evidence, but of course they don't, because people like us don't kill our associates. It's unheard of."

"The thing is, a tall person carrying a doctor's bag was seen entering Vladik's condo that night. The witness saw his car too and said it was long and dark, which isn't much of description. What's Peter's car like?"

"I suppose one might describe it as long and dark, but I'm sure there are many long, dark cars in El Paso. Still, this is very—very upsetting. If Peter was actually foolish enough to kill Vladik over that silly *Macbeth* performance, he needn't expect me to bail him out of jail. But if he simply disappears, what am I to do? I suppose the first thing is to call our lawyer and find out what my financial situation would be if any of these eventualities actually—my goodness, Carolyn. I think I'll have to get off the phone."

Poor Vivian, I thought. A husband in jail or on the run from the law was going to play havoc with her lifestyle. Not a very charitable thought on my part, but her primary concern didn't seem to be her husband's guilt or innocence, but rather how it would affect her.

42

News Al Fresco

Carolyn

It was a lovely day—clear, sunny, with temperatures in the high 60s. Feeling indolent, I took my book and cordless telephone to a lounger on the patio to enjoy more of the *Kalahari Typing School* without having to go inside should anyone care to update me on the search for and investigation of Dr. Peter Brockman. I was closing in on the end of the book and beginning to think of lunch when the telephone finally rang. My caller, Luz, said, "Hi. I'm down at headquarters. Just finished listening to the interrogation of your doctor."

"So they caught him before he could leave town?"

"How did you know what he was planning?"

"His wife told me. And why wasn't *I* invited to listen in?"

"Maybe because you don't have cop connections, and I do," she replied, laughing. "Actually, I did call you when Matalisse called me, but your phone was busy. I just barely made it to Five Points myself. So, do you want to hear what he said?"

"Of course I do. In fact, why don't you come over for lunch? We'll have snacks and sangria."

"I don't mind snacks, but that damned bottled sangria is enough to make you puke."

"I make my own," I retorted, a bit huffy. "From a recipe one of Jason's colleagues gave us. It's delicious."

"I'm on my way."

I went to the kitchen and prepared several dips, chile con queso and guacamole, and the cream-cheese-jalapeno-fruit canapés I'd fixed for the ill-fated opera party. There was a certain symmetry in finishing with the food I'd prepared when this case started, not that I'd mention that thought to Luz, who was as likely to howl with laughter as agree. She arrived as I was mixing the sangria base with red wine and soda water and pouring it over ice.

After carrying our lunch to the patio, we settled down to eat and talk, but not before Luz sampled my sangria and actually said it was good. "Great," she added, reluctantly. "Martino's used to have good sangria; my dad always let me have a little glass even when I was a kid, but I haven't ordered it there in years. After I had my first Martino's margarita, I forgot all about sangria."

"Was the sangria as good as mine?" I asked, jealous of their recipe.

"I don't know. That was years ago. Anyway, let's talk about the case. First, let me tell you about the old lady across the street. Matalisse sent someone out to interview her. Turns out she didn't tell us the whole thing. Brockman has this personalized license plate: PBMD and some numbers, and it has a light. She saw it—can you beat that? Old as she is, she could read it two houses away. Maybe she's got a spyglass. Anyway, she figures out the MD, but what does the PB mean? Since she doesn't know his name, she starts thinking up stuff—"pretty bad" MD, "pediatric butcher" MD, "peeler of bunions" MD. She was still making up names when the doctor came out. So we have a witness who can place him there at the right time. No vanity plates in Texas with those first four letters.

"They also talked to Francisco and evidently got an earful from Mrs. Escobar number two. First, she thought they were accusing Francisco, and she had a fit. Then, she caught on that it was Brockman they were interested in and

gave them a lecture on what an important community figure he is, blah, blah, blah. Poor Francisco; she doesn't
sound like much fun, but at least he got some kids out of
the marriage. Anyway, Matalisse sent the troops to Brockman's house this morning, but then you know that.

"They'd caught up with the nurse the night before—she
said he wasn't there—and with his wife, who said he was.
Case was looking good."

She poured herself more sangria, looked questioningly
at me and poured me another glass. We both dipped some
chips and filled small plates with those and canapés.

"He was gone when they went to his house, and he
might have got away, but he ran into some bad luck at the
airport." Luz started to laugh and stuffed a canapé into her
mouth. "Now, this is my kind of lunch. Anyway, he parks
in long-term parking and heads for the terminal, gets in,
and they shut it down. Security thinks there's someone in
there with a gun. Then Matalisse's guys, with your picture
of Brockman, arrive, and they get in because they're looking for a murder suspect. Poor Brockman's screwed. Cops,
airport security, even sniffer dogs all over the place.

"He hasn't got a prayer of going unnoticed. He can't
even chance waiting in line to get a ticket to somewhere.
They find him in the men's room in the booth next to the
guy with the gun, who wants to hijack a plane to Cancún.
How dumb is that? Most people who want a vacation in
Cancún save up their money. Not this guy. He steals a gun
from his brother-in-law and heads for the airport."

"Does El Paso International have flights to Cancún?" I
asked.

"How would I know? I've never been to Cancún.

"So the gunman and Brockman are hauled off. I don't
know what happened to the gunman, but they want hand
and butt prints from Brockman. He thinks that's pretty
dumb and says, 'Why not?' But he won't take down his
pants. No way. They'll have to get a warrant for his butt.

So they take a picture of his butt and a print of his hand. Guy from the basement who looks at prints comes up to give his considered opinion. He says he's no expert on butt prints, but it looks about right to him, and the hand is a good match. Says this in front of Brockman, who thinks they're just scamming him. Then they ask if he was in Gubenko's house a week ago Saturday. He say no. Where was he? they ask. Driving around thinking he'd like to get a divorce from his wife, he tells them."

My telephone rang, and Luz leaned back in her chair while I took the call. It was Vivian. She wanted me to know that her husband had been arrested, and the police told her that he had confessed. I was amazed. Luz hadn't mentioned a confession so far.

"I know that you'll be anxious about support for those Russian girls, Carolyn," said Vivian. "Now that Peter's been arrested."

"Goodness, you shouldn't have to worry about *that*," I protested.

"I know I don't have to, but my husband being accused of murder does not relieve me of my social responsibilities. Especially if he's guilty. That would make Peter responsible in part for their plight, so I wanted you to know that my lawyer assures me I'll still own Peter's half of the partnership, no matter what happens to him. I should be able to provide one day's work a week for the two girls, but probably not two."

"That's—that's so thoughtful of you, Vivian—to worry about others when you—you've had such distressing news."

"Not at all," said Vivian. "And now I must say goodbye. There are so many things to do. It's very inconvenient that this happened on Sunday when the banks are closed."

"His wife?" asked Luz when I clicked off the phone.

"Yes, she was calling to let me know that he's been arrested, but that even if he goes to jail, she'll still own half of his medical partnership and can provide part-time émployment for the two Russian girls."

Luz grinned. "That's real wifely. I tell you what. I'll never understand gringos. No wonder he was thinking about divorcing her." She drained her glass and said, "Is there any more sangria?"

Professorial Sangria

This recipe for sangria, which was provided by a professional colleague of my husband's, is not only delicious, but shows the result of scientific experimentation in the proportions. When my husband was a graduate student, we once attended a scientific watermelon party during which vodka was put into watermelons in different proportions by different methods: injection, pouring into a cut plug, etcetera. Then we sampled the melon. The sangria is definitely tastier than our watermelon experiments. Now if they'd used a fruit liqueur, the watermelon results might have been better—but more expensive.

- SANGRIA BASE: In *3 quarts water*, mix *4 cups of sugar (2 pounds)* and *3 oranges, 3 lemons* and *3 limes,* not peeled but sliced.

- Boil slowly uncovered for 2 to 3 hours until reduced by one half. Cool to room temperature. The base keeps in the refrigerator for weeks.

- SANGRIA: combine in proportions of I part base to 3 to 5 parts *Burgundy (4 liters of inexpensive red wine such as Gallo Hearty Burgundy depending on how sweet you like your sangria).*

- Before serving, add *club soda,* 1 part soda to 8 parts of the Burgundy and base mix.

- Mix and serve in a glass pitcher with ice or pour directly into glasses with ice.

- Add *sliced fresh fruit such as peaches or strawberries (optional).*

Carolyn Blue, "Have Fork, Will Travel,"
Ft. Lauderdale Weekly Sentinel.

43
Hearsay Confession

Carolyn

Gringos? Obviously Vivian and I were both gringos in Luz's eyes. But was it a pejorative term? I understood that it referred to citizens of the United States, but not Mexican American citizens. "Would a black U.S. citizen be a gringo?" I asked curiously.

"Why?" she asked. "I wouldn't have figured Brockman for having a black wife."

"He doesn't," I agreed. "I was just wondering about the word *gringo*. You called Vivian a gringo. Is that an insult?"

"Oh, for Pete's sake. You must be drunk."

"I am not," I retorted indignantly. "What were we talking about?"

"Brockman saying he wanted to divorce his wife—that was what he was doing when Gubenko died, driving around thinking about dumping his wife."

"Oh, I doubt that he'd really consider divorcing Vivian, especially if her name is on the partnership papers," I said thoughtfully. "He just had to tell them he was doing something while Vladik was dying. On the other hand, he may well have been irritated with her." I poured the last of the sangria into Luz's glass and excused myself to make another pitcher. She didn't protest.

When I returned and refilled my own glass, I said, "The police did call the Brockman's house last night to ask their whereabouts the night of the murder. Vivian said she was at home and he was doing emergency surgery. What I think happened is that Irma, that nice nurse, got worried about her job—Peter's on the hospital board—so she called him this morning to tip him off that she'd been questioned by the police about his hospital alibi."

"Well, he was on the run, for sure, and we don't know how he found out we were looking for him. Listen to me. I'm not part of that *we* anymore." She stared into her glass moodily.

I ignored Luz's sudden retirement angst and added, "Vivian called to tell me about the police wanting to talk to him this morning, and before that about a call from the hospital earlier, after which he said he had to go to Cincinnati and left without even explaining *why* he had to go to Cincinnati."

"Makes sense. So we'll assume that Irma tipped him off and he ran. Now where was I?" She took another sip of sangria, leaned forward to rub her knee, then said, "Once he had to give up the surgery alibi, they played him the tape of the old lady, talking about the tall doctor with Brockman's license plates, going into Gubenko's condo. Her saying Gubenko must have called him because he was sick."

Oh dear, I thought. *More confusing pronouns. Who in that sentence was sick and who was called?*

"So he says, yeah, Gubenko did call him on his cell phone while he was driving around thinking about divorcing his wife, and he went over there, but Gubenko was still alive when he left. He gave him a suppository to stop him from puking.

"Matalisse, who's leading the interrogation, with Guevara sitting there looking mad as hell, says, no. Nothing in the anus on autopsy. Brockman says maybe the Russian never got a chance to use the suppository. Matalisse says, they didn't find any suppositories, but there's pillow feathers and puke on the sleeves of the doctor's coat, which they got from his closet with a search warrant. The anus check on autopsy was a lie, the feathers too, but they did find puke on the coat. The wife got all upset when they wanted to take it away because she was supposed to send it to the cleaners but hadn't because she was flustered by 'harassment from one Sergeant Guevara' and forgot all about the coat."

"Do they have Vladik's DNA on the coat?" I asked, wishing that she'd stop using the word *puke*.

"Nah. Takes time for DNA, and we just got the coat."

"But the man's a doctor. Couldn't some patient, other than Vladik, have thrown up on Peter's coat?"

"While he was driving around thinking about divorcing his wife?" Luz laughed. "By then he must have figured we had him, because he said, and I quote, 'Oh very well, Lieutenant, but you'll have to agree that Vladik forced me into an unconsidered action. I'd simply come to tell him that he'd be losing his post as our artistic director, both because of his sickening *Macbeth* and because of his conduct at the party afterward.'

"I'll tell you, Caro, Brockman is one arrogant asshole, but Matalisse didn't let on. He said, 'I knew there had to be a good explanation.'

"'Exactly,' says the doctor. 'Professor Gubenko, once he finished vomiting as a result of gorging himself on guacamole, said that if we fired him, he'd sue. And then he'd sue because we poisoned him at the party. I had the most terrible vision of Opera at the Pass having to declare bankruptcy and disband because of a man who put on the worst *Macbeth* imaginable.'

"Matalisse nodded like he couldn't help but agree. Then the doctor tells us that in a moment of madness and loyalty to El Paso opera lovers, he was moved to stop Gubenko from making threats, so he put the pillow over his mouth. Imagine his surprise when the Gubenko up and expired, he said. No amount of attempts at artificial respiration could bring him back. What a load of crap that was."

My telephone rang, and Luz muttered, "Just when I get to the good part."

It was Dolly Montgomery. "Oh, Caro, I have the most exciting news. I just hope I'm not too late. Howard has been on the phone continuously since I told him you were looking for part-time work for the Russian girls, and he's managed to get a grant. Isn't that wonderful? It's to write a book called *Shakespearean Criticism: A Comparison of Russian Scholarship from the Communist and Post-Communist Eras.* And of course, he wants the young women to do the translating if they're still available. I so hope they are."

Now there's a catchy title, I thought. What I said was, "My goodness, Dolly, this couldn't have come at a better time. Vivian just told me that Peter's office may not be able to offer more that one day's work a week, and I wouldn't be surprised to hear that they'd be happy to give Howard those days as well."

"That's wonderful." Dolly, all atwitter, thanked me several times and then apologized for hanging up so soon, but she wanted to give Howard the good news.

Luz didn't even ask me about the phone call. "So Brockman thinks he has Matalisse on his side, what with the artificial respiration story and all that. That's when Matalisse turns the tables on him. He says, 'So you're saying you just wanted him to stop making threats, but had no intention of smothering him?'

" 'None whatever,' says the doctor.

" 'You didn't foresee that a man that sick to his stomach might aspirate his own vomit and die?'

" 'I wasn't really thinking that clearly,' says the doctor."

Luz was doing quite a good imitation of both men.

" 'How long would you say that you held the pillow over his face?' asks Matalisse.

" 'I couldn't say,' says the doctor. 'But you can see that it was a tragic mistake.'

"'No, sir, I can't,' says the lieutenant. 'First, you lied about where you were that night. Then you tell me that he called you, but there were no calls from his house that night, so you obviously went there of your own accord. You had motive—the lawsuits he threatened. So you put the pillow over his face and killed him. Of course, the district attorney will have to decide, but I'd say you're guilty of murder, sir.'

"All the time Matalisse is so polite. You should have seen it. I felt like cheering. And Guevara. His face kept getting redder and redder because every word they said screwed his line of investigation right into the ground. They ought to send the frigging numskull to Traffic or somewhere he can't do any harm."

"More sangria?" I asked.

"You bet," she replied enthusiastically. "This has been the best week I've had in I don't know when, and I'd never have believed it when you showed up at my door last Monday, all prissy and earnest."

"I may be earnest, Luz, but I am *not* prissy." And I passed her the guacamole.

44
He Said, She Said

Luz

Once I finished telling Carolyn about the interrogation of Peter Brockman, the two of us sat there talking, laughing, and drinking more of her great sangria. We were pretty pleased with ourselves. "Here's to catching the arrogant doctor who snuffed out Vladik Gubenko, small loss there, but justice did prevail!" I said. We clinked sangria glasses.

Giggling, Carolyn then said, "Here's to the bounty hunters of the year—us—who kidnapped the evil drug lord. His only redeeming feature was a good voice."

"Hey, give the man credit," I protested. "He would have got the prize for the most disgusting interior decoration if he'd entered the contest." We howled with laughter and drank the toast. "Did I tell you about the rewards? Should come to about forty thousand with the money for catching three alien smugglers. Gubenko counts even if he is dead. Twenty thou is yours if you want it."

"That's a lot of money," said Carolyn, awed. "On the other hand, the whole thing isn't much more than two years of your medication." She gave the matter some deep thought, if the frown on her face was any indication. "I think, on consideration, that you should have it, Luz. I'd never have dreamed of kidnapping Mr. Barrientos if you hadn't engineered it. And it *was* fun. I'll tell you what: You pay for cleaning my trunk and vacuuming Smack hair off my upholstery, and we'll call it even."

"I'll give you a chance to change your mind when you're not full of sangria," I offered, but I hoped she wouldn't; two years of medication wasn't something to pass up.

"I'm not drunk, you know," she protested. "I'm perfectly capable of renouncing twenty thousand dollars." Then she giggled. "Of course, Jason might not like it, but he won't know, will he? So let's have another toast."

"Okay," I agreed. "Here's to bringing down Boris, the white-slaving ghoul. Hey, did you know your eye is turning a very becoming yellow and lavender?"

"I don't want to hear about it," said Carolyn, and raised her glass. "To Boris the ghoul."

We drank and filled our plates with more chips and canapés. "You put on a good lunch, Caro," I said.

She nodded solemnly. "And *al fresco* too."

"What?"

"We're out doors. Look at that sunset. Do I have the best view in town or what?"

We studied a sky glowing red, streaked purple and even green, high clouds hanging over the sun's disappearance like ominous canopies. "I think it's going to rain," I said.

"That's not at all likely," Carolyn retorted. "I predict that we won't see rain until spring. Here's to El Paso and its beautiful sunsets."

"El Paso!" I agreed, and we clinked glasses.

"And here's to the rescue of the two fair maidens in distress," said Carolyn. "May they enjoy their new dorm rooms, their new used car, their donated clothes, their cans of soup, and their respectable jobs—and become great opera singers, who will mention us kindly in their memoirs." Since she'd drunk the last of her sangria, she raised a tostado dripping with chile con queso.

"Hey, I don't want runny cheese on my sangria glass," I protested. "And you were the one who saved the fair maidens in distress, if they are maidens. Doesn't seem likely after their career in exotic dancing."

"They're lesbians," said Carolyn. "But you may be right about maidenhood. I think Polya slept with at least one customer at Brazen Babes, and Irina was sexually abused by her father, so she's probably not a maiden either."

"Death to sexual abusers!" I said and poured more sangria into her glass so that she could drink the toast.

"To sexual abusers," said Carolyn, and raised the glass.

"Carolyn?" exclaimed a shocked voice.

She turned around and said, "Hi, Jason. What are you doing here?"

"My God, what happened to your eye?"

"I was punched by an evil ghoul." She grinned. "From Russia. Want some sangria? I think he's being deported."

"You've obviously been drinking quite a lot of that sangria."

"I have indeed. This is Luz Vallejo. We are El Paso's cutest crime fighters, aren't we, Luz? Luz, my husband, Jason."

"Hi, Jason." He was kinda cute himself, nice beard, but he didn't look very glad to see me. Maybe he was still obsessing about her eye. "Her eye looks a lot better today," I told him. "Yesterday it was black and purple."

"It's a comfort to know that," he said dryly. "Carolyn, maybe you'd like to tell me exactly what you've been doing while I was away?"

Oops, I thought. *Controlling husband rears ugly head.*

"What have I been doing?" Carolyn straightened up from her comfortable sprawl, put her glass down on the table, and said, "Well, I have saved the university from embarrassment by getting those two girls—excuse me, young women—out of the strip club and into a dormitory with new clothes, cans of soup, meals in the Commons, free tuition, and respectable part-time work provided by members of our ad hoc ladies' Opera at the Pass charitable committee. Then Luz and I found out who killed Vladik, and he *was* murdered—by Peter Brockman. We also kidnapped a drug dealer from Juarez and turned him in for a nifty reward, which I can have half of if I want, but I don't, and then we got Boris Stepanovich Ignatenko, owner of Brazen Babes, jailed for various crimes, among them my black eye."

She gave her husband a bright smile and said, "And what have you been doing this week, Jason, other than gamboling around Austin with a girl half your age."

"Oops," I said. "Maybe I ought to go home."

"I was not gamboling around Austin," said Jason, looking insulted. "We were consulting on research into—"

"Goodness, don't leave, Luz," said Carolyn. "Have some more sangria. You promised that I could tell you about Aztec uses, aside from nutritional uses, for chiles. Jason, sit down and have some sangria. It's amazing how much it cheers one up."

"Here's to the Aztecs," I said, raising my glass. "What else did they do with chiles? I'm all ears."

"Not at all," said Carolyn. "Your ears are quite unobtrusive. And it wasn't just the Aztecs. The Incas and Mayas also used chiles—for torture. We could have resorted to jalapenos on Mr. Barrientos instead of just threatening his genitalia with your cane."

Her husband choked on his sangria.

"They also used it to poison their arrow tips. They dusted it on food they were afraid might have spoiled and fumigated rooms with it. Do you think chiles could kill cockroaches, Jason? Maybe we should think about that as an earth-friendly substitute for insecticide. The next time I see a scorpion, I'll just shake some cayenne pepper on it."

"Scorpions are pretty fast," I pointed out. "That's kind of like trying to pour salt on a bird's tail. I tried that when I was a kid. Never had any luck at all, but it did piss my mother off. She liked birds and didn't want me wasting salt."

Carolyn nodded. "The Salt War," she said, whatever the hell she meant by that. "The Indians also thought that chiles were a cure for diarrhea. How silly is that?"

"Not silly," I protested. "My aunt says so too."

"There is a much higher rate of stomach cancer in countries that eat a lot of spicy food," said her husband.

"Exactly," Carolyn agreed, "and most interesting, they used to poison small bodies of water in order to kill the fish, which floated to the top, dead and well spiced for the pot."

"Interesting," said her husband.

"Sneaky," I said. "Here's to spicy fish," and we all clinked our sangria glasses.

Recipe Index

Adela's Guacamole 11
Recipe provided by W. Park Kerr and Norma Kerr from the
El Paso Chile Company's Texas Border Cookbook

Carolyn's Easy Eggs Ranchero 28

Tortilla Soup 65
Recipe provided by Annette Lawrence, chef-owner of the Magic Pan,
El Paso, Texas

Salpicon *(Shredded beef salad with chipotle dressing)* 85
Recipe reprinted from the El Paso Chile Company's Texas
Border Cookbook
with permission of authors W. Park Kerr and Norma Kerr

Green Enchiladas *a la Hacienda* 101
Recipe reprinted from the El Paso Chile Company's Texas
Border Cookbook
with permission of the authors

Enchiladas de Calebacitas *(Mexican Squash Enchiladas)* 246
Recipe provided by Mr. and Mrs. Henry Jurado of Casa Jurado,
El Paso, Texas

Pescado al Mojo de Ajo *(Fish Filet in Butter-Garlic Sauce)* 250
Recipe provided by the Jurados of Casa Jurado, El Paso, Texas

Mexican Crepes 251
Recipe reprinted from the El Paso Chile Company's Texas
Border Cookbook
with permission from the authors

Professorial Sangria 265
Recipe provided by Lionel Craver, Professor of Mechanical Engineering,
University of Texas at El Paso

NANCY FAIRBANKS

The Culinary Mystery series with recipes

Crime Brûlée   0-425-17918-4

Carolyn accompanies her husband to an academic conference in New Orleans. But just as she gets a taste of Creole, she gets a bite of crime when her friend Julienne disappears at a dinner party.

Truffled Feathers   0-425-18272-X

The CEO of a large pharmaceutical company has invited Carolyn and her husband to the Big Apple for some serious wining and dining. But before she gets a chance to get a true taste of New York, the CEO is dead. Was it high cholesterol or high crime?

Death à l'Orange   0-425-18524-9

It's a culinary tour de France for Carolyn Blue and her family as they travel through Normandy and the Loire valley with a group of academics. But when murder shows up on the menu, Carolyn is once again investigating crime as well as cuisine.

Chocolate Quake   0-425-18946-5

Carolyn's trip to San Francisco includes a visit to her mother-in-law, a few earthquake tremors, and a stint in prison as a murder suspect. A column about prison food might be a change of pace.

The Perils of Paella   0-425-19390-X

Carolyn is excited to be in Barcelona visiting her friend Roberta, who is the resident scholar at the modern art museum. When an actor is killed during a performance art exhibit, Carolyn must get to the bottom of the unsavory crime.